REVENGE SERVED COLD

A NOVEL

First Published in Great Britain 2019 by Mirador Publishing

First edition: 2019

A copy of this work is available through the British Library.

ISBN: 978-1-912601-93-6

Mirador Publishing
10 Greenbrook Terrace
Taunton
Somerset
TA1 1UT
UK

Revenge Served Cold

A Novel

By

Bob Ford

Author Contact
bobfordnyc@gmail.com

For
Bonnie

Revenge is a Dish Best Served Cold

When one has time to prepare vengeance
that is well-planned
or unexpected,
revenge becomes a dish that is
more satisfying when served cold.

AN EXCERPT FROM THE DIARY
OF ANDREA TRASK

Three Days Before Her Murder

I remember the look of utter disbelief on my fiancé's face when he realized he'd been tossed, fully clothed, into the swimming pool. And I recall thinking, as Max and Robby picked me up and carried me off bodily to their car, that I should at least appear to be outraged, to scream in anger and make it look as though I were trying to break free. But I did nothing; partly because I was totally mesmerized, even flattered, by the sheer audacity of what they had done, partly because I was very young with little sense of propriety, and partly because I loved them both.

Yes, I suppose I should have resisted. I should have gone back and retrieved poor Steven from the pool. After all, it was our engagement party. Thinking back, I'm sure neither Max nor Robby would have prevented me had I insisted.

The whole affair created a minor scandal, of course, my being snatched away right in the middle of the toasts to our happiness. And I didn't help matters when I returned two days later and broke off the engagement. Naturally, that bit of news set loose a flood of rumors and speculation as to what had occurred during my abduction. I could have simply told everyone the truth: We left Greenwich and drove to Max's house in the Hamptons and talked. That was all. But no one would have believed me so I said nothing and let people assume whatever they wished, which, of course, was the worst.

For months afterwards, before I married Robby, mother kept pressing me for an explanation. "Andrea Francis, whatever possessed you?" she would ask. Always those exact words. But I think she knew the answer. How would any woman of twenty-three react if two of the world's most sought-after bachelors had fallen in love with her? Exactly as I did, no doubt. I'm afraid my inflated ego simply squashed my common sense. It was all so outlandishly outrageous and I loved every minute of it. I looked forward to walking with them down Avenue Foch or the Via Veneto or Fifth Avenue with an expression on my face that said to the world, "Look at me, I've got them both!" And I know rumors were rampant that I did have them both. Only the three of us knew for sure and we would not tell. I was at such a giddy height and that made the fall so much harder to bear.

Oh, the myopia of a woman in love. What I perceived as their free spirits was, in fact, a total lack of responsibility. What I took for an engaging irrepressibility was nothing more than a snub to convention wanton abandon. It would be easy to rationalize their behavior by saying they were victims of their money. Certainly, they came into control of unconscionable amounts long before anyone could have reasonably expected them to demonstrate any maturity with it. To me, however, the money was not the cause, only the means. I believe counter to the Bard the fault lay in their stars. It seemed ordained that everything in life would come easy to them. The events which touched their lives never presented either Max or Robby with any real challenges. They never had to confront the dilemmas, the failures and adversities that, having experienced and survived them, provide balance and depth to one's character.

No, there were never any real challenges and that's why, I believe, they had to manufacture their own. Most men of fortune in search of meaningful diversion in their lives would have created foundations or undertaken social causes or satisfied political ambitions. But Max and Robby filled their void with games. Any kind of games. Contrived little competitions, contests; anything where they could pit themselves one against the other and, on occasion, against some unsuspecting target. It got to the point where they eventually reduced virtually every facet of their relationship to some sort of game. They had narrowed their world to a population of two. In their world you were either first or last. And to be last was intolerable.

I met them when I was sixteen. At first, I thought they were the best of friends. Only later did I realize they were also the worst of enemies. And God help me, once I loved them both. As I think back over all the years since then, I cannot remember a time when they talked with each other as you might expect two friends to talk. No, they parried, they prodded, they baited each other constantly. Even the most casual social get-together somehow always evolved into a mano a mano. And they thrived on it. It provided them with a high, a euphoria unmatched by anything else in their lives, including their relationship with me.

There was a time, not long after Robby and I were married, when I assumed their rabid competitiveness would fade. Instead, it intensified. I realize now they had become trapped in an ever-tightening circle of their own creation.

The tally, the wins and losses, that was what mattered. I'm sure in their own minds they always looked upon each other as victor or victim. Yet, as I think about it now, the only victim of their games has been me.

But no longer. I will have my revenge.

I
SLEEPING WITH THE ENEMY'S WIFE

1.

2 YEARS BEFORE THE MURDER
OF ANDREA TRASK

St. Jean Cap Ferrat, France

"The rich are different from you and me," F. Scott Fitzgerald wrote. Max Roarke was indeed different, but not just because, as Hemmingway quipped, "The rich have more money." Although Max Roarke's immense fortune would account for much of what made him who he was, money was by no means the only element shaping his life. To those who benefited from his largess, he seemed to have no set plan to guide him beyond the moment, moving frequently, as he did, from one place to another, from one pursuit to the next. He lived like some myopic potentate who assumes because he is financially powerful, he does not have to subscribe to the rules and accepted conventions that govern ordinary men. That being said, it must be acknowledged that everything he touched in his business life was ultimately successful. Only his martial forays had each been its own distinctive shipwreck.

It was assumed by those who knew Max, though not substantiated by any observable evidence, that he compensated for some gnawing emotional distress by permitting himself unlimited indulgences like the simultaneous maintenance of four houses on different continents, five apartments and three permanent hotel suites. He could take off for any of a dozen cities around the world carrying only his briefcase knowing that one of his cars would be waiting at plane side, that appropriate clothes for the season and locale would be pressed and hanging in his closets, that his bar would be stocked and a properly attired valet – preferably female – waiting to do his bidding. In truth, these travel appurtenances had been so much a part of his adult life, he rarely gave them much thought and would never have intimated that they were antidotes for his series of conjugal failures. Which, certainly they were not.

As the pilot of his custom-built Bombardier Global 8000 touched down on the Nice, France runway and taxied across the tarmac to the general aviation hanger, Max found himself recalling that his most recent ex-wife, Esther, had described this particular aspect of his life style as a study in unconscionable extravagance and conspicuous consumption. "He's like a spoiled little boy," she once said, "never denied his ice cream." Last month in court she had expanded and specified what she believed to be the root cause of his puerile personality. "He is a victim of self-inflicted financial insularity that has stunted his perspective of the real world and left him narcissistic, vainglorious and morally bloated."

My God, the woman did have a way with adjectives, he thought. *Call it what you like, but the sheer convenience of stepping off my plane into my car sure as hell outweighs whatever character enhancing benefits Esther might have thought I would gain by waiting for luggage to show up or subjecting myself to the calculated indignities of customs officials.*

"Get lost, Esther," he said aloud to no one through clenched teeth and then forced himself to dismiss her from his mind.

The plane rolled to a stop, the decrescendo whine of the engines told him they'd been shut down. The copilot appeared from the cockpit and immediately pulled the handle to open the door and lower the hydraulic steps. Max said a few words of thanks in his fractured French and hurried down the steps to his waiting red Lamborghini Aventador. Within four minutes of touching down, Max was driving west past the familiar white facades of the luxurious hotels that stand lined up like portiers français on the town side of the Promenade des Anglais. He glanced over at the stone beaches. He knew that a week or two ago, this place had been a human zoo and he was glad he missed it. Now, with the arrival of September, most of the lemminglike French who had converged here in August had gone home.

As he left Nice, he was more than a little surprised to find the road virtually empty and he quickly gave in to the desire to let his Aventador have its head. He eased down on the accelerator and the car responded by pushing him back into the seat. In seconds the needle was inching toward 160 kilometers. As the car leaned gracefully into the curves streaking toward Villefranche, he saw the western edge of the Cap Ferrat peninsula stretched out across the bay beckoning him home like an old friend. Oh, God, it felt good to be here, away from the turmoil and mess of the summer. With that thought he was suddenly gripped by a great burst of impatience. He wanted to be at his villa now. He wanted to be sitting on the terrace with Robby and Andrea sipping champagne or cold provincial wine. He wanted to be talking and laughing, Yes laughing, there'd been so little of that as of late.

At Beaulieu he turned onto the neck of the peninsula, drove past the turnoff to the little village of St. Jean Cap Ferrat which, like the thumb on a child's mitten, juts off at an angle pointing in the direction of Monte Carlo. He glided past the high garden walls and magnificent villas all spattered with pools of sunlight sifted by the tall, graceful umbrella pines that stood along the roadway like flying buttresses supporting the soaring vaults of some ancient Gothic cathedral.

Another two kilometers and he was at the wrought iron gates which, in anticipation of his arrival, had been opened. The creamy beige colored villa dominated the seventeen-acre estate on top of the Cap Ferrat peninsula, with ocean and mountain views in all directions. The house itself reflected some forgotten designer's fidelity to traditional 18th Century French architecture with its arched doors and windows and graceful second floor balconies.

Max got out of the car and followed the cut stone pathway to the back of the villa. In front of him were the mirrorlike rectangular ponds of his gardens surrounded by a lush lawn dotted with topiary box bushes. Beyond and to his right the azure Mediterranean, to his left St. Jean and the backdrop of the mountains which plunged dramatically to the sea. The formal gardens were laid out in a series of sections representing different architectural and planting styles. There were endless rose bushes, a Japanese garden with a pagoda, a Sevres garden, a steep dry garden planted with lavender and other herbs synonymous with Cote D'azur, and a stone garden designed around pieces of Roman and medieval bas relief carvings. In the middle was as series of dramatic reflecting ponds that, at the flick of a switch, would erupt with dozens of jets of water that would spurt and sway like choreographed ballerinas as if under the command of some invisible water elf. The ultimate effect of the estate was that of a beautiful dream conjured up for the personal pleasure of its master.

For a long moment Max simply let his surroundings invade his senses like perfume from a beautiful woman. The slight breeze was fresh and mellow and he could literally feel the tension drain from him like stale air escaping a deflating balloon. Though Max always listed the mansion in the Hamptons as his official residence, this, more than any other place, he identified as home.

His mind drifted off to the edges of nirvana where it paused, like a cliff diver contemplating his leap, before he consciously snapped himself back. *Got to call Robby and Andrea*, he thought as he turned and walked up to the large terrace that led to the grand rear entrance of the villa. As per instructions, his staff who worked at remaining virtually invisible, had maintained all the rooms exactly as he'd left them two summers before. He insisted that while the rooms should be kept clean, immaculate in fact, his personal effects were to remain exactly where he'd left them as if somehow they were to be treated like objects de arte on display in a museum. If papers had been scattered on his desk, if books had been left on his bed table, if blueprints from some project had been taped to the wall, if movie scripts for some anticipated production lay on the floor, they were to remain untouched so that, whatever the length of his absence, it would appear, and to a degree feel, as if he'd just stepped out and would return any moment. In this way, he maintained the illusion of continuity in his life.

Max picked up the phone to call Robby. A maid answered and told him that Monsieur Trask was away in Paris for several days.

"Est Madame Trask a la maison?"

"Oui. Qui est a l'appareil, s'il vous plait?"

"Monsieur Roarke."

"Une moment."

Actually, he thought, *I'm glad Robby's away. I'd really like some time with Andrea, alone.* Of all the women he'd ever known, there was none with whom he could be more honest, more fully himself. She was his oasis in a desert of drifting inconsequential sands. No pretenses needed, no affectations required, no clever repartee necessary. With Andrea he shared an emotional tie that went beyond even her marriage to Robby.

How long has it been? he wondered. *Four years? No, more than that. Let's see, did she ever meet Esther? No, no, of course not.*

"Hello, Max?" came her voice.

"Andrea, my love, why aren't you here drinking champagne with me on my terrace? How long does the prodigal have to be home before his friends come kill the Dom Perignon?"

"Max!" Her voice soared with delight. "We've been expecting you all summer. When did you get in?"

"About five minutes ago. Didn't Robby get my email? I told him I was coming,"

"He didn't say anything about it."

"Well, all I can say is that it's pretty darn inconsiderate of him to run off to Paris and spoil my homecoming."

"He'll be back Saturday. Oh, Max, I must see you this instant."

"Wrong," he countered playfully. "It is I who must see you. Do I come there or do you come here?"

"I'll come there." She paused for a moment and then asked tentatively, "Was it awful?"

"Was what awful?"

"The divorce."

"No, just your routine round of name calling, recriminations and vicious outbursts," he answered sounding very blasé and removed. "It was a little like surviving a case of shingles."

"What was she like? Esther?"

"Nondescript."

"Nondescript?" she echoed in disbelief. "A wife of yours nondescript? That's very hard to accept Max."

Max cut her off. "Andrea, hang up the phone and get your lovely tush up here and promise me there'll be no more talk about Esther."

"Then you're mine again," she teased though it sounded very much like a statement of fact.

"Absolutely, now and forever," he replied and she hung up.

Max replaced the receiver, rang for his valet and instructed him to ice the champagne and place it on the back terrace. Then he hurried upstairs to shower and change.

* ~ * ~ *

Max had a strong body, showing little of his forty-two years. His chin was still square and firm and his black hair betrayed not even the slightest hint of grey. His body language spoke of total self-assurance like some confident animal on the prowl for the next conquest. His piercing blue eyes commanded a certain deference from men and inspired the hope of an amorous encounter from more than a few women.

Max had been blessed with good health and an abundance of talent. And he had been given the wherewithal to live at the top of a world most people only dream of. He'd produced motion pictures, built and managed major corporations, bought and sold baseball and football franchises, been the financial benefactor for myriad artists and had bedded some of the world's most desirable women. Little of what he did went unnoticed by those who make it their business to notice what the elite rich do. As a result, his face and name made frequent appearances in all of the gossip laden weekly tabloids and he became as recognizable as familiar landmarks. Much of what was written about him was critical, yet even his critics were quick to admit that he possessed an incredible ability to succeed in most everything he attempted. Only as a husband had he been a failure. And three times at that.

His last marriage, while not as stormy as the previous two, was in many ways the most distressing. He had, for reasons which he could now not begin to fathom, concluded that the problem with marriages one and two had been his susceptibility to beautiful women with little intellectual depth and absolutely no interest in things domestic. Max decided what he needed was a woman who, though attractive, knew how to cook; a woman who liked to read good books; a woman of varied interests; a woman, as Robby had so delicately put it, who "knew her ass from third base." It was from this list of particulars that Max conjured up the image of Mrs. Number Three.

Enter Esther Findlay, the flower of Dayton, Ohio. His friends were frankly shocked by his choice as she possessed none of the physical attributes of his former wives. But Max simply dismissed their opinions as typical of the vapid Southampton mind which is devoted solely to the exterior peripherals of the human condition

Esther. Esther. The name lay like alum on his tongue. In the kitchen she proved to be a culinary magician, in the living room she was a repository of essential information on any subject, but in the bedroom she was simply unskilled labor. How, he asked himself, could he have so misjudged her sexual proclivity during their premarital couplings? How could he have misread her so badly? He, Max of a thousand beds. It was bad enough she proved to have all the conjugal inventiveness of a Methodist Missionary. What made it worse, as Max soon discovered, was that she was absolutely impervious to instruction. Her response to what Max regarded as an adroit and highly stimulating oral technique was an uncontrollable giggle. The fact of the matter was sex, for Esther, was simply a male intrusion like having to entertain an uninvited guest at a dinner party to which she, as a dutiful wife, would submit herself unless she could talk him out of it.

Her primary bedroom rebuff took the form of belittlement, "Why don't you read tonight Max and improve your mind? Let's give Homer," as she called it, "a little rest." Then she'd reach over and pat his member as one might a small dog, blow it a kiss and return to her book.

Max took that for about two weeks and then one night responded, "The hell with improving my mind, I want to fuck your brains out."

She sighed with the kind of resignation one expects from a mother who has given up denying her child cookies, pulled up her night gown over her breasts and said, "Well, come on, let's take care of your problem."

Max's first inclination was to file for divorce. But this was number three and somehow he had to try and make it work. There was a lot about Esther he liked outside the bedroom. So, determined to avoid the travails of another divorce, he decided to sublimate his pent-up frustrations into other pursuits. He began speculating in international real estate ventures which his advisers condemned. Yet, through the sheer power of his personality and hours of tenacious dedication, he tripled his investments. And Esther? She cooked and read and managed his houses and, when he demanded, submitted herself for his pleasure such as it was. *My God*, he found himself asking after every session, *could anyone be so backward in the 21st Century?* The answer always came back with a resounding *"yes."*

During the second year of their marriage, Max said, "to hell with sublimation" and knowing Esther would refuse to accompany him on a turkey shoot, used that excuse to cover his pursuit of several dalliances. Affairs would be too strong a word, they were simply sexual dalliances like the acts of some dog in search of random bitches in heat. Pure animal sex. Erupted passion. Pleasure greedily taken. Then one evening, after too much wine, he brought it all to a head. He confessed, as it turned out, in far more detail than good sense would dictate. He expected her to demand a divorce then and there. *Good*, he thought, *it would be a lot easier on my conscience if she were to ask for it*. But no, that was not her intent at all.

"I'm going to France for a while," she announced with cool evenness, "and think about our relationship." Slowly a note of vindictiveness crept into her voice. "Then again, maybe I won't think about us at all. Maybe I'll have an affair with some sexy Frenchman."

I pity the poor Frog, he was tempted to say.

After Esther went to bed, Max found himself fantasizing her involvement in some extramarital diddling. Who knows, maybe it would unleash the floodgates. At the very least, he concluded, an affair would put them on some kind of adulterous parity.

Esther left for Paris the next morning and landed not in the arms of a man, but on a tour of famous European Cathedrals. By her own count she visited twenty-five churches in six countries in twelve days and lit forty-three candles for Max's soul. She came back untouched, virtuous, forgiving and ready to begin again. Max filed for divorce two weeks later. The settlement she asked for, and eventually won, was substantial which seemed to appease her irate father who let it be known Max would be as welcome as locusts should he ever decide to return to Dayton, Ohio.

* ~ * ~ *

Max heard the slow crush of wheels on his washed gravel drive and quickly headed for the front door, arriving in time to see Andrea emerge from her Porsche. *My God,* he thought, *was it the memory of Esther or was Andrea truly as beautiful as she looked at that moment?* She was wearing something filmy and blue. The sun caught her from the back offering a stunning silhouette of the long lithe legs that had been indelibly etched in his memory from that summer so many years ago. Max, like every other man, never failed to be drawn to her body for she possessed a tantalizing symmetry.

What made her body all the more desirable was the prismatic facial beauty she had to go with it. There was about her a sense of sophisticated sensuality that appeared to emanate from deep behind her dark brown eyes. Her brown hair with its slight red tint seemed to invite fingers. The nape of her long neck cried for exploration and her mouth curled up slightly giving her a perpetually enigmatic smile. She was the type of woman who dominated a room and Max could imagine that even thirty years from now she would still find herself the object of admiring glances and prurient fantasies.

Why hadn't he married her? He could have. She wanted him more than Robby, there was no question in his mind about that. Why had he let the opportunity slip by? Of course, he knew why. He had let himself be coned... yes, conned was the word... into that stupid Tour de Francis with Robby.

Max would have taken another moment to simply drink her in, but now she was walking, half running toward him with arms outstretched.

"Max!" she cried falling into his arms. "Oh, Max how I've missed you."

"My God, you do look fantastic."

"It's so good... so good..." she said raising her face to his and giving him what was no more than the perfunctory greeting kiss expected between friends.

She pulled away, searching his face with her eyes and then said in a tone that was somewhere between tease and desire, "You are mine again."

She met his mouth once more, this time the kiss was full and spoke of distant remembrances. After several seconds she pulled away lowering her head to hide the embarrassment of her sudden unrestrained show of passion. Max stood inert, like a school-boy who had just been awarded an unexpected trophy, trying to formulate a proper response. She saved him the trouble, taking his hand and leading him toward the front door of the villa.

"OK, enough of the 'heavy stuff, where's my champagne?"

"Awaiting her majesty in a bucket of ice on the terrace," he said picking up the lightness of her banter.

"Where have you been, Max? You were supposed to be here in June."

"True," he said simply, holding open the door to the terrace.

"And then we got word it would be July."

"The word was correct, the facts otherwise."

"And nobody knew where you were in August."

"I couldn't tear myself away from Dayton in the summer."

"What?" she asked uncomprehending.

"That was intended to be a joke, though it totally lacks humor."

A flash of understanding crossed her face. "Oh, of course. Esther. Dayton."

Max picked up the champagne, untwisted the wire bale and pointed the top of the bottle toward the garden. "Did you know the Guinness World record for popping champagne corks is 102 feet 11 inches?"

"You are a wealth of information Max. Are we going for the record this afternoon?"

"Absolutely," he said pushing at the cork with his thumbs. "It's the only accomplishment in life that has eluded me."

"I'm almost ready to believe that."

Max popped the cork and it flew an anemic twenty feet. Andrea laughed, her voice cascading like bright tinsel across the terrace.

"And that, my love, is indicative of how things have been going for me as of late." He poured the champagne into two cut crystal glasses, handed Andrea hers and offered a toast, "To new beginnings."

Andrea's face dissolved into what appeared to Max to be a touch of melancholy, "Yes, to new beginnings," she said and turned slightly away from him.

Max was tempted to probe the meaning behind the sudden change in her mood but decided now was not the time.

They spent the rest of the afternoon catching up on the whereabouts of old friends and discussing various events back in the States. As the afternoon drifted through another bottle of champagne, Max realized they were both making a conscious effort to avoid any topic that might force them to mention Robby's name. Somewhere along the way they had tacitly agreed to bar him from their conversation. In any other situation, with anybody else, Max would have regarded this exclusion as an implicit contract between a man and woman bent on having an adulterous affair. Why chance letting an inadvertent dose of guilt spoil the carnal appetite? But in this case, here with Andrea, he was not prepared to believe she had intentionally excluded Robby for that purpose. Yet, that's what appeared to be happening and the mere thought of unspoken prospects sent ripples of longing through his body.

At seven, they got into his car and drove down to the village of St. Jean for dinner at La Voile d'Or, a quiet, one-star Michelin hotel and restaurant standing like a quiet sentinel watching the comings and goings in the small yacht harbor.

It was after ten when they finished and night had fallen over the mountains bringing out the pearl-like strands of lights that are draped along the three corniches – roadways that provide a major link between Nice and Monaco. They lingered long over Cognac and then strolled out onto the grassy terrace overlooking the water. Max found he was taking advantage of every opportunity to touch her, to place his hand on the small of her back, to grasp her arm, to press his body lightly against hers as they stood there letting the dark fill in around them. Gradually, he began to sense she wanted him as much as he wanted her. Nothing was said overtly. There was none of the fumbling, oblique references to sex or the tentative testing one hears between new acquaintances who fence with words to see if bed is their mutual objective.

As they left the hotel, Andrea took his arm and Max signaled for the hotel valet to bring his car. Her head fell lightly on his shoulder and he detected just the slightest sigh. They fell silent and in the silence Max found himself having to confront the one thing he'd been actively trying to ignore all evening. This was not just another woman he was taking to bed, this was his best friend's wife. Yes, he'd slept with her in the past more than a few times. But that was before she was married.

Yet, what he felt toward Andrea at the moment seemed to transcend the responsibilities of friendship. It was almost as if the woman beside him existed totally apart from the one that had married Robby. This was his Andrea, the one who had selected him to be her first that summer in the Hamptons, the one who had wept in his arms two nights before her wedding. This was the woman he had said would always be his only love. This was his Andrea and he needed the emotional refuge that waited in her arms. For a moment, he thought his conscience might accept this rationale, but it did not. She was, after all not two women, but one. And now, to make matters worse, Max could feel Robby's presence ready to spring upon them like some vengeful creature lying in wait beneath the veneer of the evening.

Andrea must have sensed his dilemma because as they drove away from the hotel toward his villa, she decided it was time for Robby to join them.

"I'm going to file for a divorce."

That, he hadn't been prepared for and it showed.

"Are you really that surprised?" she asked.

"I had no idea."

"Oh, I think you did," she challenged softly. "You've sensed something was wrong. How else could you explain the fact his name hasn't been mentioned more than twice since this afternoon?"

Max nodded as a concession to her point, "He hasn't exactly been the center of attention."

"And yet..." she paused and sighed in resignation, "he's been with us all evening; hovering. Making himself conspicuous by his absence."

"Is this something recent or..."

She cut him off, "I've been thinking about it for some time."

"Does he know?"

"Not yet. I've been trying to screw up my courage all summer to tell him."

"I hate to ask the obvious, but what happened?" For an instant he thought even hoped she might say, *"I never stopped loving you, Max."*

Andrea took a deep breath and looked emptily out at the night, "I don't know if I can give you an adequate answer. The problem, at least part of it, is what I call terminal indifference."

"What?"

"Indifference. He doesn't hate me, he doesn't love me, he's just indifferent. And then there's his obsessions with pushing everything he does to the edge..."she paused searching for the right word, "to the edge of wherever there's an edge. There's no feeling between us at all."

"Not even in bed?"

"In the words of the critic, 'Our performance lacks passion.'" She laughed derisively, "Yet, and this is really beyond my comprehension, unless he intends it as some kind of bizarre punishment. When he's drunk he loves to tell people 'My wife is the *best lay in the world.*' The words are his, the italics mine," she added with sarcasm.

"He's always been a master of subtlety."

"And then, there's the matter of the other women."

"Other women?" Max's response carried more surprise than he intended.

"Oh, come on, Max, spare me the pretense of shock. I'm sure you knew, everyone else does. After he bought the movie studio to compete with yours, the casting sessions on his couch or in his car or wherever he found a place to lie down were endless. I didn't so much mind the one night stands as long as he was discreet." She paused and looked away. "That's a lie. Of course, I minded. But more than that, what I can't tolerate is having to play the role of the female cuckold."

"Have you talked to him about any of this?"

"We don't talk Max. It's become an emotional impossibility. All we do is exchange information: 'I've fired this maid. I've invited these people to our next party. I'm going to be out of town for a couple of days.' It's all very mechanical."

Max pulled into his driveway and turned off the motor.

"I don't want to talk about him anymore," Andrea said firmly. "I want to make him go away. If only it had just been you on the beach that summer, how different our lives might have been?"

"If it had just been me, would you have admitted you were... ..?"

She cut him off. "Probably not. But that was then. This is now." She leaned over and put her hands on his arms and looked at him with a plea for cooperation. "Please Max, let's send him away. At least for tonight."

Max nodded his agreement but wondered if it would be possible. Robby's presence was now firmly entrenched between them like a thorn covered wedge. Then without thinking he said, "Maybe you'd like me to take you home."

Andrea said nothing in response, just looked at him with an expression which said it was unseemly and unfair of him to be testing her.

"I'm sorry," he said, "that was a bush league question. I couldn't take you home even if you wanted me to." Max leaned over and met her mouth. When they pulled away both reached automatically for their door handles and within seconds they were in the villa walking upstairs to his room.

Max snapped on the lights as she turned her back waiting for him to undo the catch on her dress. With sensual deliberateness she let it drop away. Max could not resist taking a moment to savor her full round breasts. As his eyes drifted down her body he noticed she'd been sunbathing in the nude all summer and he wondered how Robby could have become "indifferent" to this. "Please Max," her words echoed in his head, "let's send him away."

Max quickly got out of his clothes and drew her to him, their arms tightening, pulling them close. He felt her breasts against his chest and he was growing hard. Ever so slightly she began to move her hips from side to side, brushing him, teasing him. Her eyes danced with the delight of anticipation, his mouth moved closer to her parting lips and in that moment, Max succeeded in sending Robby far, far away.

2.

2 YEARS BEFORE THE MURDER
OF ANDREA TRASK

St. Jean Cap Ferrat, France

During the years in which he wasn't married to one of his three wives Max, because he was who he was, had no end of beautiful women sharing his bed. But all too often he found his ardor ebbed when he discovered their morning faces revealed the previous day's skill with makeup. That, he was sure, would never have been the case had he married Andrea. That he had not married her he regarded as the biggest mistake he'd ever made. It was that thought to which he opened his eyes and rolled over expecting to be greeted by her on the adjoining pillow. It was empty. He pushed up on an elbow and quickly glanced around the room. He found her standing just outside the French doors on the balcony overlooking his gardens. She was wearing only a large towel which she'd draped toga-style around her shoulders.

"Now that is a sight a man could look forward to waking up to."

"G'morning. I was beginning to wonder if you were going to spend the day there."

"What time is it?"

"Almost eight-thirty."

"Then my timing is perfect. I told Monique to bring up our breakfast at eight-thirty." Max positioned several pillows against the bed head and propped himself up, stretching contentedly. "You really gave me a workout last night."

"Max!" she snapped, mildly offended but also a little amused, "I would prefer to think of last night as an act of love, not a visit to a gymnasium."

He laughed and put his hands up in acquiescence, "I stand duly admonished for my tactless choice of words."

"I hope so," she responded with mock reprove.

"How long have you been up?"

"I don't know, since about seven, I guess. I couldn't get back to sleep so I came out here to enjoy the morning." Small fingers of wind caught her hair, tossing it up in the sun like silky wings. She made a reflexive, absent gesture with her hand to tame them. Her attention was riveted somewhere far in the distance. "This reminds me so much of my villa in Anasara."

"Anasara? Oh, I remember your telling me about that and your step father."

She nodded and her mouth turned up in a private smile.

"What is it?" he asked.

"Oh, I was just thinking. Mother married him fully intending to outlive him and inherit all that money. But he fooled her. He outlasted her by two years. I think I was more in love with him than she was. Such a dear sweet man."

"I assume he left you the villa."

She nodded. "It's been my refuge the last few years. Robby doesn't like it much. Mainly he doesn't care for the people. I find them very tender, very considerate. I think they'd do anything for me just out of respect for my step father." Again, the sea wind teased her in a provocative way and the wisps of hair seemed to contrive to carry her into an abstracted silence. "Max, do you ever feel alone? Really alone? As though you were drifting in a sea of people who cared about you only because you have money?"

"Well, let's just say I have no illusions as to why some people count me high on their list of friends. But I understand that. I accept it."

"I guess I can't. I often wonder what would happen if suddenly everything I owned simply evaporated."

"You'd probably get a lot fewer Christmas cards," he said with a brief laugh.

She turned away, said nothing for a moment then turned back," After that summer we first met and you went back at Yale, did you ever think of me?"

Max knew there was only one answer, "All the time. Yeah, a lot."

"Between pranks?"

"You heard about those," it was more a question than a statement.

"At almost every dinner party, after Robby has too many drinks, he rolls them out in excruciating detail like they were war stories. Frankly, I'm embarrassed every time. Actually, I'm embarrassed for you both."

"I guess you have to write them off as the product of two very bored twenty-two-year olds who had far too much time on their hands."

"You're lucky you didn't get arrested."

"At the time we never gave it any thought. I guess we should have. But then, I've done a lot of dumb things in my life ." Then in an effort to get off the subject of pranks, he added, "Like not spending more time thinking about you." When she smiled, he knew he'd been successful.

A knock on the bedroom door was followed by a maid with a breakfast tray. She had long ago accepted her role she was to see nothing, to say nothing, to be a part of the invisible staff. She set the tray on the balcony table, laid out the place settings, made a brief check of the table and left, never making eye contact with either Max or Andrea. If she was not invisible to them, they were to her.

They sat down at the table and Max poured the coffee as Andrea looked out toward the sea. She slipped away from him for several moments into a private corner and he saw a melancholy mist cloud her eyes. In an attempt to break the sullen mood that had suddenly overtaken her, he made a feeble attempt to bring her back. "Do you get to Anasara very often?"

"Sometimes. Sometimes. Whenever I need to get away and think."

"About what?"

"Oh," she sighed wistfully, "about my life. About things that might have been," she said looking directly at Max. Then she turned away, "And more recently about divorce." Again, she fell silent and gazed out over his gardens. She turned back to him. "Sometimes I feel so alone, even when Robby is as close as you are. I still feel so very much alone that it frightens me."

His response was so automatic and impromptu, that it surprised him, "Maybe I can change that."

"If only you could."

Max said nothing for several minutes as he stared at the woman across the table, thinking about their lost years. His question bordered on a non-sequitur, "When have you been the happiest?"

"Now," she said simply and the night I told you I was twenty-one."

"And when were you the least happy?"

"Now," she answered again and began to cry.

3.

2 YEARS BEFORE THE MURDER
OF ANDREA TRASK

Saint Paul de Vence, France

They left Max's Cap Ferrat villa just before noon and drove up to the walled city of Saint Paul de Vence some twenty kilometers northwest of Nice. After walking the narrow streets, visiting shops and watching the old men playing at boules, they had lunch on the garden terrace of La Colombe d'Or. The day was soft, the conversation flowed happily and they drank a great deal of cold white wine, then rented a room in the hotel and made love.

Afterwards, Andrea fell asleep and Max found a day-old copy of La Monde which he read until he too dozed off. When he awoke, Andrea was still sleeping and he found himself looking at her face and wishing he had the ability to put it on canvas. He was in love with her again, just as he had been so many times in the past.

"You were dreaming," he said as she opened her eyes.

She smiled and blinked, "How'd you know?"

"By your eyes."

"My eyes were closed."

"Yes, but they were moving beneath your lids. Eyes do that when people dream. They move as if they were following whatever it is you're seeing in the dream."

Andrea eased off the bed and walked to the window, looking out at the roof tops of St. Paul. "I was back in New York working for the magazine again. We were racing to beat the press deadline and everyone was very bus. It was wild and confusing and oh, so much fun. I'm sorry I gave it up."

"Why did you?"

"Robby insisted. During the first year he was jealous of any interest in my life that didn't include him." She smiled ironically." Funny, at first everything I did mattered to him and then, just like that, nothing about me mattered at all."

Max shook his head sympathetically but said nothing in hope she'd quickly leave the subject of Robby. She did not.

"He'll be coming home, tomorrow," she said emptily.

"And?"

"And I've made up my mind to get it over with, I'm going to tell him I'm leaving."

"Just like that?" Max asked.

"Just like that."

"What would you say if I were to ask you to marry me once the divorce is final?"

She turned toward him." What would I say?" her tone was introspective." I'd probably say, yes. But I'm not sure it would be the wisest answer."

"Then you accept?"

"Have I been asked?"

"I'm asking now."

"Yes, I guess"

"Guess?"

"No guesses. Just yes."

He got up from the bed and took her in his arms.

"Could we sustain it, Max? Or would you grow bored?" She searched his face."

"It's hard to imagine anyone growing bored with you."

"Robby apparently did."

"Then Robby's a fool. When it comes to you, I'm not. I think I'll make you a good husband. Maybe even very good."

A smile crossed her face, "Based on your past performance? I'm not sure that's a foregone conclusion," she teased.

He laughed, "I concede the point." A moment's gap, then intently, "We'll make it work. I know we will."

"I'd like it to work, Max. Oh, you can't begin to know how much."

"I do love you, Andrea and you have to know I always have."

"Ditto. I know that's not very romantic, but ditto says it all."

He gave her a simple light kiss as if to seal his proposal. "Do one thing for me," he said.

"Anything."

"It won't be easy."

"What?"

"Wait a day before you tell him. Maybe two."

"Why? The sooner I tell him the better."

"I know, but I'd like to have a chance to talk with him first – face to face. In fact, maybe it would be better if I told him about us."

"I can fight my own battles, Max."

"I know you can, and if it were somebody other than Robby." He stopped short of finishing his thought. "Let me just say that I think in this case, considering how long he and I have known each other, well... I just feel the rules of the game say it's up to me. I want to be as honorable about this as I can."

"Rules of the game? Honorable?" Max's comment had triggered a spontaneous emotional combustion. "What are you looking to do, announce to the world that you took me honorably and fairly…that you played by the rules? I can just hear you. 'Robby old pal, Andrea plans to divorce you. And oh, incidentally, because I'm an honorable guy, I feel I should tell you I've been screwing your wife for the last couple of days. What fun! But then, hey, what are friends for?" She turned abruptly away from him and buried her face in her hands. "If I had any sense, I'd put on my clothes and run as far away from you as possible."

Max crossed the room and put his hands on her shoulders attempting to turn her toward him. She refused to move. "Andréa, please understand, just because I love you doesn't mean I hate Robby. I don't know why he fell out of love with you. That's his loss. But I don't hate him for it." Her silence said more to him about his relationship with Robby than words. She pulled away and walked over to the window. He sensed they had reached a turning point and it concerned him that he did not know what they would find around the corner. "He's my best friend." His attempt at offering an explanation sounded weak.

She turned back to him, "He's your worst enemy!"

"Maybe both," he admitted.

4.

2 YEARS BEFORE THE MURDER
OF ANDREA TRASK

St. Jean Cap Ferrat, France

As they left St. Paul for the drive back to Cap Ferrat, Robby, uninvited by Max, made his way back into their conversation. Andrea's mood had turned dark and along with ignoring breakfast found it important to vent her frustration over what she perceived as the combative relationship between Max and Robby.

"I don't know what anyone would call the things that have gone on between you two, but it certainly isn't friendship. Friends are supportive and you two are totally destructive. That Picnic Mountain thing you did to him. The memory is like a festering sore."

Max was contrite, "I went too far that time. I had no idea it would be blown so much out of proportion. You can thank the goddamn press for that."

"I don't think he's ever gotten over it. You scored a direct hit on where he lives... in his ego."

"But that was over seven years ago. I can't believe he's still... ."

She cut him off, "Believe. Friends don't hurt each other that way, Max."

She was right, of course, he thought. *When he challenges me, I just don't seem to be able to refuse. Maybe I really hate him and want to hurt him. Look at what's happening here. How much more can I hurt him now? I'm sleeping with his wife and talking about divorce so I can marry her.*

For what seemed to Max like an eternity, Andrea fell silent clearly mired deep in her thoughts and Max hoped Robby had gone away. But he hadn't. He surfaced again.

"Do you know what Robby's been doing all summer?' Andrea asked as they drove into Nice. He's had a tennis pro working with him day and night. And you know what for? So he can beat you. He's been working all summer long just so that he can get you on the court and beat your brains out. It's become an obsession with him."

"I'm not surprised. For as long as I've known him, he can go overboard at times. Never satisfied unless he's the best. But when it comes to tennis, well, tennis isn't his game. He's never won a three out of five match from me in his whole life."

"Well, he will this time."

"He's gotten that good?"

"He's gotten that good," she replied and then, "There!" She pointed an accusing finger in his face. "I can see it already. I wish I had a mirror so you could have seen that expression. For an instant, I wasn't even here. You were planning how you're going to beat him. I'm right, aren't I? If you had to make a choice right now between getting Robby on the tennis court or me in bed, you'd be on the court."

Max could not hold back a smile, "Not quite true."

"It is true," she snapped, "and it's not the least funny! You do things to each other – bad things. There's a strange kind of chemistry I just don't understand. All I know is that it's bad, bad!"

"I'm sorry. I guess Robby and I've just been at it too long. It's almost instinct now."

"Well fine," she said with cutting intensity, "maybe you two can have an affair. I want no part of either of you!"

Immediately she began to cry and Max knew it was going to take a lot of words and much reassurance to undo the damage of the last several minutes. He admonished himself, *how in the hell did I let this happen? Fucking idiot!*

They drove back through Nice and made their way through Villefranche toward Cap Ferrat. Nothing was said until Andrea reached over and laid her hand on his. The look on her face spoke to distant memories. Other, better times. "Sometimes Max," she said softly, "I think about us... you and me... and I cry. I cry over what a naive, ego driven woman I was when I suggested I let you and Robby decide who I should marry. I would have chosen you right then and there, but I was so afraid I might hurt Robby's feeling. Hurt Robby's feeling?" She punctuated the question with a short self-rebuking laugh. "What a fool. I was more concerned about hurting him than I was about my own happiness. Dumb! Dumb. Twenty-three-year-old dumb."

Max found himself thinking about how much different their lives would have been had he, not Robby, married her. "You weren't the dumb one, I was."

"When all of a sudden you disappeared out of my life, I thought you had totally lost interest in me."

"No, I died a little bit every day of that year. You have no idea. But I can promise you one thing, I am not going to lose you again."

She turned toward Max, "Tell me something, two nights before my wedding when we went walking on the beach... and when we made love on the sand..."

Max finished her sentence, "I knew at that moment I was losing the one person in my life who really mattered to me. It's not often you know at the time it's happening that you're making the biggest mistake of your life."

"I would have left with you that night. You know I would have."

"Yes, I guess I knew. And don't think I wasn't tempted to ask. But I couldn't have done that to Robby. It wouldn't have been fair."

"Fair?" Andrea challenged. "We're talking about marriage, not some kind of game where you're expected to play fair. You don't marry someone because it's fair. You marry them because you're in love. Sure, I loved Robby, but not like I loved you. Oh God, I was so tempted not to show up at the church. How much easier, how much better it would have made everything if I hadn't."

She was right, of course, he thought. Being fair to Robby should never have been a consideration. But how could he explain to Andrea, even now after all these years, that thing, whatever name you might give it, which was embedded in their relationship. Then there was their tacit pact, the understanding that when you won, you won. When you lost, you lost. And the unspoken rules of the game – their game – said you had to accept that. He had lost Andrea. And Robby had won.

"Max, I promised myself I would never ask, but I have to know, what happened? After you and Robby... well kidnapped me from my engagement party, we were also so close for almost a year then, suddenly, you just disappeared. I know you said when you left us in Paris it was because of some major business problems you had to deal with. But you never came back. Was it something I did that drove you away?"

Max had expected one day she would ask for an explanation. He had considered any number of responses. He opted for a lie. "Well, I just felt that, like they say, three was beginning to be a crowd. It was pretty obvious to me that you really preferred Robby so I thought maybe it was better if I just disappeared."

Tears came to her eyes, "Oh Max... oh Max, you fool. How could you have thought that?" Andrea turned away unable to give voice to the thoughts racing through her mind.

Well, I certainly made a mess of that, he thought. If there were words that might have been right for the moment, that might have stemmed the tears, he could not find them.

Andrea's body language was negative and introspective. "I don't know, Max. I've got to be kidding myself to think there could ever be anything lasting between us. Not as long as Robby is around. Because as long as he's a part of your life, you'll always be playing your sophomoric, infantile games until one of you ends up destroying the other. What drives you two? I just can't understand it."

* ~ * ~ *

It was not the way either of them wanted to end their three days. Yet the prospect of what was before them and the dark residue of the morning had all conspired to envelop them in an oppressive grayness that rode with them all the way back to Cap Ferrat.

"Want to come in?" he asked as they drove up and parked in front of his villa.

"Need to get home," she said getting out of his car.

Max quickly got out and opened the door to her car. As she sat down he watched as her skirt pulled all the way up to her mid-thighs. *Great legs*, he thought. For a moment he considered insisting she come inside. *Maybe if we made love, I could erase this morning.* The expression on her face told him there was no chance of that. He settled for words. "I love you, Andrea. I always have and I always will. I promise, we'll put Robby out of our lives. I want to be with you for the rest of my life. I want this to work for us. And it will, I promise."

She smiled slightly indicating his words had struck home. "I want it to work too. I love you so much, Max. I love you so much it hurts." Her eyes asked him to kiss her. He leaned in through the car window. The attempt proved to be a bit awkward. Leaning in to the car, he missed her mouth and connected with her chin.

"Works better when we're in bed," he said.

"Much better," she smiled, making a quick adjustment to meet his mouth. "I do love you." The look on her face told him she was back. The morning was behind them. She started the engine and put the Porsche in gear. Max watched as she pulled out of the drive, then slowly walked into his villa, through the great hall and out onto the terrace. He sat down on one of the chairs and found it oddly curious that he was almost relieved Andrea had gone home. It was not, he knew, for any lack of love on his part, he just needed time think without the distraction of the woman he had just asked to marry him.

II
THE ENEMY OF MY ENEMY...

1.

24 YEARS BEFORE THE MURDER
OF ANDREA TRASK

Amberly Preparatory School

The first time Max Roarke spoke to Robby Trask he knew he had met the enemy. The instant animosity quickly became mutual. Max had come to Amberly Prep in his freshman year. By his junior year, he had established himself as *the* man on campus. He was the quarterback on the undefeated football team. He had won three wrestling metals and was the top scorer on the lacrosse team .

Robby did not arrive until his junior year. He had been expelled from his previous prep school for having installed a beer fountain in his room and entertaining, in blatant violation of school rules, some willing young ladies from a near-by girls' school. His father was not about to let be known the real reason for his only son's expulsion and decided to announce that Robby was transferring to Amberly Prep because of their superior athletic and academic programs. The delivery of a major financial gift to the previous prep school was all it took to expunge Robby's youthful transgressions from his record.

Robby immediately sized up the campus pecking order. First, there was Max and then, everyone else. If you weren't on the first, second or third tier list of Max's friends, you were not counted as even a peripheral member of the most important clique at the school. Robby knew that to gain the kind of recognition he felt was his due, he would have to dethrone the king. That meant he had to prove he was a better athlete or find some way to embarrass Max in the classroom or dorm.

By the spring of his first year, Robby's determination to cut Max down to size had not only failed, but his heavy-handed efforts had turned all but a few of the other boys against him. Robby was reduced to living at Amberly in social limbo. He looked upon his failure not only as frustrating, but intolerable. It was during a spring lacrosse practice that Robby found a way to release his pent-up frustration. It was only a scrimmage, but Max was on his game. Robby had been assigned to guard Max on defense. It was a disaster. Max was embarrassing him by scoring from every angle and then rubbing it in with a show of unnecessary exuberance. Like a matador waiting for the right moment to take out the bull, Robby waited for the perfect opportunity to take out Max.

Robby positioned himself in front of the goal as if daring Max to try and score. Max took the bait and ran direct at Robby then, at the last moment, faked to the left, spun around and started to pass him on the right. As he did, Robby drove the handle end of his lacrosse stick hard into Max's gut. It was hard enough to knock the wind out of Max. As there were no referees on the field, and the coach had been momentarily distracted, no foul was called. Once Max had regained his wind he turned on Robby,

"What the fuck ya doin.' Trask? One more cheap shot like that and I'll run this stick up your ass."

"Whatsamatter? Can't take it big man?" Robby taunted.

"Fuck you!" Max shouted as he ran back toward the center of the field It wasn't but a few minutes later Max had the ball again and was streaking down the right side of the field. He had drawn another defenseman who was doing his best to knock the ball out of Max's lacrosse stick. Robby waited until Max was close and focused on the goal. He then ran to Max's blind side, stuck out his foot and sent him flying with an illegal trip. Max went down hard and let out a short yelp of pain. Robby walked to his fallen foe, look down at him and said, "How's the view from down there, asshole?"

Max sprang to his feet. The sticks where dropped, the gloves came off and the two boys went after each other with a vengeance. The fight lasted less than a minute before a voice boomed, "Stop! Stop this immediately! We do not tolerate fighting at Amberly."

Both boys drew back when they recognized the voice belonged to Kimball Perkins, the Amberly Headmaster. "You two boys will be in my office in exactly five minutes."

As they leaned over to pick up their equipment, Max gave Robby a hard push. Robby kept his balance and swung his stick at Max just missing him.

"Are you boys deaf? Enough! If you would like me to call your parents and let them know you've been expelled, I will be happy to accommodate you."

The threat registered. Max and Robby agreed to an unspoken, but momentary, cessation of hostilities. Behind his back, the boys referred to the headmaster as Uriah Heap after the Dickens character in David Copperfield. Like Heap, Perkins was tall, lanky and pale with red hair and lashless brown eyes. When he walked, he looked as if none of the parts wanted to move in the same direction. Over time, the headmaster's less than affectionate nickname was shorted to "Heap."

Perkin's office was in the house Amberly provided its headmaster. He opened the front door and waited for the boys. "Into my office," he ordered sternly. Once the boys were seated in front of his desk, Perkins sat down and adjusted his glasses, which seemed to treat the bridge of his nose, which constantly glistened with perspiration, like a water slide. "I must say I was appalled by your behavior on the lacrosse field. As you well know, we do not tolerate fighting at Amberly at any time or for any reason. Amberly, has always thought of itself as a school for young gentlemen who behave like gentlemen at all times. I do not care to know the reason for your unsportsman like display on the field. That is not important. What is important is that it not happened again. Ever! At Amberly, we regard all young men as brothers. Now, I'd like to have you stand up, face each other, shake hands and promise this will not happen again."

The two boys stood up and looked at each other intently. There was no tacit truce. There was no contrition, no overt indication the headmaster's words had even dented their resolve to hate each other.

"Now shake hands," Perkins demanded.

The handshake became a bone-crushing contest. Each was determined to inflict as much pain on the other's hand as possible without giving any indication to the headmaster that the combat had resumed under the cover of their bogus pacification.

"You can leave, now," Perkins said with a confidence that bespoke his presumed success as a peacemaker. The boys picked up their equipment and left the house. They got no further than the end of the walk before they were at it again. "You son of a bitch! 'I'll get you tomorrow!" Max threatened.

"Kiss my ass!" Robby snarled.

"You'll have to mark it with an "X" because you're all ass to me," Max snapped back.

Both boys dropped their equipment and the punches began to fly, each doing his best to inflict as much damage on the other as possible. Perkins ran outside and tried to separate the two boys who had quit punching and were now trying to wrestle each other to the ground. "Stop!" he shouted. But they would not stop. Fortunately, two faculty members were within earshot and hurried over to help Perkins drag them apart.

"Back in the house!" Perkins commanded. "I can see my attempt to prevail upon your gentlemanly nature has had no effect. I think stronger measures will be necessary to assure there are no further altercations." Perkins declared their lacrosse season was over. Despite the protest and pleadings of the coach, both boys were removed from the team. Perkins decreed the only fitting punishment to correct their undisciplined aggressiveness was for the boys to report to him immediately after classes and perform various services in his yard and house. "How they hell can Heap make us pick up dog shit?" Robby growled as he and Max began the task of clearing Perkin's backyard of dog deposits.

"How many dogs does he have?"

"I've counted three."

"Look at the size of these turds."

"They're big fuckin' dogs."

"He can't make us do this?"

"You don't think so?" Max challenged.

"No."

"You want to tell your old man you've been expelled?"

"No fuckin' way."

"Then ol' Heap can make us do anything he wants."

In addition to ridding Perkins' back yard of daily dog droppings, the boys were made to perform a spring clean-up, to trim bushes, fertilize the lawn, wash windows, rake the gravel drive, clean out the basement, vacuum and dust all the rooms on the first floor. The jobs they were assigned were bad enough, but the punishment was made worse in Perkins' fastidious penchant made him near impossible to please. He was on them constantly. Nothing they did seemed to satisfy him. Jobs done once, often had to be done a second time, and even a third.

By the first week of May – the fifth week of what they regarded as their indentured servitude and two weeks before the end of the semester – they had developed a deep resentment and loathing for their headmaster. But at the same time, they had come to appreciate the truth in the old bromide 'The enemy of my enemy is my friend.'

"We got to figure a way to pay him back... big time," Robby said one afternoon as they walked back to their dorm after a particularly long work session. "Yeah, but we've got to be sure whatever we do, there is no way Heap can know it was us," Max pointed out.

A week later, while on poop patrol, Robby said," I think I've got an idea. Heap told me as of this Friday, we're done. He feels we've learned our lesson." "We've learned it alright. Now we should teach him one," Max added.

"Two weeks from now, on Saturday morning, he's hosting an alumni breakfast here at Amberly. Apparently the trustees are going to decide if they want to renew his contract for another five years."

"How do you know that?" Max asked.

"I overhead the staff talking in the administration office. This is his big show. He's pullin' out all the stops to impress the alumni with what a great shit he is as headmaster."

"So, what's the idea?" Max asked.

"The breakfast meeting is to start at 8AM. What if Heap didn't show up?" There was wily smile on Robby's face

"Why wouldn't he show up?" Max asked.

"Because he won't be able to get out of his bedroom."

"What are we doing to do, lock him in?"

"Better than that. Much better. Remember when he had me take down all his books in his library and sort them alphabetically?"

"Yeah."

"Well, I took the opportunity to liberate a key to his front door and to do a little scouting on the second floor. The night before the breakfast, say about 3AM, we let ourselves into his house and Superglue his bedroom door shut. No way he'll get out."

"Couldn't he get out through a window?"

"Not unless he's ready to drop two stories into his hydrangeas."

"What if when he wakes up he has to take a piss or a shit?"

"He'll have to hold it or take a dump in his bed."

Max broke into a full-throated laugh. "Love it. There's just one thing."

"What's that?"

"Once he gets out, you gotta know he's going to come looking for us."

"I've thought of that. He won't find us because we won't be here. At least that's what Heap will think. My mother is going to send a limo for us on Friday to take us to Boston for the weekend to see a couple Red Sox games. My mother will send Heap a letter asking for his permission to let us leave school."

"Standard procedure."

"Except the limo isn't going to take us to Boston. We'll hide out in Holyoke with a couple girls I know until Friday night and then sneak back to campus and into his house."

"What if he gets suspicious and calls your mother to check to see if we were actually in Boston ?"

"Not going to happen. The following Monday my Mom is off on some friggin' cruise. There'll be no way to reach her."

"You know, for a basic dick-head, you really are one devious son-of-a-bitch!"'

"I'll take that as a compliment."

* ~ * ~ *

They returned – or gave the impression they had returned – from Boston on Sunday night. Word of what had happen was all over the school. Apparently, no one had thought to go looking for the missing headmaster until around noon on Saturday. It took the fire department only a few minutes to chop through the door. It was reported that the moment Perkins was freed, he made a dash for the bathroom. He arrived at the alumni meeting in time to corner the trustees just before they were about to leave campus. Perkins hastily explained he had been the victim of a malicious and dastardly practical joke. When asked what he planned to do, it was said the trustees were more than a little taken aback by Perkins' response.

"I will find the little shitheads who did this and make sure the bastards not only have their asses expelled, but that no college in the universe will ever accept the sons-of-bitches."

Heap was never able to identify culprits. While Max and Robby were at the top of his list of suspects, their fake alibi was never exposed. It was the next spring the boys decided to confirm Perkin's suspicions as to who had glued him into his bedroom. They would do it at the moment when he would no longer have any ability to punish them.

It had become a tradition at Amberly for the seniors to pull some kind of benign practical joke the night before graduation. The prank the seniors settled on involved filling over a thousand paper cups with water and carefully placing them on the floor of the main school building. Then they padlocked the doors and left a note saying the keys were at the bottom of the Amberly swimming pool. At gradation, each boy agreed to carry an empty paper cup with the words. "We were all in on it" and give it to Perkins as he handed them their diplomas. Perkins expected this class, like all previous graduating classes, would pull some type of night-before-graduation practical joke and reveal it during the ceremony. He had always looked upon the senior prank with good humor.

As Perkins presented each boy his diploma, he was, per plan, handed a paper cup. Like the rest of the graduating class, Max and Robby approached with their cups to exchange for their diplomas. But, unlike the rest of the class, their cups were not empty. Inside, they had placed empty tubes of Superglue.

"I think ol' Heap would have given anything to grab our diplomas and refuse to let us graduate," Robby said as they left campus.

"No chance," Max replied. "The last thing he'd want is another year of having to deal with us."

"Right on!" Robby responded and lifted his hand to exchange a high five."

2.

20 YEARS BEFORE THE MURDER
OF ANDREA TRASK

Southampton, New York

Max watched the naked woman walk out of the sea. At least to him she momentarily appeared to be naked. She was wearing a white, one-piece bathing suit that had become virtually transparent in the water – a tribute to the marvels of fiber chemistry. At first Max was embarrassed for her, but that was quickly replaced with the carnal appetite of a twenty-one-year young man's desire to see more.

As she walked up on the beach, he was fascinated by the way she tossed her head back giving her long silken hair the freedom to blow free in the wind. He marveled at the way she moved with easy, even strides across the sand to the place where she'd spread her beach blanket. She didn't sit down, but rather it seemed to Max that she glided onto the blanket with a gracefulness and control any fashion model would have envied. Max wasn't sure if he was feeling lust or love, but whichever it was, it undulated with unfiltered passion through his body.

"Look at that fantastic piece of pulchritude," Robby said as he sat down next to Max on the mosaic of beach towels they'd laid out. "Who is she?"

"Don't know. I've never seen her before," Max answered, his eyes straining against the glare off the water.

"You can see everything!" Robby exclaimed.

"And there's a lot of everything to see," Max added appreciatively.

"Boy, if she isn't an invitation to a dance, I've never seen one."

"A dance?" Max teased. "You want to take her to a dance? You go dancing; I have other places I'd like to take her." Max picked up his towel and the ice chest with the beer and scrambled to his feet.

"Where are you going?" Robby asked.

"I don't like the sand here or the company," Max said with mock seriousness as he stood up and started to make his way through the clusters of bodies, towels, and beach umbrellas between himself and the see-through bathing suit.

"You're gonna need some expert help with that," Robby said following on his heels.

"Does Andre Agassi need help on the tennis court? Why don't you go play in the sand for a while?" He knew Robby would ignore him, but at least he was determined to get there first.

"I would, but I forgot my shovel and pail," Robby retorted as he jumped in front of Max, taking the lead in their cross-beach quest.

They were both between their junior and senior years at Yale that summer. Their hair was light from the sun, their skins a smooth bronze. Their bodies were athletically hard and the muscles in their flat stomachs rippled like heavy ropes. Each day Max led them down to the beach to bask in the female ogles. Max knew what was on the minds of the doe-eyed younger ones, but he had neither the insight nor experience to understand the meaning behind the subtle scrutiny, the appreciative gazes cast on them by the 'older women' – the prospective Mrs. Robinsons. All he truly understood, and this mostly intuitively, was that their youth and bodies gave them title to the bounty of the beach and that summer was harvest time.

As Max approached the girl in the see-through bathing suit, he felt a surge of fleshy excitement watching her apply tanning lotion to her inner thighs. His mind danced off to a concupiscent fantasy in which he saw himself performing that particular service for her. He quickly abandoned the tenuous fantasy bubble as he saw Robby flick out his towel and let it settle next to her blanket. Quickly Max sat down on the other side and immediately the assault began.

"I'm from the official beach welcoming committee," Robby said seizing the initiative. "My name is Robby Trask." He paused a moment glancing at Max and then let his eyes wander back to her face by way of the nipples which were still on prominent display under the wet suit. He leaned close to her as if to avoid Max hearing, "And that?" He nodded toward Max. "Well, if we ignore him maybe he'll go away."

"I'm Max Roarke," Max said moving closer so that he was now sitting by her feet. Immediately he had to check the urge to lay a hand on her leg.

She looked at him and smiled broadly, "I'm Andrea Francis."

"We'll have to be careful of him," Max said with a look of dead earnest as he glanced at Robby. "He hasn't been out of the juvenile correction home all that long and they tend to get a little randy when you take 'em off saltpeter."

"Humor him, Andrea," Robby injected moving closer and touching her shoulder, "it's all part of his therapy." He looked over at Max and snapped his fingers. "Now, be a good boy and show us you do have some manners after all. Offer Andrea a beer."

Max dug into the ice chest, pulled out a can, opened it, and handed it to her, "My only regret is that it isn't champagne," he said with gallant aplomb.

"Thank you," she said, obviously pleased at the attention from both of her instant suitors.

Max reached back into the chest, pulled out another, opened it, and offered it to Robby. Just as Robby was about to take it, Max's hand closed like a vice around the aluminum can forcing the beer to gush onto Robby. "Sorry," Max said with hollow sincerity, "I forget my own strength sometimes."

Robby remained in total control and shook his head sadly as he took the deformed can from Max. Slowly his eyes met hers and in a low tone said, "It's a tragic case. He has the body of a bull, but the mind of a tractor."

Andrea was unable to suppress a giggle.

"Now back to business," Robby said. "In order for you to obtain your certified beach pass you have to be able to answer 'yes' and 'eight o'clock' to the following questions."

"Yes, and eight o'clock?" she had no idea what Robby was talking about.

"Are you free tonight and what time do I pick you up?"

"You'll have to excuse Robby if he seems to come on a little fast. You see, he realizes once you get to know him there's no way you'll say 'yes.'" Max found himself wishing he could simply make Robby evaporate. As that, he knew, was not an option, he decided his best strategy was to change the subject. "Do you live in Southampton?"

"No, I'm from Greenwich, Connecticut. My mother and I are here for the summer visiting my grandmother. That's her house down there," she said pointing to one of the large mansions just off the beach. "My mother is spending the summer interviewing replacements for my father."

"Recently divorced?" Robby asked.

"Officially just a year, but she's been working on it forever," Andrea said.

"You sound a mite bitter," Max observed.

"I happen to love my father. My mother gave him a raw deal."

There was a moment of awkward silence when no one seemed to know what to say or where to take the conversation. Max sensed that any more talk about her parents could very easily derail his quest to win her for the evening. Then Robby appeared to make a discovery. "You're a Virgo, right?"

Andrea's face lit up. "Right! August 26th. I'll be... ahh, I'll be twenty-one. How did you know I was a Virgo?" She was obviously impressed.

"I just knew. All the signs where there. I'm sensitive to people's aura and yours is definitely Virgo."

Max could see Robby had scored some significant points with a lucky guess and he bit back a sudden urge to shout 'bullshit.' Instead he moved to neutralize the impact Robby's Virgo guess had had on her. With all the objectivity of a casual observer he said, "If I remember correctly, that's the first time your birth sign ploy has worked for you, isn't it Robby?"

"You guys are just too much!" she laughed. "Do you always go at each other like this?"

"Only when the favors of a beautiful woman are at stake," Robby said.

The harmless give and take went on with only occasional respite for another half hour. Max worked to check Robby's pointed gibes and to protect the inroads he felt he had made with Andrea. Finally, Max brought them back to the primary objective.

"The big question still to be answered," Max said, "is which one of us are you going out with tonight?"

"Are you both asking me?"

"We're both asking," Max replied. "But we expect you to choose only one of us. Maybe I ought to rephrase the question to give you a better perspective: Do you want to go out for dinner and dancing with a suave, good-looking, very cultured young man like myself, or..." he paused, took a deep breath and followed with a long sigh, "or, do you want to endanger your good name and reputation by being seen on the street with him?"

"Andrea," Robby countered, "before you decide, I think you should know that Max here... well, how should I put it?" Robby seemed to be struggling for a tactful explanation, then appeared to give up. "The truth," he said in what Max read as mock embarrassment. "The truth, and I'm afraid it must be told, is that Max spends an inordinate amount of time in the shower room at the "Y" with young boys."

Low blow, Max thought. *I'd really like to wipe that smirk off his fuckin' face.* Anger began to leak up like acid reflux. Immediately he fought it back knowing if he lost his cool he'd lose any chance of impressing Andrea. He decided to turn Robby's fabrication about boys in the shower room to his advantage. The look on his face and his body language said he was stepping back from the competitive banter. Max did his best to sound both serious and embarrassed for his_friend, "I must apologize for Robby. That he's crass is pitiable; that he's uncouth is unforgivable. Not the kind of talk one would expect in front of someone like you."

Robby did his best to defect Max's apology, "I'm sorry Max," he said nesting his retort in a playful laugh, "I know how the truth hurts."

Andrea could not contain her laughter. "You two are crazy. I mean you're really crazy!"

I better lighten up, Max thought. "See what you've done to us? You've driven us crazy," Max ran his fingers playfully along the inside of her foot.

"How long have you two been friends?" She asked.

"Let's see," Max said. "We've been friends for five years."

"And enemies for six," Robby added.

"What? Friends for five, enemies for six?" she echoed. "How do you explain that?"

"It's a long story, Max said. "All you need to know is that at this moment as we wait for you to decide which one of us is going to take you out tonight, we're not friends but mortal enemies."

"And to avoid our resorting to violence, you need to prevent bloodshed by making a decision. Which is it?" Robby added.

Andrea shook her head and grinned, "As I said, you're both really crazy. But I like 'crazy.' However, as far as which of you takes me out tonight, I can't make a choice with you both sitting here. Why don't you flip a coin or something?"

Robby shook his head, "Naw, that's no good. Flipping a coin would leave it to luck."

"You got a better idea?" Max asked.

"How about some kind of contest?" Robby suggested, his mind spinning through a list of possibilities. "If there was ever a prize worth competing for, it's sitting right here." He exchanged a private prurient look with Max.

"We could play a set of tennis," Max offered, hoping Robby would be fool enough to accept.

Robby's face melted into a wry smile. "Now that is a truly sportsmanlike challenge coming from a guy who was second in the Ivy League tournament."

"Okay, think of something else."

Robby's face lit up. "Given the fair damsel who is to be the prize, the contest must be the essence of chivalry."

"Which is... ?" Max asked.

"A joust."

"A joust?" Andrea and Max echoed in disbelief.

"Yep. A motorcycle joust. We'll get our Harley's, bring 'em down here to the beach and try to knock each other off."

"And for lances we'll use sharp sticks," Max said sarcastically, fully intending to ridicule Robby's suggestion and to underscore the very real chance of inflicting serious pain. "Tell you what, you keep thinking up great ideas like that while Andrea and I take a walk down the beach. If we don't come back, wait here anyway."

"Well, if you're chicken..." Robby taunted.

"Listen, if we have a joust one of us will end up skewered like a beef kabob."

Robby started to sell. Max saw that the idea had captured his imagination. "Hear me out. My mother bought a couple of big rugs the other day and they came rolled up on these long cardboard cylinders. They're hollow, about three inches round and ten feet long. They'd make perfect lances. And because I don't want you to suffer more than just abject humiliation when I plant my lance in your chest, we'll strap boxing gloves to the ends of the cylinders."

"Where are you going to get boxing gloves?"

"Leave that to me."

Max was not surprised that he immediately found himself contemplating the pleasure of humiliating Robby by knocking him on his ass in front of Andrea.

"Come on, chicken liver," Robby taunted. "No way you can get hurt..." he paused and a grin slipped across his lips, "...much!"

Andrea looked first at one boy, then the other. It was almost as if they'd forgotten she was even there, so intent was their attention on the other. "Hey, she said, "Have you forgotten I'm here?"

"Forgotten?" Robby said expansively, "How could we forget our trophy?"

"You mean me?" she asked her eyes dancing with delight.

"Absolutely," Max said. As he stared into her face he realized that love and lust had become allies. He wanted her in every way possible. And if it took winning a joust to capture the incredible trophy sitting in front of him, then losing was not an option.

"I've never been a trophy before."

"There's a first time for everything," Robby said finding an excuse to touch her arm and slowly move it to her back. He turned to Max, "So, are we on?"

Max nodded and stared intently at Robby. Not only did he want to win a date with Andrea, but he was determined to knock the cocky Robby off his bike and, at the same time, punish him…to actually hurt him. Why? Just for being Robby, who at this moment he didn't like very much. "You're on, Sir Lunch-a-lot."

Max watched as Robby's face exploded with a look of exuberant satisfaction. He knew exactly what Robby was thinking; that he'd suckered him into a mano a mano he felt sure he could win. The anticipation of combat with his friend surged through Max's body leaving a sweetness in his mouth. Boy, did he want to clean Robby's clock. He'd ride the sonofabitch into the sea if he had to. No way was he going to lose this thing.

"Wait here," Robby said to Andrea, "we'll be right back. You're going to love watching what I'm going to do to Max."

* ~ * ~ *

Within twenty minutes they returned to the beach on their motorcycles, each wearing a football helmet, shoulder pads and each with a long, narrow, cardboard cylinder which they carried under their arms like jousting lances. Boxing gloves had been affixed to the ends of the tubes. They roared back and forth in front of Andrea at the water's edge gunning their engines, purposely steering through the receding waves sending up white fantails in their wakes, all to impress the object of their combat.

Max noticed that Robby exuded a smug confidence and appeared to fully relish the attention Andrea and the others who had gathered were showering on him. *Enjoy it now, asshole*, Max thought as he pulled up next to Andrea. *Let's see how cocky you look when you're eatin' sand.* As Max looked around at the gathering spectators, he realized the joust was taking on the trappings of a major event.

"Let's do it," Robby shouted over the sound of his engine. "First guy off his bike loses."

"You want to concede now before I embarrass you?" Max did his best to appear to be savoring the challenge and project a bravado confidence. At the same time, he wondered what kind of madness he'd let himself be talked into.

Robby responded with a derisive, "Sheee-it! This isn't even going to be a contest." A thought occurred to him. "Wait a minute, I almost forgot. We've got to do this thing right." He turned off his engine and called to Andrea.

"Andrea, since you're what this joust is all about, I think it's only right you do the honors." Robby reached into his pocket and pulled out a blue silk handkerchief. "When you drop this, the joust begins."

Andrea looked at both of them with concern, "Are you sure you aren't going to hurt yourselves?"

Robby answered with an extravagant bow, "M'lady, the prize is worth the pain."

"And pain will be the only prize he gets today," Max added.

Andrea forced a little laugh in an effort to mask her concern. "Well, at least don't go too fast, Okay?"

"Just fast enough to put him on his keister, which I will be doing shortly," Max said pointing his lance toward Robby.

"Better say it all now, Maxie baby," Robby shouted, " because in a few minutes you're going to be on your ass eating sand."

Robby rode his motorcycle down the beach. Max turned his in the opposite direction for about fifty yards, then came to a stop by performing a neat "J" turn. What was this he was feeling? Excitement? No, it was fear. "This is nuts," he said under his breath. *This is really nuts,* he thought, *getting hit with the blunt end of the tube – boxing glove or not – could hurt a hell of a lot, especially if we're both closing at thirty miles an hour.*

Andrea dropped the handkerchief and the two bikes started off, gaining speed quickly. Max found he was having difficulty holding his cardboard lance steady while maintaining control of his motorcycle. Robby looked to be having the same problem. Max passed Robby well to the right and both lances missed their marks by a wide margin. Max road back to the start, reset himself and waited for Robby to do the same. Andrea picked up the handkerchief and dropped it again. The sound of the revving engines rose above the crashing waves. Max could see they were going to pass much closer this time. He could also see his lance was going to miss badly. During his effort to adjust his aim, Robby's lance caught Max on the right arm. A bolt of pain ripped through his shoulder forcing his hand off the throttle. For a moment, he thought he might lose control of his bike. But the sudden deceleration and the braking action of the wet sand gave him time to put his feet down and avoid toppling over.

Once again they set themselves. Max's arm hurt and he wanted to rub it.

Can't do it, he thought. *Can't let Robby think he's hurt me. That would give the bastard too much satisfaction.* He'd let it throb. As he waited for Andrea to retrieve the handkerchief which had sailed off in a gust of wind, he decided the trick to jousting was to sucker the opponent. Max recalled how a good boxer will drop his guard, appearing to open himself to an opponent's jab, then to counter with a right cross when the other boxer has committed himself. All at once he knew exactly what he had to do.

Andrea dropped the handkerchief and they both began to accelerate. Max sat up high on his seat, purposely giving Robby a big and tempting target. At the same time, he made it appear as if he'd lost control of his lance. He could see Robby had taken the bait and was aiming directly at his chest. Slowly Max rotated his lance so that it was virtually perpendicular to his motorcycle. Too late Robby realized was happening. Max dropped forward, hugging the bike, taking away the target. Robby found himself heading straight into the broadside of Max's cylinder. It was like being hit with a swinging gate. Max passed by and then turned back to see his friend let go of the handles, his feet flying in the air. For a long moment Robby desperately tried to balance himself like a trick rider on top of the seat. His arms and legs flailed desperately as he tried to regain control and avoid the inevitable. *No way*, Max thought. He watched as the front wheel of Robby's motorcycle veered sharply toward the ocean tumbling him off and into the surf.

Max threw up his arms in victory, turned his motorcycle around and rode back to Robby who was on his knees taking off his helmet and wiping the wet sand off his face.

As Max looked at Robby he almost felt sorry for his fallen foe. But not so sorry as to resist taking a final shot at his friend, "Since you now have the night free, you can stay home and watch the Mets on the tube. Losers love company." With that, Max claimed his trophy, helping Andrea settle in behind him on the bike.

Max started off across the beach in the direction of her grandmother's house. Robby stood up and yelled, "Come back here you asshole! If you were any kind of man you'd make it two out of three!"

No sooner were the words out of Robby's mouth than Max lifted a fist high over his head and flipped a solitary finger skyward.

3.

20 YEARS BEFORE THE MURDER OF ANDREA TRASK

Southampton, New York

Max looked up from the book he was reading as Robby burst onto the Roarke terrace overlooking a broad green lawn that rolled out to the edge of the ocean.

"Tonight is the night. I'm going to part Andrea's luscious thighs," Robby announced with a confidence that, at least to Max, defied logic. He was not about to accept that the girl they had come to know was about to give up her body to either of them…or anyone for that matter. She may have exuded sex, but Max was sure she was not about to hand it out.

"What are you going to do, tie her up?"

"Nope. The floodgates will be opened and I'll be invited to help myself to the cake."

Max greeted Robby's confident bravado with a derisive laugh. "The only way you're ever going to get any cake is to perform cunnilingus on a box of Sara Lee."

"Laugh all you want, but tonight I collect the prize. I have fooled around with this reluctant roe long enough. I am going to ply her with food, wine and one of nature's own aphrodisiacs."

"You'll never get her to eat four dozen oysters," Max quipped.

"For your information, I am going to administer a little cantharis to the lady."

"Cantharis? What's that?"

"The proper name of a sure cure for crossed thighs – Spanish Fly," Robby answered with a mildly lecherous look.

Now he understood. He'd read how Spanish Fly was supposed to work as a libido enhancer. He'd also read that it could be lethal. "Where in the hell did you get Spanish Fly?"

"I have my sources."

Max could see Robby was thoroughly enjoying himself now. "I predict we won't be out of bed for a week." He turned to Max and clapped him on the shoulder. "Do me a favor will you? Bring up food and drink now and then."

Max could feel his temper begin to curdle. "Robby, that shit can be dangerous."

"Right. To me. She might never let me out of bed."

"No, I mean it. That stuff can do a lot of harm."

"Ah, bullshit. Not if you don't overdo it."

"Look, if she invites you into her pants, that's fine with me. But no Spanish Fly." He was lying, of course. The very last thing he wanted was for Andrea to issue Robby that kind of invitation. And it certainly was in no way 'fine with him.'

Robby's eyes narrowed, "What's the matter? Afraid she'll like it so much she won't go out with you again?"

Max made no effort to temper his threat. He was fuming. "You ever made love with a broken arm?"

Robby only glared in response.

"Cause you'll have to if you even think about laying that crap on her."

"Fuck you, asshole!" Robby exploded in a petulant whine. "Who the hell do you think you are telling me what to do?"

"I'm just telling you what you can't do…to her."

"Up yours!"

Max was as cold as blue steel. "Let me tell you something Trask, if I find you've given her any of that... if I even suspect it, I'll break your fucking neck."

For a moment Robby stared back and looked as if he might try to deck Max then and there. But Max could take him, they both knew that, and Robby was anything but a fool. The tense moment seemed to stretch on for minutes, then Robby broke into a strained grin. You asshole," he said and his tone indicated it was not a challenge, but a negative form of endearment. "Do you really think I'd give her cantharis? Come on! I was just pulling your chain. I love the girl. I wanted to see if I could get a rise out of you."

Max's expression barely changed. He didn't believe him. As far as he was concerned, Robby was not pulling anyone's chain. He knew Robby was backing off to save his ego and because he knew Max meant what he'd said. There were times when Max Roarke didn't like Robert Trask very much, not very much at all.

~~*

Max discovered the truth about Andrea that same afternoon. He had stopped in a sporting goods store to pick up a racket he'd left to be re-strung. As he waited for the clerk to retrieve it from the back room, he noticed a tall middle-aged woman rapidly sorting through the racks of tennis outfits. She was wearing a yellow silk dress that seemed to delight in its grasp of her hips and buttocks, and it occurred to Max that maybe older women did have some redeeming values after all. A sales clerk approached the woman and asked if she could be of assistance.

The woman turned to acknowledge the offer, "I'm trying to find something for my daughter's birthday," she replied, mildly frustrated by her apparent failure to do so.

Max found the resemblance more than striking. It was as if he were looking at Andrea twenty years in the future. It had to be her mother.

"It's hard to know what young people like these days. Their tastes are all so," she searched for a word, "inconsistent."

The sales clerk chuckled, "How old is your daughter going to be?"

"Andrea will be seventeen on August twenty-sixth." Mrs. Francis continued to rattle on about the fickleness of Andrea's tastes.

Max barely heard any of what she was saying. The number seventeen echoed in his head followed by a ripple of panic. *Sonofabitch! Andrea's still only sixteen. She told us she was going to be twenty-one. My god, that's jailbait.*

Quickly he turned his back on Mrs. Francis, shielding his face, as if afraid she might point a finger and announce to the store, *'There's the man who has been corrupting my daughter.'* That she'd never met Max in no way lessened his apprehension. Sixteen! That, he decided, began to explain a number of things. Once or twice he had found himself wondering why there were times she acted more like a giddy pubescent teenager than a girl about to step into full womanhood. He recalled certain expressions she used along with several naiveté questions. He'd been so intent on impressing her with himself, he'd simply ignored these inconsistencies. But now they all took on a different dimension. *Damn, to think of that body and face on a sixteen-year old.*

"Shit!" he said half aloud, feeling more like a lecherous old man than a horny twenty-one-year-old. He had to tell Robby. He paid for the racket, left the store, making sure to avoid Mrs. Francis, hopped into his Corvette and headed for Robby's. Slowly, the focus of his thoughts switched from Andrea's age to the hassle he'd had with Robby that morning. Of course, he had Spanish Fly. Of course, he planned to use it. That would be like Robby. He only backed down because he knew Max never made threats unless he planned to carry them out. Max's mind presented him with images of Robby slipping the "fly" into her drink. He imagined Andrea uncontrollably aroused, grabbing Robby, pulling him down on her, begging him to make love. And there was Robby, hovering over her, his hands roaming her naked body, tantalizing her, holding back, taking sadistic pleasure from her frenzied, drug heightened passion. Max slammed his fist down on the steering wheel and jammed his foot on the brake. He seethed with anger.

"That bastard! That bastard!" he repeated again and again. He wanted to get Robby. Get him for what he knew Robby planned to do. Get him for the sleaziness of dropping Spanish Fly on a girl like Andrea. Hatred flushed through his body and he began to think of how he might punish Robby. And then it came to him. A perfect, humiliating punishment. One designed to fit the crime. Imagine, Robert Trask picked up for contributing to the delinquency of a minor. The idea raised a question: Where would Robby be planning to take her this evening? Had to be Marty's Lightfoot. It was a magnet for the college crowd and those co-eds with fake IDs. All he'd have to do was pick up the phone, call the police and suggest a visit to Marty's. Oh, what he would give to have a hidden television camera in the bar to capture the expression on Robby's face when he discovered he was corrupting a sixteen-year old.

* ~ * ~ *

The police Sergeant found them in "Marty's Lightfoot" as they stood at the bar watching the dancers on the crowded floor. The officer who received the tip knew exactly who Robby was. He wasted no time asking him the question in front of Andrea: Did he know the young lady was a minor?

Robby looked legitimately surprised by the question. "Minor? What are you talking about?" Robby's tone was harsh and feisty.

The Sergeant remained cool and unflappable. "Have you got an I.D. Miss?"

Andrea was noticeably shaking as she fumbled in her purse and produced the fake driver's license. The Sergeant could barely conceal a smile, "You're a resident of Plano, Texas are you Miss… Miss Gonzalez? Gonzalez. Is that your name?"

Robby's expression revealed he knew the cop had her, but he wasn't about to let the inquisition go any further. "OK, so she's only twenty. She's going to be twenty-one on August 26th. Now give us a break, huh? Christ, if you're looking to bust minors, this place is full of them."

The Sergeant was dispassionate, "Twenty-one on August twenty-sixth? Is that what you told him young lady?"

Andrea froze, her face turned white and she was unable to speak.

Robby persisted in their defense. "Yeah, August twenty-sixth. Now what the hell difference does a couple of weeks make?"

"Probably very little if, in fact, that's all we were talking about.." The Sergeant turned and looked at Andrea, "Do you want to tell him or should I?"

Robby stared blankly, first at the Sergeant and then at Andrea. Beads of perspiration broke out on his forehead.

Andrea lowered her eyes and it appeared if she could have sunk into the floor and disappeared, she would have willed it then and there. She had become the center of attention. The band had stopped, a crowd had gathered. All eyes were on the girl with the russet brown hair in the scooped neck blue dress.

Tears began to flow carrying the black mascara down her cheeks in tiny rivulets. Her body started to shake and the look on her face was that of someone who had just been stripped naked in front of a crowd of curious oglers. Her lip trembled; she raised her eyes only as far as Robby's chest and could go no further.

"I'll be seventeen," she said.

4.

20 YEARS BEFORE THE MURDER
OF ANDREA TRASK

Southampton, New York

Max had been anticipating this moment. He knew Robby would come running to tell him what had happened. His anger had long since abated and there was a period, just before he called the police, when he almost changed his mind. *Come on*, he said to himself, *Robby can be an asshole at times, but he's still your best friend. Why am I going to do this to him?* He didn't have to think about the answer. He knew. Max was setting him up because Robby would do the same to him if he had the chance. Somewhere, on the subconscious level of their relationship, they both understood that.

He was in bed when Robby arrived well after midnight. Max pretended to be asleep when Robby burst into his bedroom. "You're not going to believe this," he said, the words spilling from his mouth, "The cops busted her. She's fuckin' sixteen years old. Fuckin' sixteen going on seventeen. We've been trying to ball jail bait. My God, we could have been arrested for statutory rape!"

"Not we. You. Especially if you'd used Spanish Fly." Barely able to contain himself, Max shook his head somewhat theatrically to convey his shock and disbelief. "Sixteen? Wow! Hard to believe. Then again," he added, "we should have suspected she wasn't twenty-one. We both knew the body was way ahead of the mind."

"Who the hell ever looked at her mind?"

Max decided to probe for more details of the arrest feeling sure that even his friend, who was little fazed, must have suffered a large dose of humiliation. "Must have been embarrassing, the police making a big fuss like that?" He could barely conceal how much he was enjoying what he regarded as Robby receiving his just due for what he had planned to do to Andrea.

"Embarrassing? Not so much for me. Hell, I can handle anything. But Andrea! The kid was mortified. Destroyed right there in front of me and a bar full of gawkers. It would have broken your heart to see her and there was nothing I could do. The fucking cop didn't have to pull that shit of making her admit her age to me. He didn't have to make a scene. The sadistic bastard. The goddamn guy, he fuckin' humiliated her. All he had to do was ask us to come outside and Andrea wouldn't have been embarrassed in front of all those people. I really do feel sorry for her."

Robby's words fell on Max like shards of broken glass. He was immediately consumed by a shameful despondence that churned dry and deep in his stomach.

Later that day, Max learned that Robby, who he knew had been released the night before on his own recognizance, reported to the police station and was arrested on a morals charge. The case never came to court because Andrea's mother refused to let her testify.

Like the hunter who shoots at a wild animal but accidentally hits an innocent by-stander, Max was tortured with the realization that he had taken perfect aim and hit the wrong target.

$$* \sim * \sim *$$

A week later Max saw Andrea by chance on the beach near her grandmother's house. For a brief instant he thought about telling her what he'd done, but quickly realized that he lacked the courage to admit he had been the source of her humiliation. He resigned himself to offering a lame commiseration. "I was really sorry to hear about what happened to you and Robby at Marty's. I think the cop over did it."

"It was my fault," she said lowering her head. "I should have said something."

"Hey, you're not the first kid to use a fake I.D. And you won't be the last. I want you to know I think you're special. You're sweet and... and very pretty. Hopefully, one day we'll meet again." Max would like to have taken her in his arms as though the physical contact would somehow remove the embarrassing residue of what he had done.

"Maybe... when I'm twenty-one... and legal," she teased.

"I hope you'll make that a promise." He wanted her to believe he meant it. Her reply was limited to a smile. But the smile said it was a promise she would try to keep.

"Andrea! Where are you?" It was her mother calling from the house.

"My keeper. Got to go." She gave him a quick kiss on the cheek. "I love you Max, I really do," she said and ran back to the house.

As Max watched her go he found himself wondering, *if she looks like that now, what's she going to look like in five years?*

5.

20 YEARS BEFORE THE MURDER OF ANDREA TRASK

Yale

Max did not see her again before he and Robby returned to Yale, where both men had established themselves as formidable football players, as masters of co-ed seduction, and the purveyors of practical pranks – played mostly on each other.

The pranks had begun simply enough that year when Robby put a product called Manic Panic, a counter culture hair coloring, in Max's shampoo turning his hair purple. Max waited a month before he retaliated by spiking a glass of red wine with something called Neutral Red so that Robby's urine ran red. Robby thought he was dying until Max confessed to what he'd done. Robby retaliated several weeks later when he and Max went shopping in a department store. While Max wasn't looking he placed two metal strips from inside the sensomatic security store tags he'd purloined in Max's coat and pants. As they left the store Robby stood back and watched as Max set off the security alarms and drew two very large security guards who made him strip to make sure he wasn't walking out with some merchandize.

Max decided to up the ante and rigged a bucket of odoriferous slimy goop in Robby's room designed to dump on him as he opened the door. It happened, but not as planned, when Robby returned to his room with libidinal designs on a compliant red head Robby, acting the gentleman, offered to let her precede him into the room. She got most of the slop and Robby got to spend the night alone.

In response, Robby covered Max's floor with fresh cow manure, then filled the room with millions of plastic packing peanuts, making it impossible for

Max to get into his room. As final touch, before he closed the door, he turned up the heat. It took only a few days to remove the packing peanuts and manure, but the smell lingered on for weeks.

Max found a way to get even and go Robby one better. He broke into Robby's room with three buckets half full of warm water and emptied bottles of liquid dish washing detergent in each bucket. Then he dropped three pounds of crushed dry ice into the buckets and barely made it out the door before the room virtually exploded in soapsuds.

As the football season drew down to the last few games, it was apparent to close observers that the opposing teams were not the only opponents on the field. Several times Robby, playing quarterback, called for an option play designed to pitch the ball out to Max, an All-Ivy tailback if it appeared Robby was going to get tackled. Four times in the second half Robby called the option play and each time, Max, who was wide open and would have scored easily, never saw the ball. While Robby failed three times to gain any ground, the fourth time he managed to find a hole and scored what turned out to be the winning touchdown. Max was not happy he'd been totally ignored by his quarterback. Though he was tempted to confront Robby who was enjoying hero status in the locker room, he held his temper. Next day a bumper sticker appeared on Robby's Porsche:

I'm the quarterback and I'm gay.

It was a week before someone pointed out the bumper sticker to Robby and it took him three days to scrape it free from the super glue.

Robby quickly decided on his response. The program for the last game had brief bios of each of the seniors, Robby managed to bribe an employee at the company that printed the programs and had a single line added to the end of Max's bio. After lauding his record at the Yale tailback, the last line read,

Unfortunately, Max suffers from small penis anxiety.

"Enough!" Max said to Robby as they met on what Max declared as neutral ground. "We're pushing this too far. A joke is a joke and a prank should be funny, but these last two... including mine, I admit we are getting too personal."

Robby's response was not what Max had expected. "I've been thinking the same thing."

"Yeah? Then are you ready to give it a rest?"

"You mean call a truce?" Robby asked.

"A truce. An armistice. A Pax Romana. Call it what you like."

Robby nodded and then after a moment said, "You know what I've been thinking?

"I'm almost afraid to ask."

"Why are we dumping on each other when there are so many assholes out there who deserve to be our targets."

Max started to laugh. "I like the way your brain works" Max added offering his hand to seal the agreement, "'When it works."

6.

18 YEARS BEFORE THE MURDER
OF ANDREA TRASK

Yale

Max and Robby's prank truce held through graduation which took place in May, but without either of them in cap and gown as both had failed to earn enough credits for their diplomas. To graduate, the Dean told them, they would have to return for a fifth year.

That summer Max decided he and Robby owed themselves an academic break from the studies they had not completed and bum their way around Europe – if having no limit on their American Express cards can be considered 'bumming.' It was, by Max's own admission, a non-stop drunk and debauch.

In July, Max fell in love with a zaftig blond from Zurich who had found peace in Zen and decided to say goodbye to Robby and travel with her to Tibet. Unfortunately – or fortunately – he lost her in a crowd in Athens and after two days of searching, he took off on his own and met a beautiful creature who he decided had to be a direct descent of one of Homer's Sirens. But rather then luring him to her shores (read bed) with her enchanting music, she proved to be a latter-day Siren when she lured him into an alley where thugs rolled him for his wallet.

Late in August, Max met up with Robby in Rome. "Yeah. It was right here on the Via Veneto," Robby explained. "I was waiting for a rather delicious young Italian lady I'd met the night before when who do I run into? Andrea. If we thought she looked like twenty-one when she was sixteen, you should see her at eighteen. She's incredible! Apparently a couple of model agencies have been after her, but she's not interested."

"You spend much time with her?" Max certainly did not want to hear that Robby had.

"All of about three minutes. She was with her mother, unfortunately, who gave me the kind of look reserved for child molesters and then politely invited me to jump in the Tiber."

The image of what that would have looked like brought a smile to Max's face.

They were both back at Yale in September carrying a light fifth year course load to earn enough credits for graduation. As they drove back to campus after a libidinous weekend at Vassar, Max saw something that became the nascent of a passion that was to evolve over the next several years into a something neither could have imagined at the time. They had just arrived on the outskirts of New Haven when they saw what looked to be dozens of white toilets piled one atop the other in front of an apartment building. Robby jammed on the brakes," Are they what I think they are?"

"Toilets," Max said "Looks like they're being tossed out."

"There's got to be some way we can put them to use."

"Pull over, there's a guy who looks like he might belong to the building."

Robby parked the car and they both got out. Robby walked up to the man who turned out to be with building maintenance. "What's going on? What's with all the toilets?" Robby asked.

"They've just been replaced with new, low-flow units. We got a truck coming tomorrow to take them away."

As they got back into Robby's car, Max said, "I sense an opportunity here. We must not let those commodes just go to the dump."

"What are you thinking?"

"I'm thinking they may be the making of a magnificent prank"

"So long as the target is a worthy candidate."

"Does Harvard fall into that category?"

~~*

By three in the morning, they had rented a 25-foot U-Haul truck and recruited a dozen undergraduates – all of whom were susceptible to ample bribes. They pulled up to the stack of toilets and loaded them into the truck. After three weeks of reconnaissance at Harvard, they were ready to act.

The U-Haul truck, followed by a van with the same dozen commode accomplices, pulled into Harvard Yard at 3PM. They had arranged for one of the Yale recruits, who boasted he could pick any lock, to open the service door to the Abbott undergraduate dining hall. It took a good deal of heavy lifting, but four hours later, the crew had removed the 76 chairs in the eating area and replaced them with lovely, porcelain commodes. As a final touch, Robby added a sign.

"Shit where you eat. It's a Harvard tradition."

The picture of the dining room made the local Boston television stations and all the newspapers. Max and Robby experienced a heady satisfaction unequaled even by the pranks they had played on each other. But the high wore off quickly and soon they began to cast about for a new target.

"How about those assholes at the Yale Law School? The bastards wouldn't let me retake the LSAT exam I fucked up."

"Did you tell them you'd been out drinking the night before?" Max laughed. "I mean how can they expect a guy to take a test as tough as that one when he's hung over?"

By the time they were on to their third beer, they'd come up with what they considered an appropriate prank attack on the law school.

It was after midnight when Max arrived at Robby's apartment driving a large truck with the same dozen undergraduates they've recruited as commode accomplices following in a van.

As Robby climbed into the cab next to Max he asked, "Well, farmer Brown, have you got everything?"

"It's a virtual Noah's Ark back there. Two of everything. Well, most everything."

They had picked Thanksgiving night as a time when they were sure the budding lawyers would be stuffing their gullets with turkey rather than stuffing their brains with the mush of legal case histories. By four in the morning, Max was able to step back and look at how they had transformed the huge library in the Yale Law School building into a barnyard with two and a half dozen farm animals standing befuddled on mounds of straw. The recruits stacked hay bales in front of the shelves of law books.

"And this," Robby said as he pushed in a wheelbarrow full of manure, "is the final touch. The smell of authenticity."

At seven in the morning anonymous callers alerted the editors of the school and New Haven's newspapers to the barn-like environment in the Yale Law building. The headlines over the pictures the next day reflected the readership of each publication:

Barnyard Law – Chickens Challenge Ducks
Pigs and Lawyers Make Common Cause
Law School Wakes to Find Itself in Deep Shit.

"Mission accomplished!" Max said as he read the article under the headline describing the mayhem their prank had created. "That'll teach the SOBs not to let you retake the LSATs," he laughed. "Anyway, you'd have made a lousy lawyer."

The newspaper reported that stern promises had been made by both university officials and local police to find the culprits and punish them to the fullest extent of the law. No arrests were ever made.

"There's only one problem," Robby said, "we didn't get a chance to enjoy our success in person."

"I don't think it would have been a good idea for us to have been found milking one of the cows." Max pointed out.

"True, but there's got to be some way we can be more involved," he laughed. "Without getting caught."

By early spring, they had conceived a new prank. One that would enable them to participate and maybe, they assumed, take its place in the annals of truly great college pranks. It took more than a month to set it up, but with the help of a plumbing and electrical firm – both of whom were paid more than either would have billed in six months – they managed to wire the toilets in a women's dorm at a Connecticut women's college with microphones and speakers. They set up their broadcast headquarters in a rented room just off campus and launched their latest prank on a Friday night in February.

Max heard the door to the bathroom open, followed by footsteps and the opening of a toilet stall door followed by the click of the sliding door lock. He motioned for Robby to come closer to the small speaker bringing the sound from the toilet. "I do believe we have our first customer," Max said. He waited until the sound from the toilet confirmed the coed was fully 'engaged' and then turned on the microphone.

"Hello!" the voice in the toilet bowl said. "I work for a toilet paper company and we're taking a softness survey."

The shriek confirmed the girl had made a hasty exit.

For the next two hours they entertained themselves delivering impromptu comments and requests.

"Please, don't dump on me."

"Hey, don't flush. I can't swim."

"What in the hell did you have for dinner?"

"You certainly do cover all of the seat."

"The moment you sat down, I knew I was in love."

Max was fascinated by the reactions from their victims which ranged from shock, to embarrassment, to unrestrained laugher to some very un-lady-like suggestions to the voice in the toilet. Several came back for a second visit and invited the voice to climb out of the toilet and meet them later. One even repeated her phone number, twice.

As their finale, when the last girl sat down and began to relieve herself, she found herself listening to a recording of the Star-Spangled Banner. Robby's voice demanded she show some respect and stand up.

As they left their rented room command center Robby said, "You think maybe we should take that one girl up on her invitation to give her a call?"

Max laughed, "Somehow, I don't think that's a good idea, unless you're looking to get shit on."

7.

17 YEARS BEFORE THE MURDER
OF ANDREA TRASK

Southampton, New York

Max, when asked, was apt to describe his father, Arthur Roarke, as a man who dealt in absolutes and demanded control over every facet of both his life, and it seemed to Max, his afterlife. Max was told if he expected to inherit the vast array of diverse companies that made up Roarke Enterprises, he would have to attend business school. Due to his less than stellar performance at Yale, he was refused by every graduate school to which he applied. But a substantial contribution to Harvard by his father was enough to convince them to overlook Max's anemic academic achievements and concentrate on reviewing the plans for the new building Arthur Roarke's largess had made possible. At first, Max resented the stipulation his father had placed on his inheritance. Hated it, might be closer to what he felt. *Why not just give me the money?* he asked himself. Let the dozens of guys who work for Roarke Enterprises manage the fortune for me. But that attitude was to change.

Much to everyone's surprise, and not the least his, Max discovered a dormant acumen for economics and cultivated a growing interest in finance. He, whose grade point at Yale had always teetered between marginal and unacceptable, never got less than a 4.0 during the two-year MBA program. And it didn't hurt that he was freed of the distraction Robby would have created had Robby not decided to cash in a substantial part of his trust to sponsor and drive for a Formula One race team on the Grand Prix circuit.

Max had arranged for his father to attend graduation, but the day before the ceremony word came that Arthur Roarke had an inoperable cancer. Within a week of the news Max was summed to Los Angeles to be with his father in his

Bel Air home. In the days that followed, Max came to know his father as a fastidious and detail obsessed business man whose marginal trust of his subordinates meant all of his mangers were kept on a short leash. Max realized that was why his father had decided to spend so much of his remaining strength finalizing his affairs and preparing his son to take charge of Roarke Enterprises. Max did his best not to let on that he was somewhat intimidated by the prospect of taking full control of his father's enterprises. But at the same time, his mind swirled with ideas for taking the company in new directions and pursuing new opportunities. At one point he even envisioned himself as a latter-day Howard Hughes. Movies? Airlines? Women? Life without limits. Heady. Very heady.

Having exhausted himself schooling his son and feeling Max was reasonably well prepared to take his place, his father announced he intended to return to the Southampton house. His parents had died there and he would do the same.

Arthur Roarke died on August twenty-third and the funeral was held three days later. During the reception, Max found himself sitting in the huge paneled library of the Southampton house facing a room full of his father's employees, lawyers, accountants, and the men charged with managing the various companies and concerns of the vast business empire. A tacit trepidation engulfed the room as the men attempted to take the measure of the twenty-six-year-old man who was now in control of Roarke Enterprises That they knew little if anything about Arthur Roarke's son had clearly set the mood in the room on edge. Max intentionally said little, taking a kind of perverse pleasure in knowing that no one had any idea of what he was thinking or what he was planning. He felt like Al Pacino in the last scene of *The Godfather* movie as each man took his hand and paid their respects to the new Don of Roarke, Inc. By four o'clock, the last of the limousines had pulled out of the drive and disappeared. At five the owner of the catering company Max had hired to handle the reception gave him a bill and left with his serving staff.

Max was alone for the first time since he had sent word to the organization's executives that his father had died. He had not expected to feel any sadness at his father's passing, but now he was treading in a pool of despondency and unable to understand why. His father and he had never been close and it was his impression that he had never been able to measure up to his father's expectations. He walked onto the terrace facing the sea and sat down on the stone balustrade railing. It was close to seven and the setting sun had turned the ocean surface into a million silver sparkles. His mind raced along on a track of thought which, despite his effort to control it, kept being derailed with doubts about his future. He had never really thought of himself as the guiding hand of Roarke Enterprises, but there is was. Maybe, despite his father's efforts, he wasn't cut out for it. He began to wonder if there was some way he could run the enterprise by remote control. Delegate. That's what his business school professors had preached. Delegate. Demand results. And if mangers don't perform, cut 'em loose. By remote control? Maybe.

Her voice surprised him totally. "I was sorry to hear about your father," she said.

Max's head spun toward the formal garden where the sun caught her hair giving it a luminescent red glow. The slight girlish pudginess in her cheeks he remembered from that summer five years ago had disappeared leaving a perfectly sculptured face. She was wearing a yellow blouse open in a mildly tantalizing "V" and a white skirt that clung to her legs as she walked toward him. In that instant of recognition all the feelings he had for her that first summer flooded back.

"Andrea!" Max shouted in delight ignoring her condolences. "Look at you! My God, it should be illegal to look that good." He vaulted over the railing and gave her a gentle kiss on the cheek.

"Like me all grown up?" she asked in a playfully coquettish tone as she performed a demure pirouette.

"I like you a lot," Max said consuming her with an appreciative visual inspection. "You back at your grandmother's house for the summer?"

"Yes, along with my mother. She just married Arturo de Marco Spaghetti."

"Spaghetti? His name is Spaghetti?"

"No, I just call him that. It's actually Arturo Speganni."

"And you don't like him," Max added his assumption.

"No, I *do* like him. He's very sweet. We get along terrific, but I still call him Spaghetti. It's my pet name for him and he loves it."

"Where's he from?"

"Rome, mainly. But he has the most fabulous villa you have ever seen on one of the Tuscan islands just off the coast of Italy. Both the island and the villa are called Anasara. I'd never even heard of it before. He's taking us back next week."

Max found himself staring at her nakedly as she talked and only averted his eyes when she cocked her head slightly as if to ask if something were wrong.

Lust and love were back and competing. "How long has it been," he asked, "four years?"

"Five," she corrected.

"Damn, I can't believe it's been that long." Then, a little embarrassed as he remembered what he had done, said, "You destroyed us that summer."

Their conversation darted into fragmentary reminiscences of the joust, their dates, and she apologized again for having lied about her age. As the sun settled into the ocean Max suggested they go into the village for dinner and she eagerly accepted.

"I think you better call your mother and tell her where you are," he said as they were about to leave his house.

"She knows where I am... I think. Even if she doesn't, she'll approve when she finds out. You see, mother is concerned that I confine my dating to rich young men. If he's poor, I can go out, but I have to be home by ten. If he's got money, I can stay out all night. She's the only mother I know who clears all her daughter's dates through Dunn and Bradstreet." Max joined her laughter at the idea.

After dinner they returned to his house. As they walked toward the door, Andrea grabbed his hand and pulled him toward the beach. "Let's go lie on the sand and look up at the stars. It's such a beautiful night."

It was not an invitation he was about to refuse. He couldn't believe that as they stepped on the beach he was actually nervous. Max Roarke nervous with a woman? No way His breathing was shallow and his heart was actually racing with anticipation. Andrea owned him. He could not remember a time when he felt emotionally closer, more in love with a woman. She could have demanded anything of him at that moment and he would not have denied her. The sky was pebbly with stars, the wind soft and pleasantly warm. For a long time they simply lay on their backs letting their eyes roam the heavens.

"Shooting star," Max said pointing.

"Quick, make a wish."

"Do you wish on shooting stars?"

"Absolutely," she replied and again there was silence.

After several minutes she said, "There was an article about your father in the *New York Times* yesterday. I had no idea he was in so many different businesses and things. He must have been very intelligent."

"Very rich anyway," Max answered flatly.

"The paper didn't say anything about your mother. Were they divorced?"

"No, she died."

"I'm sorry."

"It was a long time ago. I was only five so I don't remember her all that well," Max's voice trailed off.

"That must have been awfully hard on you... to lose your mother that young." There was sympathy in her voice, but the statement was couched more as a confirmation than an expression of pity.

Maybe it was the residual pall of his father's funeral, or maybe it was the desolate emptiness that had crept over him with the mention of his mother, or maybe it was a basic need, unique to the moment, to ask someone to share his pain. Whichever, he felt compelled to let go. "We were in a car. It was night on the San Diego Freeway just north of Los Angeles on our way to the new house my father had bought in Bel Air. My mother was driving and my older brother, Doug, was in the front seat. I was asleep in the back. A truck coming from the other direction blew a tire and jumped the median divider hitting us head on. They were killed instantly. I was trapped in the back and it took them almost two hours to cut me out, but I didn't have a scratch."

"How awful," Andrea said sitting up in reaction to the horror of the accident. "My God, what that must have done to you. The pain from something like that can last a long time."

Max nodded. "It stayed with my father until the day he died. He never got over it."

"You must have been close after the accident."

He found her assumption unsettling and immediately felt the need to share the truth about their relationship. "No, just the opposite. You see, while I was the survivor, I was also the reminder of what he'd lost. So he made it a point to see as little of me as possible. From the first grade on, I was sent to boarding school in winter and camp in the summer. I don't suppose I saw him more than five times a year."

"How could any parent be so cruel?"

For a moment Max considered telling her how homesick he was the first year at boarding school, how he'd wake up at night screaming, how they put him in the infirmary and called his father who came up to the school and raised hell with him.

"What kind of man are you?" Arthur Roarke shouted at the seven-year-old boy. "No son of mine is going to be a homesick pansy, not when I'm paying for the finest boarding school in the country." Max took the humiliating tirade in front of several on-lookers; his head bowed, doing his best to endure the verbal lashing. That afternoon, after his father left, Max went out and picked three fights he knew he couldn't win and got himself beat up in all three. It was only much later he even began to understand why he had needed to punish himself in that way. But he didn't tell Andrea any of this. Even twenty years later the memory was still acrid, the bruises still tender.

"The day before my father died I was sitting beside his bed listening to him talk about my mother. Just talking about how he'd met her and what kind of woman she was and I realized that in all my life I'd never really heard him talk about her. Pretty soon it dawned on me how much he loved her and I began to understand, or thought I did, how her death had destroyed any sensitivity he might have had. I was sure in his roundabout way he was trying to explain a lot about why he'd kept me at such a distance, about his whole attitude toward me. For those few minutes I felt this incredible urge to put my arms around him and say, 'Dad, I love you. I understand now.' But just then, he stopped talking, looked at me without any expression at all, and said, 'I'm leaving you a fortune, Max. Try not to piss it all away before you're thirty.'"

"I can't imagine a father saying something like that to his only son. Especially not on his death bed," Andrea said.

"I'll have to admit, I was hurt. Really hurt. I felt like saying, 'Yeah and I love you too, Dad.' I was tempted to tell him to take his fucking money and stuff it up his ass. But I didn't. I just wept. I don't know if he saw the tears and frankly I don't care."

At that point Max found himself feeling self-conscious. He'd opened himself more to Andrea than he ever had to anyone and now he felt emotionally naked and vulnerable. Yet, at the same time, it felt good talking to her and he sensed he could trust her completely. *Enough,* he decided abruptly. It was time to bury the past with the past.

"Come on," he said rocking to his feet. "It's late and I don't want your mother to come after me with a shotgun."

"She won't," Andrea responded not wanting to break the mood or bring the evening to an end.

"It's after one. Come on, I'll walk you down the beach to your grandmother's."

Though she tried, Max would not let her return to the subject of his father. Instead, he quizzed her about her graduation from Vassar, about Spaghetti's home in Anasara, any thought that came to him. At her front door he gave her a kiss and said, "I'm glad you came by. You made tonight an awful lot easier for me. Plus," he hesitated and looked deep into her eyes, "it was fun falling in love with you again. You are an extraordinary looking woman." They met for another kiss, more prolonged this time, but he pulled away in a show of discipline uncharacteristic of him. "I've got to go to France tomorrow. I promised Robby I'd watch his race at Dijon. He's actually driving a Formula One in Grand Prix races."

"I know. I read about him in a sports magazine. You can get killed driving those things, can't you?"

"Yes, but chances are he'll fall off one of the mountains he's been climbing before he dies on the track. The man is really living on the edge. When he isn't driving two hundred miles an hour on some road course, he's hanging on to the side of a mountain."

"He wasn't always that way was he?"

"As long as I've known him, he's always tended to push the envelope. But more so in the last couple of years since his old man died and he took control of a virtually bottomless, and I do mean bottomless, bank account. I get the feeling he's trying to prove something."

"What?"

"Maybe that he can make the cover of every sports and celebrity magazine or maybe just to prove he's invincible. Or maybe he just feels he has to be number one in anything he does... whatever *'anything'* happens to be." Max decided he didn't want to spend any more time explaining Robby's personality to Andrea, so he changed the subject. "Hopefully, I'll get back here before Spaghetti takes you and your Mother to Anasara. I'd really like to see you again."

"Me too," she said intently, her body language offering him an unmistakable invitation.

He knew he could take her if he wanted but chose instead to martyr himself. It was, he felt, a kind of masochistic decision. But given that Andrea had, during the evening, become far more to him than a sexual conquest he'd found walking out of the sea, it felt curiously good. Max started off toward the beach with a "good night" tossed back over his shoulder. After about twenty yards, he'd begun to have second thoughts about his role as martyr and turned back hoping she'd be standing there, waiting for him. She was nowhere to be seen.

So much for missed opportunities, Max thought as he trudged back along the beach toward the huge moonlit silhouette of his father's mansion. He thought about spending the night on the sand, but the prospect of being devoured by sand flies and mosquitoes drove him inside. He walked through the living room into the kitchen and poured himself a glass of milk. He flipped on the kitchen television and gave several channels a perfunctory glance, then turned it off and made his way into the foyer and climbed the wide, formal staircase. He walked down the hall, entered his bedroom and was about to turn on the light when he stopped, startled by the presence of a figure silhouetted against one of his windows.

"Who are you?" he asked unable to think of anything more original.

The figure turned and his suspicions about it being a woman were amply confirmed. Then she spoke from the darkness. "I seem to remember, almost exactly five years ago, one Max Roarke said he'd hope we'd meet again and I said maybe when I'm twenty-one."

Max could see now that Andrea was totally naked.

"Guess what?" her voice was playful and inviting as she reached over and pulled back the sheet and let it billow parachute-like back on the bed. "Today is August twenty-sixth, my birthday and I'm twenty-one."

"Happy Birthday," Max replied peeling off his clothes. "A happy birthday for us both."

8.

16 YEARS BEFORE THE MURDER
OF ANDREA TRASK

Paris, France

Max decided it was his obligation as a friend to endure in supportive silence Robby's drug-like high over his first Formula One victory. But there were times when the braggadocio laced in Robby's every conversation with the European press, and anyone who made the mistake of asking him about the win, tested his resolve. Robby had won the Formula One race at Dijon and then declared he was through for the year. He told the press he intended to scrap his current car and had hired a group of engineers from Ferrari to build him a new engine, while another group, ex of Boeing, had been given the task of vastly improving the aerodynamics of the body design. At the same time he announced he was going to pursue his longtime dream of climbing Mr. Everest the following May and needed time to prepare.

The only thing that had threatened to mar, and possibly cost him, his Dijon victory was the claim by another driver that he had fouled him in the second to last lap.

The article Max found in the sports section of Le Monde read: *The official report filed by the race stewards notes that Mr. Trask has been involved in five incidents in four races this season. While no final determination has been made, it appears he triggered Sunday's crash at Dijon when he turned into Oswell Malegaon at the hairpin corner. Malegaon had nowhere to go and the concertina effect lifted his car into the air and skimming across the front of leader Franco Salazar, who was fortunate not to be hit on the head.*

Much to the surprise of racing fans, while the collision was regarded as an extremely serious mistake and an error of judgment by Mr. Trask that eliminated leading contenders from the race, all protests were dropped without explanation from any of the parties.

Max folded the paper and handed it back to Robby. "Well at least they spelled your name right."

"Next time I get Malegaon on a track I'll run his ass into a wall. Hate the fucker. I'll get this," Robby said handing the taxi driver twenty Euros. "Gardez la monnaie."

"I'm impressed. Now you know two phrases in French."

"Come on, I'm buying," he said as they walked through the Ritz lobby and made their way to the small intimate Hemingway bar, named after its most famous patron. As they slid onto stools in front of the bar, Max said, "Tell me the truth, did you foul Malegaon?"

A sheepish grin crept like a thief in the night over Robby's face. "Well, maybe a little. Hey, when you're in a race, you're in it to win any way you can." Then he added, "As long as you don't get caught."

"And this time, given they dropped the protest, I guess you didn't get caught."

Robby nodded toward the bartender, "Two cognacs. Your best." He turned to Max, "Let's just say there are ways to deal with protests off the track."

"Meaning?"

"Meaning this topic of conversation is closed for the night."

"You're obsessed, you know."

"I'm a winner," he smiled victoriously. "And speaking of winners… "

Max was interrupted by a loud, "Howdy ya'all! I'm buyin' drinks all around."

"Where'd he come from?" Max nodded in the direction of a middle-aged man wearing a cowboy hat and boots who had just entered the bar.

"He's a loud son-of-bitch." Robby turned away in mild disgust." Let's hope Tex left his horse outside."

Max figured it took 'Tex' but a split second to decide he'd like to rope two French women sitting at one of the tables. When they saw the large Texan homing in on their table, they did their best to ignore him. He had no intention of being ignored.

"Looks to me like wherever Tex has been tonight, he was definitely over-served."

Max laughed, "I'm surprised he can even stand up."

"I've got a 100 Euros he falls off his cowboy boots in fifteen minutes."

As they watched, Tex pulled up a chair next to the women and almost missed planting his ample behind on it. Max said. "I'll take the bet. I'll say he never makes it past ten."

Both men shared a short laugh and turned back to the bar leaving the women to fend for themselves.

"Good cognac," Robby said taking a sip.

"You'll never guess who I ran into after my father's funeral."

"Andrea."

"How you'd know?"

"Who else would be worth running into after a funeral in Southampton? And... ?"

"And what?"

"And what happened? I mean is there still a prize to be had or have you collected?"

"Does your mind ever get out of your pants?"

"Got a better place for it to be?" Robby didn't wait for an answer. "So, what happened?"

"She and I..." he inserted a long and deliberately teasing pause, "and her mother, the jailer Mrs. Francis, went to dinner to celebrate her twenty-first birthday."

"And?"

"We had cake."

"You had both of them?" Robby joked.

"Will you stop?"

"Has our Andrea bloomed?"

"If you're asking me how she looks, the answer is fantastic. The woman could go on the cover of any fashion magazine tomorrow."

"And... did you have some time alone with her? You know, for a proper twenty-first birthday celebration?" he asked lasciviously.

Max just shook his head as if he could not believe Robby's line of questioning.

Robby leaned close to Max and began to whisper in his ear, "Did you get her, you bastard? Why do I have the feeling that if you got her in bed and you're not about to tell me? That's one trophy I'd certainly want to brag about. Then again, it could be mama Francis wasn't about to let her out of her sight knowing the kind of lascivious predator you are."

Max, who had elevated Andrea into an elite list of one, had no intention of revealing anything about their night together. It was special, it was his, and not to be shared. So he told Robby what he knew he really wanted to hear. "Let's just say her mother never travels without a Biretta in her purse, a Doberman in her car and two very large eunuchs who look to be refugees from some wrestling organization."

"A guess your reputation had preceded you," Robby chided.

"I guess."

"You know what I'm thinking?"

"I'm afraid you're going to tell me."

"I'm thinking that you..."

"I'm talkin' to ya'all! Goddamn it! Yer not leavin' me after I paid for them drinks!"

Tex's outburst cut Robby short and both he and Max turned around. One of the women began to swing her purse at Tex, while the other was fighting to free herself from his grasp.

"It's time for ya'll to re... cip... ro... cate!" Tex stood up and began to teeter on his boots. Max thought he looked like a giant tree about to be felled by a woodsman's axe. He did not fall. He crumbled, landing at the foot of the woman he had been trying to prevent from leaving. As he went down he flailed the air hoping to grab something to break his fall. All he could find was a handful of skirt, which ripped off, exposing her legs. She responded by placing a hard kick into Tex's ribs, then yanked the tablecloth off the table, wrapped it around her waist and quickly followed the other woman out of the bar.

"I think you owe me a 100 Euros," Max said, "He was out in less than ten minutes."

"Put it on my tab," he laughed.

"Colin," Max said to the barman as he looked down at Tex, "Do you want us to prop him up in the corner?"

"No, no, no," the barman answered." Please do not bother. He has a suite here in the hotel. I will call the manager and have him send porters to help him to his room."

Max looked at Robby and saw the look of a man with mayhem on his mind. "Don't bother, Colin. Since he's our countryman, we'll take care of him."

"We will? I'm not sure what's swirling in the devious mind, but he's not our problem," Max said.

"True. But he *is* our opportunity and you're going to love it. Why don't you just rest your bones here for a moment while I go get a luggage cart?"

Robby was back in less than two minutes with a cart. "I've got his room key. Management was more than happy to enlist our services."

Max was reasonably sure he knew what Robby was up to. Together they loaded Tex on the cart and wheeled him out of the bar.

"Charge our cognacs to his room," Max said as they left. "I'm sure he'd want to pick up our tab as a thank you for taking care of him." As they left the bar, Max said, "You are thinking what I'm thinking, right?"

"Of course. You know I am. Elevator is over there."

"Our only decision is how he should be dressed."

"I vote for the boots and the hat."

"I second that. Perfect nighttime attire for ol' Tex."

They wheeled him through the lobby into the elevator and up to his suite where they prepared him for the night.

Once Tex was in place, Max and Robby sat in the lobby across from the elevators to enjoy the shocked looks and vocal expressions of disgust by hotel guests waiting to be lifted to their rooms. When the elevator doors opened they were treated to the sight of a large man, asleep on a mattress, in the bottom of the elevator wearing only boots and a cowboy hat. Max and Robby did their best to look both shocked and disgusted when, in fact, they could barely contain themselves.

It took almost a half hour before someone from the hotel staff arrived to hang an 'Hors Service' sign on the elevator and tend to the removal of the naked Texan. Satisfied that Tex would never be forgotten by the Ritz staff, Max said, "Enough of this fun. I'm bored. How about a short walk down to Sank Roo Doe Noo?"

"And New York Harry's Bar. Next to Tex," Robby added, "is the second-best idea all night. Tex being the best idea and that was mine."

A five-minute walk from the Ritz is what Max often touted to friends as the best bar in Paris. Not so much for its drinks or food – hot dogs being a main stay – but because of its history. In 1911, a New York City bar was dismantled and shipped to Paris and reassembled at number 5 Rue Daunou . The first barman was a man name Harry MacElhone and it was his name given to the bar.

"Every time I come in here," Max said as they made their way to a table beyond the long bar, "I expect to see the ghosts of people like Scott Fitzgerald or Hemingway or Sinclair Lewis or George Gershwin."

"Number one hangout for those folks back in the twenties," Robby added. "And the home of the original Bloody Mary. You up for one?"

"Not at this hour. Beer is fine."

"Deux bières," Robby said to the waiter. After the waiter returned with their beers, he said, "You know what I'm thinking?"

Max immediately sensed he would rather not know. "Haven't you done enough thinking for one night?"

"No, seriously. What's the one thing missing from our pranks.?"

"I don't know, what?"

"Competition. Going all the way back to prep school, our victims have never really offered us much of a challenge."

"What did you expect them to offer? Retaliation?"

"I mean it was fun with the farm animals and the toilet thing and if we were still at Yale, I'm sure we would be dreaming up all kinds of things. My feeling is there has got to be a way for us to make pranks a competitive sport."

"You thinking we should try and qualify it for the Olympics?"

"I'm serious about this."

"Ok, I'll be serious," Max said making no effort to indicate he meant it.

"Who are the two brightest, most inventive and ingenious guys you know when it comes to practical jokes?"

"Present company."

"Right. And between you and me, we are the only two people I know who represent any kind of competition."

"You just lost me," Max said.

"Here's what I'm thinking: What if you and I took turns trying to pull off the perfect prank on each other before the other guy can figure it out?"

"Haven't we already done that. We have a truce, remember?"

"Come on, those things we did we're amateur night. Kid's stuff. I want to elevate the game to a whole new level."

"How much have you had to drink?" Max had no idea where Robby was going with this.

Robby ignored him and began to lay out the *new level*. "Let's say you were to go first. Your objective would be to dream up some really, I mean off-the-charts, practical joke to pull on me. If you're successful, if you can do it, then you claim a win and get a point. But… and this is what will make this interesting – if I'm able to figure out what you're up to *before* you pull it off, then I score the point."

Max began to shake his head, "Let me see if I understand what you're saying: if I expose your prank before you pull it off I score a point and you don't."

"Sort of like when you fault on your tennis serve."

"Only I don't ever fault. *Maybe it was the Cognac*, Max thought, but he was beginning to find himself intrigued by the idea. "But if the prank works, if one of us pulls it off, that's an ace and scores a point."

"Like in tennis. And we'll use tennis scoring: 15, 30, 40, Game. First guy to game, wins."

"Wins what?" Max asked.

"I don't know. Bragging rights. Some sort of trophy. The right to hold the win over the other guy's head. Whatever. We'll figure it out later."

Max thought for a moment, then raised what he saw as a potential flaw in Robby's game, "Just one thing, if it's your turn and you're trying to pull something on me you gotta know I'm going to be on guard. I'm going to be suspect of everything you do."

"That's what makes this such a brilliant and interesting competition. In order to score a point we'll have to be extremely clever, really inventive. We'll have to spring it on the other guy when he least expects it. And that doesn't mean doing something humiliating to each other like we did to Tex tonight. This has got to be just between us. A mano a mano. The victim, whether it's you or me, has to be awake and at least mostly sober."

"Agreed. Otherwise, how the hell are we going to know we've been had?"

Robby added a caveat, "Oh, and no fair killing the other guy."

"That's an excellent rule," Max said laughing.

"Maxie, this is going to be fun. This is going to take imagination, cunning and skill."

"Which means there's no way you're gonna win."

"Says you," he challenged.

"Just thought of something. We've got to give this a name," Max said.

"Ok. How would you describe the game?" Robby answered his own question," It's the ultimate completion. That's not a bad name."

"No, it's got to have more class." Max thought for a moment, "How about something in French, Le Jeu Ultime? The Ultimate Game."

"Perfect. Perfect name for a competition in which the world's two best and only players go head to head."

"Are we going to have a time limit between serves?"

"No. We can take as long as we want. A month, a year or even a couple of years."

"Really? No time limit?"

"Yeah. Makes it a lot tougher to stay on your guard if there no time limit."

"And the game ends when... ?"

"The first guy gets to game. Just like in tennis."

"This is crazy, you know that don't you?" Max said.

"Of course it is, but it'll be fun. You got anything better to do?" Robby tossed out the bait. " Unless you're not up for this kind of competition...."

Max took it. "How do we decide who goes first?"

"Ahhh…see the young woman who just walked in?" Robby said pointing to an attractive woman who looked as if she might be taking a break from her work on the street.

"Yeah. Definitely a femme de joie."

"What if we were to ask her to decide?"

"Will she know what she's deciding?"

Robby shook his head. "She doesn't need to know. What's more, she probably wouldn't understand or care."

"Ok, we'll ask her to pick one of us."

"And the one she doesn't pick gets to take her to bed," Robby added.

"Not unless she's got a doctor's certificate."

"How's this going to work?"

Robby opened his wallet, pulled out a hundred Euro note and rolled it up in his hand. "We tell her it's a game. The object is to pick which one of us is holding the Euro. If she picks me, she gets the Euro and I go first. If she picks you, then you go first."

"But we still give her the hundred."

"Absolutely. It'll be the fastest hundred she'll make tonight."

They approached the woman who looked as if she was expecting to negotiate for a ménage à trois. Max explained in French what they wanted her to do. At first, she looked at them suspiciously. Max assured her they wanted nothing more than for her to choose which man she thought was holding the Euro.

Robby and Max held up their closed fists in front of her. She looked first at Max and then at Robby. She continued to study their hands, glancing now and again at their faces. Max thought he saw Robby wink at her. He was sure he did. For a moment he was going to protest but decided it didn't really matter. *So, he goes first, who cares?* The woman took Robby's cue and instantly pointed to him.

"Merci" he said and handed her the hundred Euros.

Max added his thanks and they started to walk back to their table. The woman, believing she recognize another profit opportunity, followed them. She touched Robby on the shoulder, "Voulez-vous me baiser?"

Max immediately understood her business proposition. "Do you know what she just asked you?"

"Pas ce soir." Robby said.

"Not tonight? Wow, you are really expanding your French." Max teased.

"When it comes to sex, I'm a linguist in any language," he said with bravado.

Having been refused by Robby, the woman turned her attention to Max. She sat down beside him pressing her thigh against his.

"If at first you don't succeed," Robby said as he watched the woman slide her hand onto Max's lap.

"I think the lady is trying to sell me something?" Max laughed.

With the look of a man about to undertake an urgent mission, Robby stood up and started to back away from the table toward the front door.

"You leaving?"

"Far be it from me to interfere with two people in love," he joked.

"When I'm done, I'll send her up to your room."

"No thanks. Don't like seconds," he smiled as he looked at the woman then turned to leave. He had taken only a few steps when he turned around looking like a salesman who had forgotten to ask for the order. "It's a deal, right? We're 'go' for Le Jeu Ultime?"

"We're go." Max held out his hand and they shook. But knowing how mercurial and capricious Robby could be and how easily distracted by the next "great" idea or challenge, he doubted if they really were "go.".

"Good." Robby said emphatically, "Then game on. And it's my serve."

~~*

It was three months later that Robby called Max, "Pack your bags, Max ol' boy, and warm up the jets on your plane. I'd take mine but it's in for an overhaul."

"Where are we going?" Max asked.

"We're taking four young lovelies, two French, one Italian, and one who I think might be….I don't know what the hell she is, to Baden Baden this weekend."

"We are?" Max asked sounding ready to accept.

"Absolutely. A weekend at the invitation of the four "Bs.""

"The four "Bs?"

"Booze, Bathes, Baccarat and Broads."

"An invitation I'm not about to refuse."

9.

15 YEARS BEFORE THE MURDER OF ANDREA TRASK

Baden Baden, Germany

Robby made all the arrangements for the weekend in Baden Baden. In addition to the four women, Robby had invited six other friends to join them "Hey, your plane seats twelve. Why not fill it up?"

They left Orly early on Friday and landed at the Baden Airpark in less than an hour. Max thought the six limos waiting to take them into the city was overdoing it a bit, but as this was Robby's show he said nothing.

In the mid-1800s, Baden Baden was a favorite destination of royalty and aristocracy who would arrive from all corners of the continent to gamble in one of the world's top casinos and take the 'Cure" – a mixture of sauna, massage and the supposed curative properties of the mineral water.

Immediately after they had checked in, Max, Robby and the two French women headed for Baths of Caracalla, a huge wonderland of steamy pools, waterfalls, neck showers, Jacuzzis, hot springs, cold pools, saunas and a bar. They began by taking a couple laps around the fake river, then opted for a few minutes of 'water spankings' under a waterfall. After several minutes of being pummeled by the water, they made their way to the central cauldron where all modesty and clothing are abandoned with the only cover being the misty hot steam.

Later that evening Max looked up and saw Robby making his way through the large group of spectators who were watching Max hold forth in single handed combat against the dealer at one of the Baccarat tables.

"I see you've got the table all to yourself."

"I bought the table because I like playing against the house."

"I don't know why you like Baccarat. At least poker involves strategy. There's no skill to this game."

"Right. That's why I like it. Baccarat is a hundred percent luck, zero percent skill. Which means when you are as drunk as I am right now, you don't have to think. He deals and I count."

"How are you doing?" Robby asked as he pulled up a chair next to Max.

"Well, I'm up sixty-thousand Euros."

"Now for the most important question: How many scalps have you taken?"

"Scalps? What are you talking about?"

"That's what I call the women I've had so far."

"You sound like some kind of perverted Indian?"

"Got three so far," Robby announced with unmasked pride.

"You're scalping tool must be blunt by this time," Max chided.

"Sharp as ever. You're going to have to go some to keep up."

"I didn't know we were having a scalping contest."

"I think you need a drink," Robby said.

"If I have any more to drink I'll float or pass out. One or the other. I can barely make out the cards."

"Mind if I watch?"

"So long as you don't jinx me."

"Never."

It was moments later when Max's attention was diverted from the cards to an approaching woman who looked like she had just stepped out of a James Bond movie. She was blond and dressed in a slinky, form fitting, low cut, black dress that Max thought to be having some difficulty containing her breasts. She paused at one end of the Baccarat table, her gaze fixed on Robby.

"And what have we here?" Max said to Robby as he nodded toward the woman.

"She's gorgeous. Sex on a stick," Robby said, "A potential scalp if I ever saw one."

The woman slowly made her way over to where the two men were sitting and tapped Robby on the shoulder. "You are Robert Trask, no?" she asked in a low, throaty voice, her face expressionless.

Robby stood up, "I certainly am. And you are... ?"

"Lily Marlene," she answered flatly.

"Like the song," Max said, somewhat bemused by her name. "By your accent, I'd say you are from Switzerland or maybe Austria."

She ignored Max and directed her full attention to Robby. "You are the same Robert Trask that races Grand Prix?"

"One in the same," Robby appeared to be delighted to have been recognized.

"I do not like Grand Prix drivers. They are all pigs." She did not attempt to hide her disgust.

Max broke into spasms of laugher. "Not exactly one of your fans, is she Robby?" Max stood up. "Lily Marlene, you are clearly a woman of refined tastes. And your assessment of my friend here is quite correct. He is a pig. But you, on the other hand have clearly improved the decor of this room."

"I think she's your scalp," Robby said backing away.

"Scalp?" Lily asked. "What is scalp?"

Max improvised a quick response, "It's a term Americans use to indicate it will be my privilege to buy you a drink. Champagne?"

"That would be lovely," she responded pressing close to Max and exploring his face. It was the kind of look intended to offer unlimited opportunity. "But can we go somewhere private? Away from..." she glanced at Robby, "him?"

"Yes. Far away from him," Max said shooting a triumphant glance at Robby. "I have a lovely suite. It's very private and ideal for sipping champagne." Max took a moment to quickly assess the physical attributes of his intended conquest. "You are a beautiful woman. I can hardly wait to get to know you better."

"You flatter me."

"You deserved to be flattered, and more," he said suggestively.

She leaned in to him, pressing her breasts into his arm and putting her mouth to his ear and whispering, "I am always ready for *more*."

Max took her arm and was about to usher her away when he stopped and looked back at Robby. "Why don't you take my place at the table? And try not to lose all my money."

Robby just smiled as he sat down. "Don't worry, I don't lose."

Once in Max's suite, they didn't bother to wait for the champagne. Lily knew why she was there and immediately dropped her dress exposing her breasts. She was naked except for some uncharacteristic frilly and seemingly oversize panties. She lay down on the bed, her arms outstretched.

Max took off his coat, pulled off his tie, and kicked off his shoes. His ardor, combined with the previous three hours of alcohol, causing him to neglect his shirt and pants. Immediately he approached the bed and with both hands took hold of her panties pulling them off in one swift motion.

"Oh **SHIT!**" He bellowed in disgust.

Lily released a deep throaty giggle. "What's the matter, you don't' like what Lily has for you?"

What he saw was not what he had expected to find between her legs. She... *he* was whatever gender sex transvestites bestow on themselves. What he also saw was a small note card tied to her substantial member with a pink ribbon, it read:

Score is 15- Love.

Trask

"That son of a bitch!" Lily Marlene looked up at him with a silly grin, pursing her lips, inviting a kiss. "Get the fuck out of my room!" he shouted jumping off the bed, her panties still in his hand. He picked up his shoes and retreated to the door. He looked back at Lily who had propped herself up with pillows and appeared to be settling in for the night. "If you're not out of here in ten minutes, I'm going to send up a couple of guys to bust your *balls!*" The threat was enough to motivate Lily. The last thing he saw was the half woman-half man slide out of his bed. *Shit,* he thought, *I've got to call room service and have them change the sheets.*

It took Max less than two minutes to find Robby in the bar. He greeted Max with a smile akin to the cat who had just consumed the classic canary.

"You son-of a bitch," There was no rancor or anger in Max's voice. Rather, it sounded more like a concession and reluctant acknowledgement of Robby's first point in La Jeu Ultime. He'd been caught totally off guard. He really hadn't believed that Robby was actually serious about the game, but obviously he was.

"Did we get a scalp?" Robby asked laughing.

"You played that well," Max said sitting down next to him, "I have to admit, I never saw it coming."

"And that, my friend, is the key to winning this game. You have to spring it when the other least expects it. And I'd say tonight, you did not expect it."

"How could anyone look so beautiful and be a chick with a dick?"

"Not that I've had a lot of experience with transvestites, but some of them, like Lily, are amazing. You'd never know what they are, until you..." Robby could not check a laugh, "get into their shorts."

"It was not a pretty sight. I need a drink."

"Already ordered for you," Robby said pushing a scotch on the rocks in front of Max.

"I have a question for you."

"Shoot."

He reached into his pocket, pulled out Lily's panties and tossed them into Robby's lap. "Does that count as a scalp?"

Robby burst into laughter. "Good God man," he said gingerly holding up the scalp between two fingers as if he expected something nasty to crawl out of the underwear. "I think this should count as two." He laughed.

"My turn now, right?" Max asked.

"Just like the sign on his dick said. Your turn. But let me suggest that scoring on me won't be easy."

"Yeah? Why's that?"

"Because unlike you, I'll be expecting it."

Max took a sip of his drink and stared off into space for several moments, then turned back to Robby, his face plastered with a wide grin, "Maybe you will and maybe you won't."

10.

15 YEARS BEFORE THE MURDER OF ANDREA TRASK

Greenwich, Connecticut

Max was back in Southampton when the call came. "I just found out. We need to do something." It was Robby.

"Just found out what?" Max asked.

"Andrea. She's engaged. Mrs. Francis is throwing an engagement party next Saturday at their place in Greenwich."

"How'd you find out?"

"I happened to be, shall we say, entertaining a woman at the Plaza last night who turned out to be a friend of Andrea's. Going to be one of her bridesmaids. She said Andrea's mother has essentially arranged the marriage with the Earl of SomethingOrOther in England. Mrs. Francis wants her to marry royalty so she'll have a title and Mama's ready to pay for it."

"What do you mean, pay for it?"

"Turns out the Earl is all but broke and needs Andrea's money to bail out his estate."

A tsunami of panic rolled over Max at the thought of Andrea marrying some broken-down Earl. "He gets the cash and she gets the title," Max said derisively.

"Right. Per my lady-of-the-one-night-stands, Andrea likes the guy, but she's not exactly doing cartwheels over having to marry him. Sounds like mother-pressure in the extreme."

Max made an instant decision. He would not let it happen. He agreed with Robby, it was her mother's doing. "What I hear you saying is we've got to save her from making the mistake of her life. No way we can let her marry the Earl of Goingbroke."

"Absolutely not."

"What do we do?" Robby asked.

"I suggest we invite ourselves to the engagement party."

"As party crashers?"

"No, as kidnappers."

* ~ * ~ *

They arrived at the Francis estate mid-afternoon. To Max, the lawn behind the house looked like a used car lot for late model luxury cars.

"Got to be over two-hundred people here," Robby said.

"That's good for us. Nothing like staying invisible in a crowd."

"Main thing is to steer clear of Mrs. Francis. I'm pretty sure she knows we're not on the guest list."

"We need to find some way to get Andrea alone," Max said.

"You're serious about kidnapping her?"

"Totally. If she doesn't want to marry the Earl of Goingbroke we'll be doing her a favor."

"And if her mother calls the cops and we get caught, we'll claim the kidnap was just a practical joke between old friends."

"Absolutely. I've got an idea," Max said, "I'll kidnap Andrea and you kidnap the Earl and hold him for ransom. Who knows how much you might get for him?"

Robby was willing to play, "Won't work. If the Earl is broke his title won't be worth much on the ransom market."

"Maybe the two of you... well, you know... could become *real good* friends."

"Up yours," Robby grinned and gave Max a playful push.

"There she is," Max said coming to a stop.

"Where?"

"Over there by the swimming pool."

"That must be the Earl next to her."

"Look," Max said. "You said your bed friend said she really doesn't want to marry the guy, right?"

"That's what she said."

"I want to be sure. I think we need to hear it directly from her. If, for some crazy reason, Andrea loves him then we owe it to her to disappear. If she's doing it because her mother..."

"We'll fuck the Earl so she won't have to." Robby could not hold back a full-throated laugh which drew curious glances from several guests walking nearby.

"How much do you know about the Earl?" Max asked.

"Looked him up on the Internet. Found a pretty good write-up,"

"Think you could find enough to talk about with him for a few minutes?"

"I can pump up his ego so much he'll all but float off like a gas balloon. What are you planning to do?"

"I'm going to play like a cowboy and see if I can cut Andrea out of the herd for a couple of minutes," Max said. "If I decide she's ripe for a kidnap, we'll dump the Earl in the pool and get the hell out of here as fast as we can."

"Sounds like a plan."

"Okay."

"There she is on the terrace," Robby said. "She looks pretty well occupied with several of the guests."

Max waited until they saw the Earl wander off to talk with a group of people who looked as if they wanted to be impressed with the Earl's attention. "Go get him," Max said giving Robby a gentle push in the direction of the Earl. "He's all yours,"

As Robby zeroed in on the Earl, Max slowly made his way toward Andrea. When he was within about fifteen feet, she saw him. She was wearing something filmy and blue. The sun caught her from the back offering a stunning silhouette of the long lithe legs that had been indelibly etched in his memory from that summer night three years ago.

"Max!" she made no effort to hide her surprise and immediately ran toward him. She was about to throw her arms around him, but caught herself, pulled up short and just held out her hand. "What are you doing here?"

"Robby and I have come to find out if... well if this," he said indicating the engagement party, "is what you want. I mean, do you want to marry the Earl?"

She ignored his question. "Where have you been?"

"The question is where have *you* been? I wrote you letters, tried to track you through your grandmother and even came up here once. They said you were in England but wouldn't tell me where. I'm guessing your mother has been hiding you."

"You wrote me letters?" Max could see her surprise was genuine.

"I didn't have your telephone number or your cell so I wrote at least a dozen. The last ones came back."

She lowered her head and provided a one-word answer as to why she had never gotten them. "Mother."

"You think your mother intercepted my letters?"

She nodded sadly, "Somehow she found out I was with you that night at your house. She wasn't ever going to let me see you again. Next thing I knew we were living in England and watching the Earl play cricket."

"Well, at least now I know you weren't tearing them up. I wondered if after... well, you know, after we were together you decided you didn't want to see me again."

"Oh, God, no! I wanted to be with you so bad. When I didn't hear from you, I thought maybe all I was to you was..."

"Stop," he said putting his finger to her mouth. "You were and are everything to me." He took her arm and pulled her further away from the few guests who, he suspected, might be tempted to listen in on their conversation. "I want you to be completely honest with me. If you love this Earl and really want to marry him, Robby and I will immediately get lost."

"Robby's here too?"

"He's talking to your Earl. On the other hand, if this is your mother's idea and you'd like an excuse to... well, to have forces beyond your control, meaning Robby and me, help you find a way to disappear, all you have to say is 'yes.'"

Andrea stared at Max for a long moment. "Mother will never forgive me, but yes, oh, yes."

"Okay!" It was a controlled explosion of glee. "You are about to be kidnapped by two very good-looking young men and your whereabouts will be a national secret."

"Where are we going?"

"Kidnap victims don't ask questions. Wait here."

Andrea said nothing, but the smile on her face said she was ready for whatever Max and Robby had in mind.

Robby, who had been feeding the Earl's ego with insipid social pabulum, saw Max approaching. The look on his face asked, "Well?"

Max responded with a grin, a nod and a victorious fist pump.

"And who might you be?" the Earl asked as Max joined Robby and him.

"Robby and I are old friends of Andrea's."

"Well, a friend of Andrea's is..." he stopped. "By the way, what's happened to her?"

Max answered, "The question my dear Earl, is not what *has* happened to her, but what's *about* to happen to you." Then in his most formal English accent, "And that, my dear fellow, I am not at liberty to reveal."

The Earl was instantly put off by Max. "What the duce are you talking about?"

"I'm talking about swimming lessons." Max said.

"Swimming lessons?" he asked incredulously.

"Yes. My friend here and I are instructors." Robby said. "And we've come to give you a swimming lesson."

"The devil you are!" The Earl said taking a defensive step backward. "I will have to inform Andrea I'm not sure I approve of her friends." The Earl caught a glimpse of Andrea.

Before he could call out to her, the two men who had just offered swimming instructions picked him up, took a few quick steps to poolside, and tossed the Earl of Goingbroke into the deep end. The splash, followed by his pleas for help, drew the immediate attention of the guests standing around the pool. There was a general clamor of confusion and concern as one of the waiters took off his coat, dived into the pool and swam toward the Earl. The commotion in the pool set off a chain reaction and several young men jumped in to help with the rescue. Three others, including one young woman in an inebriated condition, joined the Earl and added themselves to the pool. General chaos followed providing Max and Robby with the diversion they needed to make their escape with the bride-to-be.

Max quickly looked for Andrea. She was standing where he left her doing her best not to let anyone see she was enjoying the pandemonium. Max picked her up like a groom carrying his wife over the threshold and followed Robby as he led them across the lawn, down the drive to where they had parked the car. Robby slid in behind the wheel and Max carefully put Andrea in the back. Robby floored the accelerator spinning gravel in his wake. Down North Avenue they roared onto the Merritt Parkway, then on to I-95 toward the Throgs Neck Bridge and Long Island.

"Poor Stephen, I'm not sure he can swim," she said.

"Well, we did offer him swimming lessons," Max laughed.

* ~ * ~ *

Max was not surprised her apparent abduction was the kind of story that made all the society media. When Andrea reappeared after permitting herself to be held hostage on Long Island, she admitted to anyone who asked that she had been with two men she adored. The wedding was called off and the poor Earl was left to peddle his title elsewhere.

Mrs. Francis, Max was told, declared herself terminally mortified. Not only was she forced to watch the waterlogged Earl pulled from the swimming pool, but she had to endure the society page coverage which had a field day speculating on the kidnapping. She knew, of course, her daughter would never become a Countess and once word got back to the Isles, no other English title would ever be available to her. To escape the endless enquiries from friends and the tabloids, she booked herself on a six-month cruise with no possible means of contact.

The weather for late September was warm and the two kidnappers with their hostage returned to the beach where they had staged the motorcycle joust. They spent the rest of the day just talking. At some point Max found himself contemplating the possible consequences of their abduction. Certainly, there would be repercussions and for the first time he worried what kind of damage they might have done to her reputation. "Any regrets?" Max asked. "You would have made a beautiful Countess.".

"But a miserable wife," she said with a smile that Max took as confirmation they had done the right thing.

As their eyes met, there was an unspoken electric connection that might have lasted much longer had Robby not short-circuited the moment. "Now, other than eventually marrying one of us, what do you think you'll do?" Robby asked.

"I've already decided."

"Smart girl" Robby said, "We'll have the wedding right here on this beach."

"You're talking about *our* wedding, right Robby?" Max put his arm around Andrea and gave her a hug.

"Maybe you two should have another joust," she teased.

"Been there, done that," Robby said

"So, what is it you've decided?" Max asked.

"On my twenty-third birthday I came into my trust which, I think, was what Stephen loved most about me. I'm not ashamed to tell you I could have rescued his estate with a lot left over. But now, since I won't have to support him, I'm going to move to Paris and live the life of a La Boèhme bohemian."

"On Avenue Foch, no doubt," Max offered.

"You mean in the high rent district?" she asked.

"Hey, nothing like being a rich bohemian." Robby said.

Had Max taken some time to consider what he was about to say, he might not have made the suggestion so all inclusive. "And you know what we're going to do?"

"No, what are we going to do?" Robby echoed.

"You and I are going to buy apartments on either side of wherever Andrea lives and the three of us are going to bring Europe to its knees."

"Meaning?" Andrea asked.

"We're going to have our own moveable feast. Like Hemingway wrote about in the twenties," Max said. "There's a great Hemingway quote which, a long time ago, I memorized for a report at prep school. It goes, 'If you are lucky enough to have lived in Paris as a young man, then wherever you go for the rest of your life it stays with you, for Paris is a moveable feast.'"

"Ditto for young women. At least to this one." Andrea said glowing with anticipation.

11.

15 YEARS BEFORE THE MURDER
OF ANDREA TRASK

Europe

They were inseparable. They lived by whim. Planning was forbidden. Caprice dictated their days. They roamed Europe as if driven by a rogue wind. It was a year of conspicuous extravagance. For Max, his relationship with Robby quickly evolved into an acknowledged, but unscripted contest to see who could outdo the other as they competed for their beautiful trophy.

Robby booked the Palace at St Moritiz and had them helicoptered in from Paris so they could be skiing on the Corviglia the same day. For New Years, Max arranged for rooms at the Adlon Hotel in Berlin that cost as much as a Volkswagen Golf. After more skiing at Zurs, they flew to St. Barts to thaw out. In February, Max arranged for them to attend the ball at Vienna State Opera which is transformed into the most festive and most famous ballroom in the world.

Robby had initially planned to compete on the Grand Prix circuit, but knowing the amount of time it would require, he told Max the last thing he wanted was to leave him alone with Andrea.

Paparazzi from both the European and American tabloids followed the uber-rich Americans as they flaunted their wealth in dozens of cities in England and Europe. They were seen at the Monaco Grand Prix, at the Palio, the famous horse race around the central square in Siena, Italy, and at Wimbledon where they learned the Earl of Goingbroke had landed an heiress ten years his senior.

In July, Andrea finished reading the 'Sun Also Rises' and challenged Robby and Max to run with the Bulls a Pamplona. They installed her in a hotel room at Callejon, a dangerous bottleneck in the run, where she could watch her daredevils pass on their way to the Plaza de Toros. But it was well before the bulls ran from the Plaza del Ayuntamiento to the Curva de Mercaderes that Robby learned to respect the sharpness of a bulls' horns. Max, choosing discretion over valor, had elected to find refuge off the course. As he looked back for his friend, he saw Robby take a horn in his rear. Max jumped down, ran against the flow of runners and bulls and pulled Robby off to the side.

"Are we having fun, yet?" Robby asked as he looked up at Max.

"Not yet," Max answered

Robby laid a hand on the right cheek of his behind and groaned in pain, "Much more to the left and I think that would have qualified as colonoscopy."

"Much higher and you'd have been a kidney donor."

Robby spent three days in the Pamplona Hospital on his stomach. With his friend incapacitated and, as Max put it, "not exactly in a position to go dancing," Max decided Andrea should see the Costa del Sol and a very private boutique hotel. They returned the day Robby was released from the hospital and Max did his best to convince Robby that he had inadvertently forgotten to tell him where he and Andrea we're going.

"Bullshit," was Robby's response.

That night, they met in the restaurant at the Grand Hotel La Peral. "While you two were leaving me deserted, without friends and unable to speak Spanish to any of the nurses who I think were part of the original Spanish Inquisition, I had time to make plans for us to visit a surprise destination. I've arranged for my plane to leave from the Pamplona airport at 3PM sharp.

As Max discovered the next morning, Robby, suffering from the same attack of inadvertent forgetfulness, forgot to tell Max he had changed the takeoff time to 11AM.

* ~ * ~ *

Robby and Andrea landed at Nice and immediately drove to Cap Ferrat to show her the impressive villa he had bought a month earlier. This little castle will be your home should you have the good sense and good taste to become Andrea Trask."

"Does it have a name?" she asked.

"That's for you to decide. I'd like you to name it."

"There," she pointed to at a bird that had just landed on one of the sculptures on either side of the entrance. It's Blue Bird. I think the name of your villa should be after that bird. But in French of course. Oiseau Bleu.

It took Max only six hours after having discovered Robby had retaliated for having absconded with Andrea to the Costa del Sol to follow in a charted plane. He landed in Nice the next morning and, learning Robby had secured Andrea in his new villa, did what any avid billionaire competitor would have done. He told the local real estate broker to go Robby one better. Within the month, Max was showing Andrea his villa and gardens overlooking the sea and the village of St. Jean Cap Ferrat. "I'd like to have you name it," he said.

"Maybe I should make this a career. First Robby's villa and now yours. I love your gardens and when you stand here... it looks almost as if they are rising up out of the Mediterranean. How about Jardin de la Mer?"

"That's what it is."

Back in Paris, neither man let the other out of his sight. They continued to bounce around Europe with seeming abandon. They chartered a sailboat and crew for the Greek Isles. Then flew back to France to follow parts of the Tour de France and stood on the Champs Elysee for the finale. Next day, Max and Robby discovered Andrea was not in her apartment. It wasn't until late afternoon that she left them a voice mail saying she had been invited to celebrate with one of the riders of the winning team and had no idea when she would return.

When she returned to her apartment a day later, she found both Robby and Max waiting at her door. They demanded to know if it was true she had let herself be flaunted all over Paris with some bicycle rider. "He not just some bicycle rider, he's one of the best riders in France. They say he's sure to win the Tour de France one day." She smiled in a way designed to prove she knew she had them both wrapped tightly around her little finger. "Jealous?" She asked as she went into her apartment. Before she closed her door, she announced, "Champagne, at seven... here."

By September, Max and Robby knew they were in a battle for Andrea that neither was going to win easily. She had not given either of them any indication she preferred one to the other. She seemed to be enjoying their threesome arrangement too much to let marriage bring an end to the fun. Max, who was feeling more desperate each day to claim what he felt was rightfully his, decided not to approach her with a proposal, not so much out of fear of rejection as much as having to cope with her being unable to make a decision.

It was late one night after they had dropped Andrea at her apartment that

Max suggested they stop in at Harry's Bar. The bar was mostly empty. They chose a table in the back and ordered two beers.

"I think it's time," Max began once the beers were served.

"Time for what?" Robby asked

"Time for one of us to disappear."

"Be my guest. Vanish tonight, if you like."

Max ignored the suggestion." Look, we both love Andrea, right?"

"Right."

"And we'd both like to marry her. But knowing her as we do, I think it's safe to say she'll put off making any decision if she thinks saying 'yes' to one of us is going to hurt the other. But if one of us were to disappear... and I mean drop out of her life totally and completely, it would make her choice a hell of a lot easier."

"You have my vote. I'll miss you, of course." Robby's faux sincerity was clearly not intended to sound convincing. He clapped Max on the back, "But I want you to know Andrea would will be happy to have you as my best man at the wedding."

"I'm serious about this," Max said, clearly annoyed by Robby's flip response to his suggestion.

"Well I'm serious about not taking you serious," Robby retorted.

"Look," Max continued, "all I'm saying is with the way things are now when it comes to putting a ring on her finger you and I are at a stalemate." Max's hand flailed aimlessly in the air as if he were looking to rake in the right words from some unseen source. "Running around like we have been for the last year is getting us nowhere as far as Andrea is concerned. I don't know about you, but this seems like a no win situation for either of us until one of us drops out. You know I'm right." Max waited for a response from Robby who had seemed to find something in his beer that commanded his attention. After a long moment Max said himself, *Waste of time. I should never have brought this up with him. He's not going to take this seriously.*

Finally Robby looked up, "Maybe you're right."

"About...?

"Love triangles don't work." Robby stared off to the front of the bar then turned back to Max. "Let's say...just for the sake of discussion...if I were to agree with you that one of us needs to get lost. How would we decide? I'm not about to leave it to something like a coin flip."

"Me either."

"We've got to come up with some sort of competition."

"Why am I not surprised you'd want to reduce Andrea to a trophy."

"She makes a damn fine prize. Short of one of us just handing her over to the other, we've got to find a way to decide."

You want to play games? Max decided to toss out a suggestion he knew Robby would refuse. "Why don't we settle it on the tennis court? Best three out of five sets?

"Given I've never won a set from you in all the time we've known each other, that's a definitely 'no.'"

"Well, we could opt for dueling pistols. That would certainly solve the problem of which one of us goes."

"Only if I get to shoot first," he laughed and then got serious. "If we do something competitive, it's got to be something where we really start even."

"So if dueling pistols and tennis are out, I guess you're not up for swords either?"

Robby let Max's humor bounce off him without even the slightest verbal or facial response. "I got an idea. Andrea loved the Tour de France. How about a Tour de Francis?"

"You talking about a bike race?" Max asked.

"Yeah, why not?"

"When was the last time you were on a bike?" Max asked.

"The only bike I've ever ridden was the stationary one in my gym."

"I think you'll find there's a difference."

"I suppose you had a bike when you were a kid?"

"Go carts. Never had a bike."

"Well, at least neither of us will have an advantage," Robby said

"And if you want to use training wheels, I won't object," Max said.

"Where are we going to have this race?"

Max couldn't believe he was agreeing to make Andrea the trophy in a bike race. This was not the way he had hoped their conversation to play out. Did he think Robby would just fold up his tent and leave? Of course not. But he had to admit that he was beginning to like the idea. He'd won the joust on the beach years before, why not a bike race? "We'll lay out a course like they do for the Tour," Max said now fully ready to accept the challenge..

"How long should it be?" Robby asked.

"Long enough to make it a real contest, but short enough so I don't wear you out."

"Wear me out? I'll ride your ass into the ground." Robby's boast expanded to fill the space between them.

"I'm thinking thirty miles?"

"I was thinking double."

"Double it is."

The longer the race, the more time I'll spend waiting for you at the finish," Robby said.

"In your dreams!" Max snapped.

"So when do we do this?"

"I think the first of October should be perfect, weather-wise.

"That's just two weeks from now."

"Hey, if you're going to need more time to learn how to ride a bike, pick a date that works. Ideally, sometime before it snows."

"Three weeks."

"Done," Max said.

"What do we tell Andrea?" Robby asked.

"Well, we sure as hell aren't going to tell her she's about to become the prize of a bike race."

"I agree. She's got to think the loser simply lost interest. We'll work out the details of your graceful exit after the race."

"Don't worry, I'm sure I can come up with some reason why you fell off the face of the earth that she'll believe," Max said with smug confidence.

"You really are one cocky son-of-a-bitch." Robby said through a thin smile.

"Not cocky. Positive," Max answered. "Considering the prize, this is one contest I'm not about to lose. You can take it to the bank."

"Ha! We'll see what we see. So, are we agreed?" Robby held out his hand to Max.

"Agreed. Winner takes all," Max said as they shook hands.

"In this case, Andrea is the 'all.' I'll buy the bikes. Exactly the same." Robby volunteered.

"If you're going to get the bikes, then I get first choice on the day of the race," Max's tone said this was non-negotiable.

"What? You don't trust me? You think I'd give you a faulty bike?"

Max nodded "Yeah, given what this is all about, I think you would. Just because you're my best friend, doesn't mean I trust you."

"Ah, the foundation of our friendship. A total lack of mutual trust."

"Hey, that's the one reason we've been friends for so long," Max said laughing.

"Okay, you mistrusting son-of-a-bitch, I'll buy the bikes and you get to choose which one you want to ride."

"On the day of the race," Max added.

"Any day you wish," Robby said. Then a question occurred to him, "When Andrea asks what we're doing and why we've bought two bikes, what do we tell her?"

"She won't ask, but if she does we'll tell her we're thinking about qualifying for next year's Tour de France."

* ~ * ~ *

They had agreed the race would both begin and end at hotel in San Remy. The route they chose through the Luberon lay between the Alpes-de-Haute-Provence and the plain of the Vaucluse. Fields of lavender, oakwood, ochre rock and limestone outcrops at every turn in the road. In the villages, medieval castles and hilltop villages, most bearing the "Loveliest Villages in France" label, succeed one another in the triangle formed by Gordes, Bonnieux and Ménerbes.

The first leg took them west toward Tarascon, the second south down the route de Fontvieille where they turned east toward Le Baux and then north for the final leg to Saint-Remy. For much of the race, they took turns trading the lead, allowing the rider in the back to benefit from the draft created by the man in front. It was on the Avenue Vincent Van Gogh about three kilometers to Saint Remy that Max broke away with a burst of energy he was sure would leave Robby, who'd been laboring, well behind.

As he rode toward the finish Max guessed he had but two kilometers to go. He was going to win.

The bang caught him totally by surprise.

The rear tire seemed to have exploded and wrap itself around the chain. While he was able to avoid falling off, it was immediately obvious to him that he wasn't going to be able to ride any further. Max pulled his bike off to the side. "What the hell," he exclaimed examining the tire. "I can't believe this – perfect road, no glass, no nails." He sat down dejected on the side of the road. It wasn't more than a few minutes later that he saw Robby riding toward him. It seemed to Max that Robby wasn't surprised to see him sitting with his crippled bike. His expression and tone already reflected his certain victory.

"Tough luck, guy. You'll still be my best man, right?" Robby shouted as he rode on.

Max took off his helmet and threw to the ground in disgust, "For what it's worth," he shouted as Robby disappeared around a curve "I know she loves me more."

12.

13 YEARS BEFORE THE MURDER
OF ANDREA TRASK

New York City

"Can a girl entice you to buy her lunch?"

"Andrea! You bet I can be enticed." Max virtually shouted into the phone. "It's been almost a year. Where are you?"

"At my mother's apartment."

"What are you doing in New York?"

"Quitting my job at the magazine and finalizing the wedding plans."

"I Robby with you?

"No, he's in LA talking to ABC about a televised mountain climb. Not sure."

"A televised mountain climb?"

"I'll tell you about it at lunch."

"Then the good news is I have you to myself."

"Is that a problem?"

"Not for me it's not. I just might kidnap you and hide you from Mr. Trask."

"Is that a threat or a promise?"

"To be determined," he laughed. "How long are you in town?"

"I have an 8PM flight to Rome tonight. I'm meeting my stepfather and we're going on to Anasara?"

"Good old Spaghetti, right?"

"You have a good memory."

"Where's your mother's apartment?"

"720 Park. At 71st Street."

"I'll pick you up at noon," he said and hung up.

It took him only three phone calls and a promised donation to the Central Park Conservatory to assure their lunch would more than just a lunch. By eleven he had everything planned and in place. At exactly twelve noon, a horse drawn carriage pulled up in front of 720 Park, its driver formally dressed all the way to his top hat. Andrea was waiting just outside the front of the apartment building. "Max! I love it!" she called as Max hopped down from the carriage. They met at the curb and he gave her a brief 'hello' kiss. "If I'd had more time I would have flown in the Queen's coronation coach."

"I almost believe you would have. Where are you taking me?"

"To a special place that will require three modes of transportation starting with this carriage."

"What, no jet?"

"No, retro transportation all the way." Max helped her into the carriage and the driver guided the horse around the corner onto 72nd and headed west toward the Fifth Avenue entrance to Central Park.

"You know, in all the years I've come to New York, this is the first time I've ever been in one of these carriages."

"I'm glad to be with you for a first."

Andrea gave him a knowing look. "We've had several 'firsts' together."

"My only regret is there haven't been more," he said.

As the carriage crossed Fifth Avenue and onto the Terrace Drive that crosses the park, Andrea glanced down at the Model Boat Pond. "I'd always hoped one day I'd have a son or a daughter and sit down there watching them sail one of those little boats." She drew down a and a veil of sadness and for a long moment fell silent. And then, "I learned several months ago I can't have children. Somethings missing inside and I can't even pronounce it.

"Robby never said anything about..."

"I'm not surprised. He didn't take it well. I guess he felt I'd let him down."

"Let *him* down?" Max made no effort to hide his surprise. "He must have been a real comfort to you," he said sarcastically.

Andrea looked as if she was about to respond, but immediately stuffed whatever it was she was going to say back into its private place. "Let's change the subject. I don't want to ruin this special day. I want us only to talk about happy things. And speaking of that, how is your new wife? Her name is Hillary, isn't it? Oh, and where is she?"

Max began to laugh. "I thought you said we were going to talk about happy things? I'm sorry to report my marriage has…shall we say disintegrated.. Totally kaput."

"But you've only been married for six months."

"Four," he corrected. "You know what they say, 'What happens in Vegas stays in Vegas.' Unfortunately, I should have left her in Vegas at her father's casino and _I_ should have left Vegas before I married her. Sadly, I didn't. My lawyer is in the process of working out a settlement."

"What was she like?"

Max shook his head as he considered his answer. "Let's just say her looks made up for what she lacked in intellect. In court Hillary tried to convince the judge she was an art aficionado. Some aficionado. The woman wouldn't know a Degas from a Disney. However, she was smart enough to know the art work I inherited from my father could be converted to cash faster than dollars can be changed into poker chips. So she tells the court she wants the Renoir, the Rembrandt, the Rubens and several others as part of her settlement. She left out the Modigliani because she couldn't pronounce it. . So her lawyer said it for her."

"No money, just paintings?"

"Money _and_ the paintings. Fortunately the court decided my offer to donate them to the National Gallery pre-empted hanging them in a Law Vegas casino."

"Didn't you have a pre-nuptial agreement?"

"Oh, we had one. But as I have learned, just because they claim it's a pre-nup, doesn't mean an angry spouse with an expensive lawyer can't find a way out of it. As it turns out, breaking a pre-nup comes down to how you answer three questions about the agreement: "When was it signed? Where was it signed? And under what conditions was it signed? Her lawyer contends the conditions… we were both, shall we say, were inebriated when we signed it… made the whole thing void. I told my lawyer to give her whatever it takes, absent the paintings, to make the whole unfortunate affair history."

The carriage came to a stop on the overpass over the Bethesda Terrace. "Mr. Roarke, we're here."

"And here is… ?" Andrea asked.

The second stage of our journey. This will be on foot. But as you can see from the stairway, it will be mostly downhill."

The Bethesda Terrace is actually two terraces, both an upper and a lower, which are connected by two grand staircases. The lower terrace extends to the edge of the Central Park Lake which, one-hundred and fifty years ago, was nothing more than a large, untamed swamp. In the middle of the lower terrace stands The Angel of the Waters fountain.

As they stepped off the staircase onto the lower terrace, Andrea said, "Look, the fountain is playing."

"When I told the park you were coming, they made sure to turn it on."

"Just for me?" she said in a playful challenge to his claim.

"Just for you," he said.

They walked across the terrace to the edge of the lake, which was dotted here and there with amateur oarsmen doing their best to avoid collisions with other rowboats.

"Is that for us?" Andrea asked pointing toward the gondola pulled up next to the Terrace.

"The last stage of our journey," Max said.

"Don't tell me you had it brought in?" Andrea said ready to be impressed.

"I wish I could say I had. Actually, it's been on The Lake and for hire since the mid-eighties. But I did arrange to have it waiting for us."

"The Roarke party?" the gondolier asked.

"A small party, as you can see."

As Max helped Andrea step into the gondola, she nodded toward the gondolier. "Does he sing Italian songs?"

"Giovanni," Max said to the man, "do you sing Italian songs?".

"My name is Klaus... I'm German. But I can fake a little O Solo Mio for you."

"Perfect."

As it turned out, Klaus did a reasonably good impression of an Italian gondolier.

"I take it the Boathouse is our destination. I love that place."

"Yes, but not the main restaurant, I've rented the Lake Room."

"The entire Lake Room? Isn't the Lake Room for large parties?"

"And in this case, a large party for two."

The gondola was maneuvered next to the edge of the restaurant. Max stood up and helped Andrea onto the landing. Their table had been placed overlooking the lake. A waiter stood nearby holding a bottle of champagne.

"Champagne? My, my, Mr. Roarke, you do think of everything."

Max motioned for the waiter to pour. "I hope this meets with your approval. It's Bollinger's Blanc de Noirs Vieilles Vignes Francaises 1997. They didn't have it on their wine list so I had it delivered."

"You continue to dazzle me Mr. Roarke," she said glowing. They waited for the champagne to be poured then Max raised his glass. "A toast. To you.

"No," she said, "to us."

"To all three of us?" he asked.

"No... just to us." she said softly. Her voice was tinged with purposeful intent. Yet, no sooner had the words passed her lips than she seemed to realize she had opened a private door and quickly closed it

Two waiters arrived with covered dishes and set them in front of Andrea and Max. "I hope you don't mind, I ordered for you."

"When the three of us were roaming around Europe, you always ordered for me. And it was always perfect. I wish I could say the same about Robby. To this day, he still has very little idea of what I like and don't like."

"Speaking as we are of my friend, tell me about Robby televising one of his climbs."

"It's something he's talking about with ABC. They're thinking about doing a series of climbing specials and Robby would be their first. It's not going to happen anytime soon. Maybe a couple years from now."

"He's done Everest. What's left for him to climb?"

"Peru. It's called Pinnacle Cumbre and it's really more of a giant slab of granite than your typical mountain. He told me it soars almost straight up for about 9000 feet. According to Robby, it's one of those mountains every Alpine climber worth his salt would like to climb."

"But nine thousand feet isn't all that high."

"No, but I guess from a technical standpoint it's considered one of the ten toughest climbs. According to Robby they're going to shoot the climb live because the producer feels there will be a lot more viewer tension if people know what they're seeing is happening as they watch."

"There will definitely be a hell of a lot of tension if he falls off or gets himself stuck some place where they can't get at him."

"What can I say? Much as I've tried, there's no talking him out of it. As you know better than anyone, Robby lives on the edge. It feeds his ego and his ego requires a lot of feeding. He hopes the climb will get his picture on the cover of Sports Illustrated."

"Well for sure he's never going to make the cover in the swim suit issue."

"That would make an interesting cover," she said joining Max in a brief laugh.

There was a momentary lull in the conversation, as both Max and Andrea appeared to be looking for the best way to disinvite Robby from their conversation. Max broke the silence. "You know what I forgot today?" Max said his eyes fixed on her with laser preciseness.

"What?

"An artist."

"An artist? What for?"

"To paint you. You are truly a work of art. And if I can't have the original... at least I'd have the copy... albeit in oil. God Andrea, every time I see you I realize I've forgotten just how truly beautiful you are."

"Is that the Champagne speaking, Max? I don't know if you've noticed, but we're most of the way through our second bottle."

He leaned back, realizing he had been less than discreet. He felt it best to offer an apology, "No, it's not the champagne, it's Max Roarke stepping way out of bounds."

Andrea reached over and laid her hand on his. The look on her face spoke to sweet memories. "Sometimes Max," she said softly, as if afraid somewhere in the empty room there might be ears, "I think about us... you and me... and I cry. I cry over what might have been."

"I think about that too."

"Max, I promised myself I would never ask, but I have to know, what happened? Why did you just... well, disappear? I know you said when you left us in Paris it was because of some major business problems you had to deal with. But you never came back. Was it something I did that drove you away?"

Max had expected one day she would ask for an explanation. He had considered any number of responses. Certainly, he could not tell her about the Tour de Francis. To admit he had abandoned the one person he loved more than any other because he'd lost a bike race, and to admit he had felt it necessary to honor his agreement with Robby would not only be demeaning and an insult to her but would confirm the worst about him. The last thing she needed to know was that Robby and he had made her little more than a trophy to be won or lost. No, his ego would not permit him to admit what a fool he had been. That the whole thing had been the biggest mistake of his life, so he opted for a lie. "Well, I just felt... at least I thought... like they say, three was beginning to be a crowd. It was pretty obvious you really preferred Robby. I thought maybe it was better if I just disappeared."

Tears came to her eyes, "Oh Max... oh Max, you fool. How could you have thought that?" Andrea turned away unable to give voice to the thoughts racing through her mind.

Well, I certainly made a mess of that, he thought. If there were words that might have been right for the moment, that might have stemmed the tears, he could not find them.

It was full a minute before she turned back to him, dabbed at her eyes with a handkerchief and took Max's hand.

"This has been special, Max," she said standing up.

"You're not leaving?" It wasn't a question but a plea. "Please stay a little longer," Max urged.

"It's after two. I have to go. I still have things to do before I leave for the airport." She paused, her face full of sadness and longing, "And it would hurt too much to stay here any longer."

Max stood up, but he realized there was no way he was going to keep her from leaving. "Andrea, let me call you a car service."

"No... no... I want to walk a bit.."

"Andrea... you've got to know..." Max started to speak.

She cut him off as she turned back to him. "Please. Don't say what I think you're going to say. If you do, I won't be able to leave... and we both know I have to." She backed away from the table. "I love you Max. I loved you then and God help me I still do." She turned and hurried toward the door.

Max watched her go. A torrent of depression swept over him. He'd never felt emptier or more alone. She had been like the brass ring on a merry-go-round. She had come around and invited him to grab it... and he'd let it go. He could not imagine it would ever come around again.

13.

12 YEARS BEFORE THE MURDER
OF ANDREA TRASK

Greenwich, Connecticut

Robby opened his eyes. "Son-of-a-bitch! Where the hell am I?" He looked up at Max who was standing next to the bed looking down at him.

"Stanwich Hospital. Take it easy. We'll get you out in time for the wedding."

"What the fuck is this?" He had just discovered his right arm was in a full shoulder and arm plaster cast. "My arm! My God! It's dead! I can't feel a thing all the way up to my shoulder!"

"That's because the Doctor shot you full of Demerol. You won't feel a thing for hours."

"How did this happen? I don't remember breaking my arm." He said looking at his enormous cast.

"Let's just say you're not a natural when it comes to skateboarding."

"Skateboarding? Who me?" He asked in utter disbelief.

"Yeah, you."

"I've never been on a skateboard," he protested.

"You're tellin' me. However, I will say for the first five minutes you looked like a pro."

"When did I get on a skateboard?" He almost shouted

"Must have been after two. Some dude came into the bar with his skateboard and you paid him a hundred dollars for it. Then, after a skating down Greenwich Avenue, you decided to show us you could take the steps on the Greenwich Town Hall. But what did you in was when you decided to hop your board on the railing."

"Shit! I don't remember doing any of that. How could I not remember?"

"Because of the red head you were hitting on in the bar. The one falling out of her dress."

"Redhead? Oh, yeah, he said with a tinge of guilt. "What did she have to do with this?" he asked looking at his cast. There was panic in his eyes.

"Well, I discovered she slipped you a Rohypnol."

"What's a Rohyphol?

"A roofie. Basically, it's a date rape drug. Although, given your condition, I don't know why she would have wanted to rape you. Plus, you were too busy showing her what an expert skateboarder you are."

"I don't remember any of that."

Max smiled sympathetically, "Maybe it's better you don't. After you crashed and burned, you were in a hell of a lot of pain. Screaming your head off. The EMT people really had a tough time getting you in the ambulance."

"What the hell did I break?"

"According to the x-rays, you cracked your collarbone, and broke your forearm. The break is a nasty one."

"How they hell am I going to get married with..." he nodded toward the cast on his arm, "with this?"

"All you have to do is stand up in front of the minister. I will hold you up, if necessary, and answer 'I do.'"

"What time is it?"

"About one."

"Shit, the weddings at three."

"Not to worry. I've got your tux and I'll get you dressed and drive you to the church in plenty of time."

Robby struggled to sit up and found the cast was forcing his arm to extend out almost perpendicular to his body. He looked like a waiter carrying a tray without the tray. "Shit! Andrea is really going to be pissed."

"Hey, if you want to postpone it, I'm sure Andrea will understand."

"No fucking way. I don't care if I have to get married from a stretcher."

"That could be arranged," Max said with a smile.

* ~ * ~ *

There was a shocked and muffled reaction to the arrival of the groom at the church wearing a large plaster cast in place of the missing right sleeve on his tuxedo.

Andrea had been told about Robby's accident and was warned to be prepared to find a man in a very large cast on his right arm and shoulder waiting for her at the altar. As she walked into the church, the initial look on her face said the preparation had been inadequate. Halfway down the aisle she managed to regain her composure and effect an expression intended to give the guests the idea she found nothing out of the ordinary waiting to greet her.

"What happened?" she whispered as she stepped up to his side.

"I slipped"

"On what"

"Ahhh, a skateboard."

"A skateboard? What were you doing on a skateboard?"

"Long story."

"Give me the short version."

Robby, in need of rescue, was saved any more explanation when the minister began. "Deadly beloved, we are gathered here... ."

~~*

During the reception, Robby managed to sidestep, deflect and ignore most of the questions about his cast with a short "I slipped." "I tripped." Or "I fell." Andrea tried several times to probe for a more details but gave up when he put her off with a "Later."

It was after eleven Robby stood in the bathroom of the large suite of rooms at the Pierre Hotel on Fifth Avenue looking at himself in the mirror and wondering how he was supposed to have any kind of conjugal consummation with the huge cast on his arm and shoulder. *So far no pain*, he thought. *Didn't Max say the Doctor had said his painkiller would wear off by about this time? Wait a minute, the Doctor didn't say it. Max did. In fact, I never saw a doctor.* He began to wiggle his fingers, to rotate his shoulder, to the move and extend his arm as much as the cast permitted. "Fuck me!" he shouted. "Bastard. That son-of-a-bitch!"

"What's wrong?" Andrea said as she opened the bathroom door. "Does it hurt?"

"Not in the way you might think." Then more to himself, "I can't believe he suckered me into this."

"What are you talking about?"

"Give me a minute and I'll show you." He picked up the phone in the bathroom and called the front desk. "This is Robby Trask in the Penthouse Suite. I need a hammer and maybe a saw up here right away. And tell whoever brings it, there's hundred bucks if he gets it here in the next five minutes."

It took less than two for Robby to break up the plaster and free himself from the cast. As the last of the plaster fell away from his forearm, he saw the message.

The Score is 15-15
Max
Your serve.

Andrea started to laugh, then turned away hoping Robby hadn't noticed.

III
Le JEU ULTIME

1.

2 YEARS BEFORE THE MURDER
OF ANDREA TRASK

Cap Ferrat, France

He had dreamed all night of Andrea and awaken to the sad realization that she was not there in the bed next to him. After her divorce, he decided, even if they held off getting married for an appropriate amount of time, they could at least live together. Maybe at Anasara. To have her perfumed smell, her wonderful skin next to his... it could not happen soon enough. He dressed, went downstairs and asked his breakfast to be served on the terrace so he could enjoy the morning freshness and savor the views of his gardens. *I would love to see her here when I wake in the morning,* he said to himself. He imagined walking out on the terrace to join her as she lifted her face to his and kissed him with the same passion they had shared the past two days. *God, I want her. I want her with me now. Today.*

After a moment he found his thoughts turned to wondering what he would say to Robby. How would he say it? *Did I mention Andrea wants a divorce? Oh, and by the way, once it's final we plan to get married.' Nothing like coming straight out and smashing him over the head with the fact I'm about to run off with his wife,* he chided himself. Even if Robby should decide to accept the inevitable, Max could imagine him saying something snide and maybe even belittling, *Max this reminds me of the guy who decides not to buy a new car, but to save money and settle for one coming off lease. It may be a bit used, slightly depreciated, some scratches in the paint and a few too many miles on it, but hey, it's still very serviceable.*

Knowing Robby, Max could imagine a response like that would not be out of the question, especially if the divorce comes as a total surprise. *No telling how he'll react. Angry? Maybe. Physical? Not his style. Shocked? Possibly. Passive? Doubtful. Whatever, it's bound to get messy. Even if what Andrea says is true, that there's nothing left in their marriage, the fact remains he won her. She's been in his trophy case for almost ten years. He's not one to give up one of his prize trophies without a fight. No, this is not going to be easy and it sure as hell isn't going to pleasant.* For a moment he thought how much different his return to Cap Ferret would have been had Robby been home that first day. None of this would have happened and he was surprised to find himself wondering if maybe that would have been better. *No. No,* he corrected himself. *Andrea and I were meant to be together. I'll do what I have to do.*

At first he wasn't sure what it was he'd just seen. He had but a brief glimpse but felt sure he had seen something white appear at the far end of his garden then disappear. Maybe a reflection? No. There it was again. Now he was sure what he had seen was a woman in a long, nearly diaphanous white dress moving quickly though the distant trees. Then nothing. He waited a moment and like the finale of a magic act, she suddenly seemed to materialize in the middle of his pavilion alongside one of the statues. Max stood up and started down the terrace steps onto the washed gravel path calling a "Hello." Even at a distance he could see she was young and had long, flowing blond hair. It may have been the way the sun was striking the pavilion or maybe a reflection off one of the ponds, but she seemed bathed in an ethereal and opalescent glow. As he drew closer, he got the impression she was waiting for him.

"Hello," he called again. No response. He was still maybe a hundred feet from her, but close enough to make out her features. *That is one very good-looking woman*, he thought. He called to her, "You're welcome to walk around, if you like." A forlorn smile formed on her lips for the briefest of moments, then, for no apparent reason, she started to weep.

"Pelléas. Pelléas!" He heard her say. Though Max spoke passable French, he had no idea what she was saying. He was about to ask who she was, when she simply disappeared.

Where the hell did she go? Max could not believe what he had just seen. *Damn, I'm looking at her and she just vanishes. And I haven't even been drinking.* He waited for several minutes, thinking she might show herself again. When she did not, he turned and walked back to his villa terrace. He found himself looking around several times to see if she might have reappeared. No sign of her. Where had she come from? And how had she gotten in? The entire seventeen acres of his villa were surrounded by a high stone wall. It would take a pole vaulter to get over. The only entrance to the property was though the front gate. Or at least so he thought. As she clearly did not seem to represent any kind of danger – at least not to himself – he decided she'd have to find her way out the same way she found her way in. He did, however, make a mental note to tell his head groundskeeper to check the perimeter of the property for some break in the wall, some place where the stones might have given way during his absence. *Wouldn't do to the place overrun with beautiful women*, he mused, and then laughed at the thought.

* ~ * ~ *

Max had not been in his library since he had returned to Cap Ferrat. His time and interest had been totally devoted to Andrea. The room, per his instructions, was exactly as he had left it two years ago. He checked his shoes for dirt then crossed the 18th century Savonnerie rug he had bought at a French auction years before and sat down at his desk that faced the large window overlooking his gardens. He began to shuffle through the stack of papers on the desk and stopped when it came to the brochure the National Museum of Art had created to announce his donation of five of his father classic paintings. As a member of the Museum Board and a major benefactor, it was understood than his divorce settlement had included his promise to donate some of the priceless paintings his father had collected. Most, if not all of the collection, had not been seen in public for decades. As he thumbed through the pages a pained smile crossed his face as he remembered how Robby had succeeded in humiliating him and creating a Museum scandal witnessed by the hundreds of press, art aficionados and spurious connoisseurs assembled to witness the unveilings.

The main hall in the museum had been set up for the presentation. All five paintings were placed on easels and covered with black velvet drapes. The program called for Winnifred Manfuso, the imperious, self-important president and chief curator of the museum, to reveal them one at a time and make brief comments on the long-hidden treasures. Although she had openly expressed her dislike for Max and frequently made it known she did not think a man with his profligate reputation had any place a board of such distinguished men and women, she was overruled by the majority of directors who recognized their need of his financial largess. They decided to overlook the fact that he seemed to enjoy irritating the imperious Winnifred by caustically finding fault with her proposals and decisions. She, in turn, would dismiss his opposition by making it clear she found him a cultural dilettante who had had to buy his seat on the board. Despite her obvious dislike for Max, she had nevertheless been more than happy to accept the gifts of his father's paintings. She even overcame her tacit reluctance to displaying the paintings in a separate room designated as a memorial to his father and the Roarke estate.

After a much too long an introduction, Winifred began the unveiling. First the Renoir – applause. Then the Modigliani – appreciative murmurs. Followed by the Rembrandt and the Matisse – more "ahs and applause." The last and potentially most impressive was the Venus of Urbino, a reclining nude by Titian. When the velvet cover slipped away, the audience was greeted not with the Titian's Venus, but with a huge pornographic blow up of would-be Venus performing fellacio on an extremely hairy man undressed as Neptune.

Winnifred turned crimson and then turned sharply to Max spewing a series of non-artistic invectives accusing him of deliberately intending to humiliate both her and the National Museum of Art with this disgusting prank. Max's shook his head and held out his hands to protest his innocence. As he attempted to plead his innocence to the audience, he caught sight or Robby in the back of the hall raising his arms in triumph as he slipped out of the hall. Looking back at the nude, Max noticed the fine print on the right buttock of the woman:

30 -15 Me
Your serve

The reaction of the museum crowd was what one would have expected. It took several hours to quell the outrage of the museum directors and for Max to find the missing Titian hanging sedately in an adjacent gallery. Max's denials that he had anything to do with the pornography fell on deaf ears. Certainly, there was no way to explain Le Jeu Ultime to Winifred, the board and the press. After the Titan was returned and the pornography dispose of, Max resigned from the board and knew he had but one option. He would have to even the score.

When a year later Robby let it be known ABC sports was going to broadcast his climb of Pinnacle Cumber, the pillar of granite in Peru that no one had ever climbed successfully, Max saw it as his opportunity to "return serve." On the night before Robby's climb, Max hired a helicopter to land on the flat top of Pinnacle and place two park benches, a dozen empty whisky bottles, and two totally inert rummies asleep on the benches surrounded by assorted props which made it look like the two inebriants had climbed up the mountain for a booze-drenched picnic.

The next day, after what was a reported as a spectacular climb, Robby was greeted at the top by the sight of two sober, but frightened derelicts wondering how they got there and asking in Spanish if Robby could get them down. Attached to one of the benches was a large sign that read:

The score is now 30-30 – All
Let's call it a draw

The sporting press made sport of the event and headlined Robby's accomplishment as *The Daring Assault of Picnic Mountain.* In another article the headline read: *Rummies Beat Climber to Top of Pinnacle Cumbre.* He became the punch line to a joke at the Alpine Club. The climb became the kind of legend to which no man would ever want to attach his name.

As Andrea had said, "He embarrassed you at the National Museum and then you turned around and humiliated him with your Picnic Mountain thing. I don't think he's every really forgiven you. Max had to admit, if only to himself, *it was over the top, But,* he rationalized, w*hen he challenges me, no way I won't accept. Maybe subconsciously I really do want to humiliate him. Look at what I've been doing with Andrea the last three days. And she's not even part of the game. No, with Andrea it's no game. I love her and always have. Was stupid of me to give into Robby's bike race victory. I should have married her and said to hell with friendship.*

As his thoughts rummaged through their four Le Jeu Ultimes, Max had to admit that what had started out years ago as a mostly vacuous series of inane college pranks had somehow morphed into a bizarre and essentially demented competition.

I should have let it end at the museum, Max thought, and then made no effort to hold back a chuckle. *No way I could let him walk away a winner. But it's all behind us now.*

* ~ * ~ *

The cell phone call began not with a 'Welcome home,' but with a verbal baiting. "Max, unless you've become soft in your old age and are afraid to take me on, you'll get your sorry carcass over to my house at three o'clock and be prepared to have me wipe your ass all over my tennis court."

Given what Andrea had told him about Robby working with a pro all summer, Max was not surprised by the call or the challenge. As Max had not played more than a couple times all summer, he knew the match would have to begin off the court in order for him to overcome whatever advantage Robby might have as a result of his work with the instructor

Max immediately decided on a four-step strategy calculated to destroy Robby's game. Step one: Demean and Degrade the challenge of the baiter. "The only way you'll wipe my ass is with toilet paper and while you may be into that kind of anal perversion, I'm not. However, I will take great pleasure in proving once again when it comes to playing tennis with me, you are totally out classed."

"I'll show you out-classed, Maxie. Wait till you see how I've elevated my game."

"You'd need a fork lift to do that."

"You want to put money on it?"

"Money? Bet money? A bit pedestrian for the two of us, don't you think? If we're going to bet, let's get serious."

"Serious as in, what do you have in mind?"

"The payoff of the bet needs to be at least semi-humiliating," Max said

"Agreed," Robby responded and then paused a moment before he said, "How about this? I'm hosting a dinner tonight for you and a dozen or so vague acquaintances at the Voile d'Or. There'll be enough bodies for a proper audience."

"Audience?"

"For the performance. At some point during the meal, the loser has to stand up on his chair, ask for everyone's undivided attention, drop his pants and recite a poem."

"What poem?" Max asked.

"Any poem."

"Works for me."

"Good. You're on."

"You will be wearing shorts under your pants, I hope," Max said.

"It's what you'll be wearing that worries me. Spare us having to look at you in bikini briefs?"

"Given I won't be the one dropping my trousers, it won't matter what kind of underwear I'll be wearing."

"To be on the safe side wear boxer shorts, OK? Oh, and one more thing," Robby added. "No one must know the loser is paying off a bet. For all they know, one of us has simply gone off the deep end. Blame it in the champagne, if you have to, but not the bet. It has to stay between us. We won't even tell Andrea."

"I'm sure she'll be very proud of her husband's ability to recite poetry sans his pants."

"But she won't, because it will be you reciting poetry."

"You're delusional, you know. No way you're going to beat me."

"Three o'clock. On the court, dick head." Then with true affection, "God, I'm glad your back. Life around here has been really dull this summer," he said and hung up.

Well, it won't be very dull once I tell you about Andrea and me, he thought. Then to an empty room he asked, "How the hell do I tell my best friend I have been sleeping with his wife who wants a divorce so she can marry me?"

* ~ * ~ *

Robby's tennis court was cut into the side of the bluff beneath Robby's enormous villa and just a few feet above the water. A spiral stairway led from the lawn in front of his villa down to the court and the small tennis hut. Max made his way to the edge of the bluff and found a place where he was able to look down on the court as Robby warmed up with what he presumed was his tennis coach. With his wavy blond hair and chiseled features, dressed as he was in his Nike Solitaire Kicks and his custom-made Eton shirt, he looked as if he'd just stepped out of a tennis magazine ad. And the graphite racket? Max was sure he'd had it custom made. Not only did he look the part of a pro, but his racket control was excellent and his return shots were deep. His cut dinks over the net all but bounced back, the lobs to the back line seemed to have eyes and his serves were rockets. Andrea was right. He had really improved his game.

Max immediately realized their match was not going to be like those in years past when Max usually let Robby win a game or two so as not to send him into a total post-match funk. Maybe if he were able to bring his "A" game to the court he could beat Robby. But given that he had played so little while untangling his life from the flower of Dayton, Ohio, there was no "A" game to bring.

"Now for step two," Max said to himself. "Get into the Robby's head before the first serve." His mind quickly settled on what he had to do. *I've got to find a way to push the right buttons as soon as I walk onto the court. If I can do that, I'll destroy his concentration and piss him off so instead of thinking about placing his shots, all he'll want to do is slam the ball down my throat. And I know exactly what it's going to take to mess up your head, Robby ol' friend.* Max began to smile and it was all he could do to choke back a laugh. *I'm going to own you today.* he thought as he looked down at the court. *I am absolutely going to* own *you! Just like I always have.*

He drove back to his villa and began to dress for the match. He put on a flowered Hawaiian muumuu shirt that had been stored away years ago. He found a torn and faded pair of madras Bermuda shorts and then decided to put on black socks – one longer than the other. *Tennis shoes? Not for this game. How about a pair of brand-new Gucci loafers?* He looked at himself in the mirror. Outrageous. Ridiculous. In no way did he resemble a tennis player. One more thing. *I need a beret.* He found one left by some long ago guest in the foyer closet. *Ah... rose tinted granny glasses... they will complete the look.*

* ~ * ~ *

For a moment, Robby acted as if he didn't even recognize the man walking on his court.

"I'm ready,' Max shouted. "You need to warm up or shall we just play?"

"What the hell are you wearing? Are we playing tennis or are you going to a costume party? You can't play in that."

"Why not? Do you have a dress code on your court?"

"Come on Max, get serious. If you're afraid to play me, just say so. We can cancel our bet."

"Who's afraid? I'm ready. Before we begin, I think you should know I have played three times in the last six months." It sounded as if he were issuing a friendly warning.

"So, what are you telling me? You want me to spot you a couple games?"

"No. The other way around. I thought you might want me to spot *you* a couple of games to make the match more even, I'll be happy to start with you up two games to love if you think it will help."

"You bastard," Robby shot back making no effort to hide the fact Max's needle had found its mark. "We start even. And since it's my court, I'll serve first." Robby was about to serve when he noticed Max did not have a racket. "Where the hell is your racket?"

"Couldn't find mine. Can I borrow one of yours?" *Oh,* he thought, *to beat him with a borrowed racket will be icing on the cake.*

"Take you pick," Robby growled.

Max walked over to the side of the court where Robby had left several rackets on a bench. He picked one up, looked at it, took a couple of swings, pounded the strings and then walked back onto the court.

Step three. Frustrate the hell out of him.

"Wait a minute. Don't like this one," he said and walked off the court again. He took his time selecting another racket. Out of the corner of his eye, he could see Robby's impatience was growing exponentially. *Good*, he thought. *He's really getting pissed. I guess I had better take a couple minutes to clean my sunglasses.*

"Are we going to play today?" Robby's frustration had surfaced and was spilling over.

"Would you rather play some other time?" Max's tone was both solicitous and patronizing at the same time."

"No, God dam it! Get your ass on the court!"

He's almost primed, Max mused. Slowly Max ambled back on the court and dropped his racket. He stooped to pick it up and then settled down on one knee to adjust his black socks. As he stood up and took his position to receive Robby's serve he said. "Ready? Need some warm up serves?"

Robby said nothing but tossed the ball over his head and blasted it over the net. It was well long.

"Just long," Max said knowing Robby could see the ball landed almost five feet out of the box.

Robby's second serve was just at hard and it wound up in the net. "Damn!" He quickly moved to the other side of the court, placed a bullet of a serve in the middle of the box and rushed the net to cut off the return. Max hit it with top spin and the ball shot back to Robby's right and landed just inside the end line. Had he been pressed, he would have had to admit it was a very lucky shot. But given the circumstances and the opponent, he said nothing knowing it had the desired effect. *Now to rub it in.* "Was that in?"

"You know goddamn well it was, you bastard! How the hell did you even get your racket on the serve?"

"It sort of like riding a bicycle," he said in a tone intended to insert yet another needle, "Once you've mastered the game, you never forget how to hit winners."

Max's pedantic, master-talking-to-pupil superior tone drew an immediate and heated response, "Yeah? Well let me see if I can knock you off your god dam bicycle." He faulted twice and bounced his racket hard off the ground.

"I think we're Love-40, right?" Max asked intending to sound as if he'd lost track of the score.

"Right!" he spat and muttered something about the legitimacy of Max's birth. Robby retrieved the ball at the base of the net and turned his back as he walked slowly to the base line doing his best to regain his composure.

He's really starting to lose it, Max decided. *Let's see if I can help him along.* Max pulled out a pack of cigarettes and lit up. When Robby turned around to serve, he saw the cigarette between Max's lips.

"Since when in the hell did you start smoking?" Robby asked clearly vexed.

"Just started. Helps me stay relaxed when I play tennis.."

From that point on the game was essentially over. Max had succeeded, as Robby would have put it, 'in messing with his head.' All Robby wanted to do was pound the ball at Max. Max on the other hand was on his game. He lobbed him, dinked him, hit winners down the side and ran Robby all over the court. Max served at 40-15 in the sixth game. Robby returned the serve deep and then rushed the net in hopes of cutting off Max's return. Max lifted a high lob over Robby head. He turned, ran back to the base line to set up for a smash of the lob

Step four: The coup de grace. The final affront to the opponent's game.

Max turned his back on Robby, bent over, dropped his Bermudas and mooned him.

"Hit this, asshole!" Robby shouted, putting every fiber of his frame into what he intended to be a rocket of a smash. He whiffed. He totally missed the ball which fell well within the backline for the winning point. His temper flared and he threw his racket over the court fence into the Mediterranean and followed it with a string of expletives.

As he scored the final point he shouted, "Game and Set. I believe per our bet, it's you who will be dropping 'trou' at dinner tonight. I do hope you'll choose a short poem."

"You son of a bitch." Robby said with an 'I-don't-believe-it-grin' that seemed to concede the fact he'd been had. "You rotten son of a bitch. You really fucked with my head and, goddamn it, I let you do it. God, I don't know how I can hate a guy as much as I do you and love him at the same time. Now, get the fuck off my court and take off that goddamn outfit. Burn it." Robby walked over to the side of the court, slumped into a chair and started to take off his shoes. "I'll see you tonight. Seven at the Voile d'Or. And let me warn you, I may not wear any underpants."

"That'll be a treat." Max said laughing. He crossed the court to pick up the balls. As he did, he happened to glance out on the rocky seawall that was busy holding back the waves rolling in off the Mediterranean. She was well over fifty yards from where he stood, but he was sure it was the woman he had seen in his garden that morning. She was wearing the same long, diaphanous white dress, which responded to a gust of sea breeze and billowed up revealing her long perfectly shaped legs. He looked back at Robby, "Do you know who she is?"

"Who you talking about?

"The woman standing there on the rock wall. Come here and take a look."

Robby pulled off his last shoe and walked across the court in his stocking feet.

"Damn, she's gone," Max said.

"Where was she?"

"Right down there on the rocks."

"You're imagining things. No way anyone, especially a woman, could get herself down there without risking breaking her neck."

"Well, she got down there somehow. I'm sure it was the same woman I saw walking around in my gardens this morning. She was dressed in the same white dress. Actually, it was more of a gown than a dress. Long blond hair. Great body... or at least what I could see of it. Had a real ethereal look about her."

"Well, if you see her again, bring her to the Voile d'Or tonight. Other than Andrea, there's not a decent looking woman in the lot."

2.

2 YEARS BEFORE THE MURDER
OF ANDREA TRASK

Cap Ferrat, France

Max pulled up to the Voile d'Or just as Robby and Andrea were going inside. Max handed his keys to the valet as Robby reappeared out of the front door.

"We *are* going to have a rematch?" It was more of a demand than a question. "And without any of that shit you pulled today." He began to laugh. "I don't know where you found that outfit, but I wish I had a picture."

"I can wear it again, if you like?"

"Not on my court, you won't. Next time..."

Before Robby could continue, Max broke in. "Listen, I'm going to let you off the hook on our bet. You don't have to drop your pants tonight. Pushing your buttons today was all the reward I need."

Robby's expression suddenly turned dark and there was intensity in his voice. "A bet is a bet and I always pay my bets. Believe me, if I had won, I would have demanded to collect from you."

Max was slightly taken aback by Robby tone and could sense there was no way he was going to change his mind, so he simply acquiesced with a shrug and said, "I hope the poem is short."

"It is," Robby said. For a moment he just stared off into space as though taking a moment to collect his thoughts then clapped Max on the back and grinned, "Come on inside, Andrea is dying to see you. How long has it been since we were all together? A couple years?"

"I've lost track," Max answered quickly. *Well, some of us have been together a little more recently than that*, he thought already feeling conflicted over what he and Andrea had decided.

Andrea was waiting in the small lobby. As if by some prior agreement, they immediately fell into the roles of two old friends greeting each other after a long absence. "Well, finally and at last you've come home," she said.

"Yes, and for the sole purpose of seeing you. Andrea, you get more beautiful each time I see you. Come here and give me my welcome home hug."

She put her arms around him and pressed her body into his. Max could see Robby take the arms of two of his guests and start to escort them out of the lobby into the restaurant. For a moment he was tempted to follow his cursory buss on her cheek with a full mouth kiss, but seeing they were not alone, he restrained himself at the last minute. "God, I love you, Andrea," he whispered in her ear. "Think we could just duck out of here and not be missed?"

"Not likely," she laughed

"Talking to Robby about..." he hesitated, "about us, isn't going to be easy."

"I know. Maybe you should let me tell him."

"No. I think it's better if I do it. If he's going to get mad, let him take it out on me."

"When do you plan to have your," she searched for a word, "your chat?"

"I think later tonight. Knowing Robby, he will want to close the place and I'll stay with him. Hopefully, he will have had enough champagne so things won't get too ugly. Thank God he's always been a mellow drunk."

"Good evening Andrea dear. Could my eyes deceive me or is that Maximillian Roarke in your embrace?" The syrupy voice belonged to Ellenorita Pulinzie de Torsan, the Cap Ferrat purveyor of malicious gossip. To Max, the greeting sounded more like, 'Ah ha! Caught you two in the act!'

"Andrea, I can see at the very least, you are exceedingly happy to see Max has finally come home." Her tone was heavy with innuendo.

What did she mean by 'at the very least,' he wondered? The haughty smirk on her face suggested this was a woman who had just come upon juicy fodder for her next rumor.

Andrea quickly turned away toward her guest. "Ellenorita, so good of you to come," Andrea said doing her best to project a modicum of sincerity. "Yes, having Max home is a little like discovering the missing brother you thought had been lost at sea has finally been rescued. Now, you must tell me, where *did* you find that most *interesting* dress." The word 'interesting' hung ambiguously between them so that depending on the listener's interpretation it could be construed either as 'I must know whose haute couture you're wearing?' Or

'How anyone with taste would be caught dead in the outfit?' She pasted a smile on her face which gave Ellenorita no clue as to her intent.

"Just something I picked up in Paris..."

Before she could finish, Andrea turned her back on the woman to greet two guests who had just entered the front door of the hotel lobby.

Max, as the guest of honor, had been placed opposite Robby on the other end of the rectangular table. Once everyone had been seated, Robby stood up and addressed his guests, "I can't tell you how much I'm looking toward to our dinner together this evening.

Andrea was to Max's his right. She leaned over to him and whispered, "He's about to dazzle our guests with his checkbook."

Max responded with an expression which asked for an explanation.

"Wait, you'll see," she said.

"I'm happy to announce that, for your enjoyment this evening, I have selected from my wine cellar one of the world's most extraordinary – and needless to say *expensive*," – he let the word expensive linger on his lips' – champagnes. However, before I have Philippe and his staff start pouring, let me tell you a little about the history of this liquid gem. At the beginning of the twentieth century, Heidsieck was the champagne of the House of Kings. And every year between 1900 and 1916, Tsar Nicolas II of Russia ordered 250,000 bottles. Unfortunately, at least for him, the last shipment never arrived because on November 3, 1916 at 5.30 a.m., a German U-22 submarine torpedoed the Swedish ketch carrying the shipment of Heidsieck. It all sank to the bottom just off the coast of Finland and was presumed lost forever. Then, some eighty years later, deep-sea divers discovered a sparkling treasure on the sea floor of the Gulf of Finland; 2000 of bottles of the 1907 Heidsieck champagne, well preserved and nicely chilled. Now, you might ask, where are those bottles today? Well, happily some are here with us tonight, but most are in Moscow in the wine cellar of the Ritz-Carlton where they can be purchased for the most reasonable price of $275,000 a bottle. Because of its history, this brave little champagne is known by its current name, Shipwreck 1907 Heidsieck. It is my pleasure to share with my dear friends several bottles of this French jewel from the bottom of the Baltic Sea. Philippe," he said to the captain, "will you and your staff please pour?"

The staff appeared with several bottles and began to pour.

"And now," Robby continued, "before we lift our glasses, let me offer a toast. As you know, this little end of season gathering is for the purpose of welcoming back our prodigal neighbor, Max Roarke. While appearing to be charming, gracious as well as recently made available for any of you ladies planning to leave your husbands, he is at heart a miserable son-of-a bitch whose tennis court attire shows a complete lack of class and taste. But aside from that and his many personal unsavory habits, trespasses and failings, he remains my best friend," he paused and let an enigmatic smile creep across his face. "Except at those times when he chooses to be my number one foe. So, here's to you Max, my friend. Great to have you back. And I'm sure my lovely wife shares my sentiment. Now that you're back, I look forward to whatever surprises we have in store for one another. And I'm sure there will be surprises." He lifted his glass in salute and brought it to his lips.

Max found himself wondering if Robby had purposely inserted hints in his toast suggesting he suspected, or possibly knew, what was going on between his friend and his wife. Max decided the tinge of guilt bubbling up in his conscience was forcing him to read too much into the toast. He took a long sip of Robby's champagne. "So, this is what money, tastes like."

Other voices chimed in.

"Incredible."

"If silk had a taste this would be it."

"Marvelous."

"Lucky us!"

"Wonderful treat, Robby," Max said. "A toast to the U-Boat Captain for making this possible."

The meal progressed and the Shipwreck 1907 Heidsieck flowed like Cold Duck at a college fraternity party.

After they'd finished the flambé, Robby tapped his glass and singled for Philippe to refill the glasses one last time. He pushed back his chair and stepped up on it. The expression on the faces of the guests varied from shock to outright laughter.

"What in the hell are you doing, Trask?" one of the guests asked.

"I am about to entertain you by reciting a poem. And lest you think I might be subjecting you to a long and tedious recital of one of those lengthy tomes we all recall from our school days, this just happens to be the world's shortest poem. And so that I can be assured of your undivided attention, I will lower my pants."

Max glanced at Andrea who's unsettled expression said she could not believe what was taking place.

Robby dropped his trousers around his ankles revealing white shorts covered with images of red ants. "I give you Fleas, by the poet Anonymous. He paused, took a deep breath and with a flourish recited the poem.

Adam
Had 'em.

Robby bowed, looked at everyone at the table inviting their applause. Max accommodated him. Two or three other men joined him accompanied by their bellicose laugher and shouts of "Well done!" The rest of the table seemed frozen in a state of mild shock. After a moment, Robby reached down and pulled up his pants.

Andrea, making no effort to hide her disgust, leaned over toward Max and whispered, "He's just paid off a bet, right?"

Max pretended not to hear her question.

"Come on, you heard me," she challenged. Her tone was accusatory.

"It could have been me."

"Tennis?"

"Tennis," he confirmed.

"I watched part of your match today."

"I didn't see you."

"I was up on the cliff. I thought dropping your pants to moon Robby showed a lot of maturity and class on your part. Something I'd expect from a sixteen-year-old." she said her voice tinged with mild derision.

"It worked. I won." Then in an effort to make light of his set point ploy he added, "And because I won, I was not the one standing on a chair reciting poetry."

Andrea shook her head. "Will you two ever grow up?" The tone of her voice suggested she did not expect an affirmative answer.

"Philippe," Robby said gesturing toward the Maître D', please bring me my box of Montecristos. I think the Shipwreck 1907 deserves a fitting finale."

Andrea pushed her chair back and stood up.

"Are we leaving?" Robby asked in a tone that made it clear he was not.

"Not *we*. Me. I invite those of you who find cigars as offensive as I do, to join me. But before I go, I want to apologize for my husband's chair-top performance just now. As you witnessed, sans-culotte, my husband lacks a certain degree of literary and cultural sophistication. I had hoped we would hear something from Tennyson or Lord Bryon or at the very least, Robert Frost. But alas, all we got was... Anonymous. You'll forgive me if I leave you here in the company of your puerile host."

The table broke into laugher.

Robby smiled and nodded his appreciation for her response "Well said, my dear," he said nodding in her direction. Then looking at his guests, he added, "I'm not sure what the word puerile means, but I have hunch it's not a compliment." He laughed doing his best to make light of the moment.

"Very perceptive of you, dear,' she said mockingly and then to the men at the table, "And be careful, for all I know those cigars might be loaded."

"Not a chance," Robby said. "I'm far too classy a guy to pass out loaded cigars," again he laughed but it lacked conviction.

Andrea turned and leaned down to give Max the expected good-bye kiss on his cheek. As she did she whispered, "I'll come by tomorrow. I'm really afraid how he might respond when you tell him." She stood up and gestured for the other women to follow.

"Don't wait up for me, dear," Robby called after her. Then to the rest of the table, "Somehow, I don't think she thought much of my poetry performance," he laughed in a way that said he really didn't care what she thought.

Philippe delivered the box of cigars and Robby started to pass them out to the men who remained at the table.

As he offered the box to his friend, Max handed Robby a cigar cutter sandwiched between an old Napoleon coin. "Remember this?"

"Ahhh, how could I forget?' Robby turned the cigar cutter over and saw an inscription on the back. He held it up and read: "*Max Roarke Number One! Robby Trask Not Number One*. When did you put this bullshit on the back?"

"Not bullshit. Fact. I won our race. So I added it to commemorate my win."

"I can't believe you still have this thing," Robby said using it to cut the end of his cigar.

"Are you kidding? I carry it all the time. It's like having an Olympic Gold Medal."

"Of course, you know I had the slower boat."

"Slower boat? The hell you did. Your boat just had the slower guy rowing it. My win was totally legit."

The remembrance of their race brought smiles to their faces. "What a night. Drunk as skunks. Nobody thought we'd dare race two rowboats on the Seine in the middle of the night. That was one funny race."

"The Parisian gendarmes didn't think it was so funny," Max said.

"Those Frogs had no sense of humor and a total lack of competitive spirit. What did we pay them not to lock us up?"

"A lot, as I remember."

"What was the girl's name who offered this as the prize?"

"Monique something or other. Forget her last name."

"A girl with a body like hers didn't need a last name." Robby said. "There's one thing about the race I never told you."

"What's that?"

"She might have put this cigar cutter up as first prize, but Monique put her body up as second prize." He inserted a pause for emphasis, "And I did collect." He broke into a wide grin.

"Didn't Monique, give you the clap?" Max teased.

"It wasn't clap, it was a round of applause," he said with bravado." I took her to school in the finer points in the art of bedroom performance." Robby took one last look at the inscription on the back of the cigar cutter, shook his head and handed it back to Max. "I may have come in second in our boat race, but not on our bicycle race."

"Only because you got lucky and I had the bad luck to blow a tire." *But once you find out about Andrea and me,* Max thought, *the race results will be null and void.*

Robby seemed to purposely ignore Max's blown tire defense and turned away calling out to the captain. "Philippe, would you be so kind, sir, as to produce another bottle of Shipwreck 1907?. I think my friend here is dying of thirst."

"Much more of this champagne and I'll be a shipwreck in the morning," Once his glass was filled, he raised it in silent salute to this friend. Nothing was said for several minutes. Robby took his seat at the head of the table and seemed to be savoring his cigar. As the smoke curled up over his head, Max became aware his friend was staring holes in him. *I know that look*, he thought. *We're not done. He's thinking, and what he's thinking is how to even the score for what I did to him on the tennis court.*

Max did not have to wait long for the baiting to begin.

~~*

"So Max, when did you stop working out?" Robby said. He took a long drag on his cigar, formed an oval with his mouth and blew out three perfect smoke rings which floated over the table.

"What are you talking about?" Max suspected this was not some idle, inconsequential question. The bait was on the hook.

"It may be my imagination, but it looks to me like you've lost a bit."

"A bit of what?"

"The old arm strength. But then, a lot of guys our age start to go soft."

"Soft?"

"You know, every year they lose a step. They find it easier to crash on the couch than to hit the gym every day."

Where is he going with this?, Max wondered. "What are you saying, Robby?"

"I'm not saying anything. I'm just asking. Have you lost some of the old arm muscle?" It was clearly more of a taunt than a question.

"Don't think so."

"How are we going to find out?"

Max decided to take the bait, "I have a feeling you have an idea."

"Maybe a little mano a mano arm wrestling."

"You think maybe we're too drunk for that?" Max knew he was and was hoping Robby would give his challenge a pass.

"Can't hold your liquor, eh?"

"Ok. We're not too drunk. Where do you want to do this?

"On the bar."

"You're on."

The two men excused themselves from the table and made their way to the bar. Robby said, "Philippe, bring me two short candles. Really short."

"What are the candles for?"

"We put one on each side of our arms so the winner is the one who drives the other's hand into the fame. First guy's candle to be put out by the back of his hand, loses."

"Let's make this a little more interesting," Max said. "With our free hand, we should be downing snifters of cognac at a rate of one every three minutes. That way we not only test strength, but our alcoholic endurance."

"Love it." Robby said.

"But, it will not be just any cognac, Max boasted. "Philippe break out the Henri IV Dudognon Heritage. I would like to prove to my friend that I too am a man of impeccable taste."

"At least a man of expensive taste. What's ol' Henri IV go for?"

"Even more than your Shipwreck."

"One upping me are you!" Robby grinned.

"Every chance I get."

"Well, let's see how you do when there's no money, just muscle involved."

"I'm going to put your lights and your candle out."

Both men removed their sport coats and stood on opposite sides of the bar. Philippe placed the two short votive candles on the bar positioned so the loser's hand would smash into one of the flames. The bartender filled their snifters. By this time, the remaining guests and some of the other diners had been drawn to the bar to watch the competition. They two men locked their hands ready for combat. "Who will give us the start?" Robby asked the onlookers.

"What are you two doing," a young woman seated at the bar asked.

Robby glanced over at the woman and gave her a silent, but appreciative assessment of her obvious assets. "Ah, what better than to have a beautiful woman initiate this epic test of strength? Do us the honor of giving us a count down."

"I'd love to. You two ready?"

"Anytime," Robby said.

"Three, two, one... Go!" she shouted and both men immediately tightened their grips and began to pull. Neither man was able to budge the other more than a couple of inches off center. After ten minutes and three cognacs, neither man seemed to have gained any advantage though each kept goading the other with taunts intended to do with words that which neither seemed to be able to do with their arms.

"Doesn't feel like you got much left."

"More than enough."

"You know I can take you at any time? Right?"

"Bullshit. Not a chance."

After the fourth Henri IV Dudognon Heritage, Max began slowly to bend Robby's hand back driving it ever closer to the candle flame. *God, what is that?* The unmistakable odor of burning flesh.

"Damn! Your hand is burning," Max shouted, simultaneously easing up on the pressure he was putting on Robby's hand. The momentary lapse was all Robby needed to slam Max's hand back onto his candle.

"I win!" Robby shouted throwing both hands in the air. Quickly he searched for an ice bucket and thrust his burned hand into the cold water.

"You did that on purpose!" Max said. He was incredulous. "You're demented!"

"But I won!" Robby shot back through an absurdly triumphant grin.

"I'm sorry man, but that was nuts."

"Whatever it takes to win," he answered with an intensity Max found unsettling.

"Next time I'll just let you burn the skin off."

Robby shook his head, "No you won't. I know you too well. After all, you are my best friend. And friends don't burn friend's hands, do they?"

"You never know," Max answered and punctuated it with a laugh intended to lighten the moment. Robby pulled his hand out of the ice bucket. Max stared at the rising blister. "That's going to scar."

"I'll wear it as a badge of victory," Robby said proudly.

"You're absolutely fucking crazy," Max said laughing.

"You both are," the young woman who had served as starter observed as she lit a cigarette.

"Maybe we are," Robby added making no effort to hide the fact he was picking up where he'd left off assessing the woman's ample charms, "but I won didn't I?" And then, "Since you were kind enough to be the starter for our little competition, maybe now you'd like to be the prize for the winner?"

All eyes fell on the woman who suddenly found herself the focus of attention in what, for her, had become an uncomfortable situation. "You'll have to ask my husband about that," she said doing her best to make a graceful escape.

The bar rippled with laugher.

"Too bad," Robby said. "But then, had she agreed, I'm not sure my wife would have approved."

More laugher.

Robby turned toward the bartender who did little to hide he was not happy at having his bar turned into an arm-wrestling venue. "Come on Pierre or whateverthehell your name is, tell Philippe to bring up another bottle of my 1907 to celebrate my victory. Oh Christ, that was sweet!"

"How much 1907 do you have?" Max asked.

"A lot."

After a round of less than sincere congratulations from the few on-lookers who had remained for the duration of the match, Robby and Max staggered into an adjacent lounge area. Max collapsed onto one of the couches. "I am wasted," Max said closing his eyes for a moment.t

"What's that?" Robby asked cocking his head as if it would help him hear better.

"What's what?"

"The music they're playing."

Max paused to focus on the music coming over the hotel's sound system." Something from some opera."

"It's Andrea Bocelli. The blind Italian singer. You're not into opera, are you Max?"

"Too heavy for me."

"That's what I thought."

"Why do you ask?"

"No reason."

"Bull. With you there's always a reason."

"You're right. And in this case I'm just proving to myself what a cultural vagrant you are."

"What do you want to do, go one-on-one matching IQs?"

"God Max, you take the bait like a hungry shark."

"You trying to set me up again?"

Robby smiled a champagne and cognac-induced sleepy smile and shook his head 'no." Once is enough for a night." Then he glanced around the room. "What happened to Andrea?"

"Don't you remember? She went home after she apologized for your performance on the chair."

"Oh, she'll be pissed. I'm going to hear it tonight."

For several minutes, neither man said anything as if their ability to speak coherently had been significantly encumbered by the amount of alcohol they had consumed. Max began to wonder if he was in any condition to talk to him about Andrea. *Why in hell did I feel it was up to me tell him she wanted a divorce? How do you tell your best friend you've been banging his wife?* Immediately he admonished himself. *That's a crappy way of putting it. You don't 'bang' someone you love. Shit! My head feels like it's coming unscrewed. God, how much champagne and cognac have I had tonight? Don't think this is either the time or place to... ."* he was cut off in mid thought.

"Max, I need to talk to you about Andrea." Robby was leaning forward, his arms on his knees, looking very serious, his eyes fixed on Max.

Does he know something? Max wondered. *Has Andrea said anything?* "You need to talk to me about Andrea?" he repeated, What about?" Max asked, hoping the surprise in his voice revealed none of what he had been debating with himself.

"I was just thinking what great times the three of us had before she and I got married. Nothing was out of bounds. Too bad we couldn't have cloned her. Then she could have married us both."

"But then we would have fought over which one got the original."

"In the end, that wasn't a problem, was it?" The solemnity in Robby's voice brought a quick and unexpected end to what, up to that moment, had been casual banter.

Max had the feeling Robby's question was loaded with intended portent. Maybe it was meant not so much as a question but a probe. *But for what?* Max wondered. He decided it best not to try reading something into what was probably unintended. "No," he agreed, "in the end it wasn't a problem. You're the one she married and I was the one left holding the short end of the stick."

"It's not working."

It sounded to Max like a non-sequitur. "What's not working?" Max asked.

"Us."

"Us ? What are you talking about? You and me?"

"No, not you and me. I'm talking about my marriage. If it's not on the rocks, it's damn close. She's been seeing a divorce lawyer."

How the hell did he find out? Max did his best to conceal his surprise. "A divorce lawyer? Are you sure? How do you know?"

"I have many eyes," he said making no attempt to explain whose 'eyes' they might be.

I'm not sure I want to go wherever this going, Max thought. He decided that given his condition and the concern he might reveal something he would regret, it was best to get up, call it a night and go home.

"I also found out she's seeing someone. She's having an affair!"

Divorce! Affair! It was as if Robby had fired both barrels and Max could not decide if the shots were intended for him or were no more just the pained discharge from a friend. "What makes you think she's having an affair?"

"I told you, I have eyes... everywhere?"

"Who's she having it with?"

"Don't know. But I have suspicions."

"Korman Swenson?"

"Good God, no. That dick head? If she's going to have an affair, I'd hope she'd have better taste than Swenson."

A wild idea. *Got to find what he knows.* "Maybe it's me?"

Robby laughed. "Naw. Not you. No way."

"Why not me?" Max knew he was stepping out on to what might prove to be the high wire of truth.

There was a curious look of passiveness on Robby's face as he said, "Because a Max Roarke would not screw his best friend's wife. At least not until after she's divorced."

Wrong, Max found himself confronting a tsunami of guilt.

For a moment, Robby said nothing as he pondered his glass like a medium focused on her crystal ball looking for answers.

"I really hate to think I'm going to lose her." Robby's tone was distant and sullen.

Max was sure he saw tears well up in his eyes and one tear escaped down his cheek before Robby could wipe it away.

"I guess if she wants to leave me because I'm a rotten husband and an asshole, I can accept that." Then as if some internal switch had been thrown, his morose tone turned to rancor. "But if she wants to leave me for some other guy... that I couldn't take." He repeated himself making no effort to hold back his anger. "That I could not and would not take!" He then added something which caught Max totally by surprise. There was no anger in his voice when he said, "Unless it was you."

"Me?" he was incredulous.

Robby nodded, "She belongs to us... only to us."

"Us? Belongs to us? I think the marriage certificate reads Trask."

"You know what I mean. We both found her and at one time she loved us both. There was never anyone else for Andrea. Just us."

Where is this going? Max wondered. *Is he testing me or does he believe she belongs to 'us'? How the hell am I ever going to tell him she just wants to belong to me?* Max noticed something or someone behind him had attracted Robby's attention. He made a gesture as if to dismiss whatever it was he saw.

"Who you waving at? " Max asked without turning to look.

Robby fumbled for a moment, "Ah... uh... nobody."

"Nobody?"

"A waiter," he said almost defensively. Robby's mood changed again. It was as if the drunk had suddenly been struck sober. "Look, let's talk about Andrea tomorrow. I'm in no condition to have an intelligent conversation and neither are you."

"That's about the first rationale thing you've said."

Robby stood up and Max attempted to get up as well, but Robby put a hand on his shoulder and gently pushed him back. "There's still about $15,000 worth of Shipwreck left in the bottle," he said pointing to the ice bucket next to Max. "Someone's got to finish it and I'm appointing you to do the honors."

"Appointment accepted," Max said realizingbby's departure meant an end to any further discussion of Andrea. *Thank god, this was about to get sticky.*

"Call you tomorrow," he said leaving.

As Max watched Robby leave, he decided it was long past time for him to go home. He managed to lift himself a few inches off the couch before he gave up and sank back. No way was he going to get himself vertical. Not in his current condition. The champagne and cognac had taken its toll. *Well, if I can't stand up, I might as well sit here and finish the Shipwreck 1907.* He pulled the bottle out of the ice bucket and looked at it. *Hard to image there's at least $15,000 left in this bottle. I wonder if they could re-cork it. Wouldn't work. Needs to be drunk now.* He aimed the mouth of the bottle at his glass but missed and poured some of it in his lap. "Ooo, a thousand-dollar spill. Doesn't feel like money. Just wet." The next try was successful. He took a sip and realized the room had suddenly become unglued. "Somebody please nail it down," he pleaded to the empty lounge.*" I think they classify this as being totally shit faced. How the hell am I going to drive home much less walk out of here? I'm going to need a little help. No, a lot of help. I haven't been this snockered in years.* He looked around the room. No one in sight. The couch on which he was sitting began to look like his only option for the night. *I could die here and no one would find me until they started to serve breakfast.* For some reason the thought of the breakfast staff finding him dead or unconscious seemed very funny. He closed his eyes and started to laugh.

"Pourquoi riez-vous?" Her voice was almost a whisper.

"Why am I laughing?" He repeated the question in English almost reflectively. He opened his eyes and for an instant thought he might be dreaming. She was standing over him in the same diaphanous white gown he had seen her in before. A silk shawl was draped over her shoulders. He studied her for a moment then said, "Are you real or are you just a champagne and cognac induced illusion?"

"I'm real, Pelléas" she said in English but with a heavy French accent. Slowly she sank down beside him, pressed her body into his and kissed him on the mouth.

He, the seducer of many women, never had one of his potential conquests come on to him like this. Her kiss was warm and passionate and affected him in a way he would not have thought possible given his current numbed condition. "Yes, you are very real," he said clearly impressed. "There's only one problem."

"Oui?"

"I am not Pelléas."

She pulled back looking at him as if she had just realized she was being accosted by a stranger. She was at once angry and afraid and expressed her disbelief at what he'd told her, "Non, vous n'êtes pas, Pelléas?"

"I think that's what I just said. I am not Pelléas, whoever he is."

She moved to the other end of the couch and began to weep. "If you are not Pelléas, who are you?"

"Max Roarke, at your service," he said making a sweeping gesture with his arm. He was not surprised she continued to switch from French to English and back. Many multi-lingual Europeans frequently hold conversations in more than one language.

"Que voulez-vous?" she asked.

"Me? I don't want anything." He was too tired to make the effort to hold up his end in French.

She stopped crying and moved next to him searching his face. She looked as if she was about to say something, but only continued to stare.

God, what a beautiful creature, he thought. "Who are you?"

After what seemed to him to be an extraordinary long time she answered, "Qui voulez-vous que je sois?"

"Who do I want you to be?" he repeated clearly confused by the oddity of her question. "I'm not sure if I'm just very drunk, dreaming, hallucinating or God knows what, but I'm a little confused."

Again she repeated her question, "Qui voulez-vous que je suis?"

"I want you to be whoever you are? I assume you have a name?"

"Oui."

"And it is...?"

"Mélisande."

"Mélisande," he repeated, "Pretty name. Where are you from?"

Immediately her expression turned gloomy." Someplace... someplace far from here."

"How did you get here?

"I do not remember."

"Are you visiting somebody on Cap Ferrat?"

"No. I do not know anyone here."

"You said you thought I was somebody named Pelléas."

"He is looking for me."

"Looking for you here?"

"No."

"Where?"

"Please take me home."

The room was not only spinning now, it was going in and out of focus. "I don't think I can take myself home." Max looked at her with a bemused smile. *Maybe it's me or the booze, but this conversation isn't making a lot of sense.* Suddenly his stomach began sending signals that the Shipwreck 1907 and Henri IV Dudognon Heritage were not getting along and contemplating an unwanted reappearance. *God, please do not let me get sick.*

"Why are you looking at me like that?" she asked.

"Like what?" His head bobbed and he caught himself before his chin dropped to his chest.

She appeared frightened, "Allez-vous me faire du mal?"

"No, I am not going to hurt you." *Feel like shit! Really fading fast.* "I'm not capable of hurting you or anyone else tonight. I assure you."

"What have you done with Pelléas?"

"Young lady, I know don't know who..." the words were so slurred he could barely understand himself. "...this Pelléas person is, but..." The uncontrollable demand for sleep pulled heavily on his eyelids. Consciousness was hanging on by a thread. Her face, drawing close to his, was the last thing he remembered before he passed out.

3.

2 YEARS BEFORE THE MURDER
OF ANDREA TRASK

Cap Ferrat, France

The ceiling looked familiar. Of course, it was his. This was his bed. And he was alone. He lifted his head slightly and looked out the French doors opposite the end of his bed. He could tell by the direction of the sunlight it had to be mid-morning.

Have I been dreaming? He began to try to reconstruct last night. *The conversation with Robby. Then the woman... Meli... something... was it a dream? And how did I get here? Who brought me home? Maybe someone at the hotel,* he reasoned. His thought process was a muddle.

The knock on his bedroom door was followed by the entrance of Jacques carrying a tray with coffee, juice and a small pastry. He placed it at the foot of Max's bed. "I thought you might want to get up, sir. Mrs. Trask called and said to tell you she was on her way"

"Thanks, Jacques," he said pulling himself into a sitting position "Do you have any idea how I got home last night?"

Jacques seemed somewhat surprised by the question. "I presume you drove, sir. Your car is in the driveway."

Max decided not to press the mystery further. "Oh, yeah, I forgot." Max felt the need to explain himself to his valet. "Over did it a little last night, I'm afraid. Please, let me know when Mrs. Trask arrives."

Max hoped the juice and coffee might help him unscrambled his memory of last night and maybe help shrink his head which felt twice its size. The juice and coffee had little positive effect. *I've had hangovers before,* he thought, *but this one has to be at the top of the list. Damn, everything hurts.* He laid back and the next thing he knew Andrea stood over him, hands on her hips, a critical look on her face.

"Look at you! You don't look like the man I've been waking up to the last several mornings."

"And I don't feel like that man, either." Max's head was pounding. "Afraid I really over did it last night. How's Robby?"

"I don't know. He never came home last night."

"Never came home? I wonder if maybe he took a room at the Voile d'Or. He was pretty drunk and maybe he figured... ."

"I checked. He wasn't there. Oh, and that's another thing; the two of you have become legends at the Voile d'Or bar. I think maybe they might even put up a plaque in your honor," her voice was heavy with sarcasm. "The staff is talking about your arm-wrestling bout and how Robby let his hand get burned in order to win. I'll tell you truth, Max, I do think he needs some... some help. I'm talking serious psychiatric help. But I don't want to talk about Robby. The only thing that matters to me now is us. Did you talk to him?"

"We talked. But not really about us."

"About what, then?"

"He knows you've been talking to a divorce lawyer."

"He does? How did he find out?"

"All he said was he has 'eyes.' I guess that means he's been spying on you."

"If he knows, why hasn't he said anything?"

"Good question."

"So what did he say?"

"Just that he would hate to lose you. Said if he found you were leaving him for some other guy... that's he couldn't take."

"And you know why? Because to him it would be like losing a trophy to a competitor. A trophy is all I am to him Max, something he put up on his shelf a long time ago and takes down now and again to look at."

"Maybe, but believe it or not, I saw him start to cry when he said he was afraid he was going to lose you."

"Cry? Robby cry? Those must have been Champaign tears. I've been down this road before with him. The tears are new, but believe me Max, it was all an act. There's no love there."

"Something else. He says he knows you've been seeing someone."

"Did you ask him who?"

"Says he doesn't know."

"Of course he does," she said with conviction. "He knows it's you. Robby's not stupid. Who else could it be? He's trying to lay a guilt trip on you. You should have said, 'Yes, it is me. Andrea and I love each other. We always have and we're going to correct a mistake we both made years ago.' Why didn't you just tell him the truth?" The frown on her face demanded an answer.

Max realized her question had put him on the defensive. He would like to have explained that you do not just raise a glass of Shipwreck 1907 to your best friend and then announce you've been screwing his wife and plan to marry her when she gets a divorce. Immediately he realized that would be stoking the fire. The pounding in his head was making it difficult for him to come up with a safe answer. He had to avoid saying something he knew would drive them into a conversational sinkhole. But that is exactly what he did. "I don't know, Andrea. I don't know why I didn't just come right out and admit everything. Somehow, it just didn't feel right to tell him his best friend has been sleeping with his wife. I mean, I want you and me to be together, but, if I can, I'd like to find some way not to hurt Robby." Big mistake. Sink hole ahead.

Andrea exploded. "Hurt Robby? Hurt Robby? You mean like damaging his precious ego? Like depriving him of one of his trophies? Is that the kind of hurt you're talking about?" She was angry. Deep down angry and it was all she could do to contain herself. "Has it ever occurred to you what your trying not to hurt Robby is doing to me? And more important, to us? If we are going to go through with this, if we are going to have a life together, Robby has got to become past tense. Out of our lives. Forgotten!"

The pain in Max's head throbbed like endless electric shock therapy. He realized he'd just lost control of the conversation. "Andrea, I love you. I want to marry you, but..."

"But nothing! You can't have us both. One of us has to go. It's either him or me. Our lives are not going to be some kind of ménage a tois." She turned and walked quickly to the bedroom door. "When you make up your mind, let me know."

"Wait. Where are you going?" Max called.

"I need to get away. Away from you both. I'm going to Anasara. I'll give you a week to settle things with Robby. I want you to tell him about us. If you don't, then I will be happy to tell him. I don't intend to go sneaking around like illicit lovers trying to hide the truth. If you decide to choose me over him, then you have to promise neither you nor I will ever see Robert Trask again. I want him out of my life. If you can't do that... then," she hesitated as though considering the potential consequence of what she was about to say, "then, I want you out my life as well. It's your serve Max. Let's hope you don't double fault." She opened the door and was about to leave when she turned and looked back at Max. He could see that some of the heat of her anger had begun to cool leaving her emotionally spent and disconsolate. There was resignation in her voice, "Somehow I get the feeling the two of you will be the death of me yet." And then she left.

Max watched her go. *I can't win*, he realized, feeling the weight of the conundrum, *no matter what I do, I'm going to lose one of them. Or maybe both.* For a moment, he thought about going after her, but his head threatened to explode and his body had become like one large toothache. *I have to think*, he said to himself. *But I can't think. Need an Aspirin. Maybe a whole handful.* Slowly he pulled himself out of bed and walked unsteadily to the bathroom. He found the Aspirin bottle, which, for a moment, refused to let itself, be opened. *Goddamn this kid protection packaging.* Finally, it gave up three pills which he popped in his mouth and follow them with a glass of water. He glanced at the morning-after image staring back at him in the mirror. I look like I've been hit by a truck. He set down the glass and staggered back to his bed. Within minutes, he was asleep.

~~*

The clock next to his bed read 4:22. *Damn,* he thought, *I've been asleep most of the day. No more nights like last light,* he vowed. *Wonder if Robby is as wrecked as I am?* He pulled himself up in bed and braced himself with pillows. The French doors that overlooked his front gardens stood open. The wind was blowing softly into the sheer curtains puffing them up then letting them float back like twin parachutes.

Slowly he lowered his feet to the floor, crossed over to the doors, and looked down in the garden. "What the..." he said aloud. She was sitting by the edge of one of the ponds, wearing the same white dress, her hand in the water as if she was searching for something she might have dropped.

"Hello? Bon jour!" he called. If she heard him, she gave no indication.

Max slipped into a pair of pants and a t-shirt and ran downstairs. "Jacques!" he called as left the staircase and headed for the front door. No answer, "Jacques?" *Never mind,* he thought and hurried out the front door, across the terrace and into the garden. As he approached her, he realized she was far more

~ 140 ~

beautiful than the woman his alcoholic haze had permitted him to remember. When she looked up he saw she was crying. "You OK?"

"Please, you must help me find it. It fell into the water."

"What did? What fell?"

"It was a present from Pelléas?"

Max took a step closer to the pond. "What kind of present? I'll help you look."

"No, no. You will not find it." She looked up at him with great sadness in her eyes, "Je suis perdu."

"You're lost? What do you mean you're lost?"

"Tu ne vas pas me toucher, êtes-vous?"

"No, I'm not going to touch you. Not if you don't want me to." He took a step back as added reassurance.

"I don't think I do. Not yet."

"Last night. I think you said your name was..." he drew a blank.

"Tu m'as appelé Mélisande."

"I called you Mélisande?"

"You don't remember," she said sadly. "I thought you would remember.""I thought..." he was about to say given his condition, there was a good chance he did not remember anything. *Why fight it?"* Ok, Mélisande. That's your name." He said it in a way intended as confirmation.

"If you say it I," she whispered.

Max shook his head, *Whoa! This is one very confused young lady in my garden. I think somebody has let her off her leash.* Around her neck he noticed a diamond necklace with matching diamond earrings. *But what kind of nut case dresses like that? Not likely an escaped mental patient. Not with those jewels,*

"Why are you staring at me?" A look of concern erupted on her face.

Max sensed he needed to be delicate. "I'm looking at you like this because you are extremely nice to look at." A faint, shy smile crossed her face. "And second, while I'm delighted you've come into my gardens, I'm afraid I really don't understand why you are here."

She seemed confused, "I'm not sure why I'm here. I'm just... here."

"Can I get you something? A coffee maybe?"

"Can you take me home?"

"Where is home?"

"I have no home anymore. Once I did. But there was a fire... ."

"A fire?" *She needs help. Who should I call?* He wondered. *Maybe the hospital in Nice*, he thought. *I'll have to make some calls. But I can't leave her sitting out here.* "Mélisande, it's so hot. Why don't we go inside? I'll have someone in the kitchen fix you a cold drink."

Suddenly she stood up. "I must leave you now. It's time."

"Time? Time for what? Can I call someone for you?"

"There is no one to call. I must hurry. Goloud does not know and if he finds out he will kill Pelléas. I must warn him." She began to run toward the rear of the garden. As she ran, the shawl she had around her shoulders blew off and floated gently to the ground.

"Can I come with you," he called starting to walk toward her.

She stopped and turned back to him. "No, not yet. Not yet."

"Will I see you again?" he asked.

"I think so. Maybe. Yes. When the time is right."

"And when will the time be right?"

"I do not know. Maybe tomorrow. Maybe not. I hope you will remember me." She turned away, ran up the steps to the marble pavilion.

Max walked over to where her shawl lay flat upon the ground. He picked it up and shouted, "You dropped your shawl."

She did not answer. She stood inside the pillars near the back of the pavilion, turned, looked at him and, as before, just vanished.

What in the..." He looked at the shawl, then at the empty pavilion. *Maybe it's me who needs the help.*

4.

2 YEARS BEFORE THE MURDER
OF ANDREA TRASK

Cap Ferrat, France

Robby arrived just after eleven the next day. "Bone Jure Jacko," he said in his murderous French. He had refused to learn even the most rudimentary phrases. When asked why he had refused to learn the language of his adopted country he would reply, "When you have as much money as I have, it's up to the Frogs to speak to me in English if they want any of it. When you're rich you can do and say just about anything and everyone will forgive you for it." His attitude did not earn him many friends in France or anywhere else for that matter, but his willingness to reward compliant waiters, servants, employees and even friends – all of who hoped for his continued largess – was more than enough for them to overlook his boorishness with servile and even groveling tolerance. Robby stood in the middle of the enormous foyer and shouted, "Where the hell is he?"

Somewhat startled by his abrupt entrance, Jacques kept his composure. "Bon jour monsieur Roarke. He is in the library," he pointed towards a door across the foyer

Robby nodded with what passed for a 'thank you," made no effort to knock on the library door, went inside and tossed himself on a large sofa. Max, seated at his desk looking at his computer, showed little surprise. Not much Robby did ever-surprised Max. "Asseyez-vous que vous. That means have a seat, Max said."

"As you can see, I just did. Don't know about you, but I was really trashed for all of yesterday. Never got out of bed."

I thought Andrea said he hadn't come home. He was about to say something but cut himself off. The only way he could have known Robby didn't come home was to reveal that Andrea had come to see him. *Not a good idea.*

"It's almost noon and the day is wasting. What are you doin' cooped up here?"

"Doing a Google search."

"A search? For what?"

"I'm trying to find the nearest psychiatric hospital."

"Thinking about committing yourself? About time." Robby laughed.

Max ignored the question. "Do you remember the woman I saw on the rocks below your court?"

"The one that wasn't there."

"The one that *was* there, but *you* didn't see," Max corrected

"What about her?"

"She keeps showing up?"

"Showing up where?"

"After you left the Voile d'Or the other right I hadn't moved from the couch and wasn't sure I ever would. I was just sitting there, totally paralyzed with half a bottle of Shipwreck in my lap. I closed my eyes, started to laugh at the thought I might die there and not be found before breakfast. All of a sudden, I hear this woman's voice. I open my eyes and she's asking me why I'm laughing. Next thing I know this gorgeous creature sits down beside me and puts a yard of tongue in my mouth."

"And naturally after you got through choking you said, 'Voulez-vous coucher avec moi?'"

Max shook his head," Robby, I'm really impressed how well you're adding to your extensive French vocabulary."

"That's all the French I've ever needed to know. But enough my excellent command of the language. What happened?"

"Suddenly she pulls back, looks at me and says, 'You're not Pelléas."

"What's Pelléas? A person or something to eat?" Robby seemed to think his question was funny.

"He's some guy. Right then our conversation went off the deep end. Not much of what she said made any sense. Tell you the truth, she was either drunk as I was or some kind of head case. She had no idea where she was from or even how she got there. The whole thing was bizarre."

"So, did you take her to bed?"

"I couldn't have taken her anywhere. I couldn't have taken myself to bed.

Which raises another question. I'm ashamed to admit it, but I guess I passed out in the lounge. At least I think I did. Next thing I know it's morning and I'm in my own bed. I have no idea how I got there."

"Was she with you?"

"Nope. All by myself."

Not exactly the kind of performance I'd expect from the stud master. Who knows, maybe she'll show up again."

"She already has."

"Really?"

"Yesterday afternoon, must have been after four, I find her sitting on the grass next to one of my reflecting pools. She was wearing the same white dress she had on the night before. So I go outside, just sort of stroll up to her and sit down to talk We have the same kind of disoriented conversation. Then she gets up to leave saying she has to find Pelléas because if Goloud, whoever he is, finds out, he will kill Pelléas."

"Finds out what?"

"I have no idea. Whatever it is she doesn't want him to find out. As I said, not much of what she said made any sense."

"She sounds like some kind of nut," Robby offered.

"Clearly, she needs help, if she's not getting some already. I began to wonder if maybe she was a psychiatric patient somewhere and had, well... escaped. Before I know it, she gets up, runs off to my pavilion and disappears. I know it sounds crazy, but I do mean disappears. Poof. Gone. No sign of her."

"Has anybody else seen your lady in white?"

"Not that I know of. But here. This is hers." Max got up from his desk and picked up Mélisande's shawl which he had laid over a chair. "She dropped it when she took off running." He handed it to Robby

Robby looked at it for a moment and then began to examine the corners. "This is Andrea's," he announced.

"You sure?" Max asked.

"Yeah. This belongs to Andrea. Or at least it did, anyway."

"How do you know?"

"Andrea has just about everything she wears made by this guy Gianna Banana or whaterthehell his name is. He's a haute couture designer and makes all her clothes. Puts this little mark in everything he does for Andrea."

"Where would Mélisande get Andrea's shawl?"

Robby shook his head, "You sure Andrea didn't leave it here?"

Max was tempted to respond by denying she'd been in his house since he returned. But what if she'd told Robby she'd come up for a visit 'with an old friend' the night he arrived? *Don't get caught in a lie that could lead to places he was not yet ready to go.* Max opted to deflect the question. "Was Andrea wearing this at the Voile d'Or the other right?"

"Maybe. Don't remember."

"Mélisande might have picked it up there."

"Yeah, probably." Robby appeared to accept the possibility and tossed the shawl on a chair. "Well, life is full of strange things. Maybe your girlfriend is a thief."

"She's not my girlfriend," Max assured him. "I've already had my share of weirdos in my life. Don't need another one."

Robby stood up. "Let's get out of here. I'm in the mood for Chevre d'Or at Eze. I'll buy lunch."

"Maybe you'd like to arm wrestle for the check."

"The old right paw is a little sore for arm combat," he said pointing to the large dressing on the burn wound, "but we'll come up with something else."

"We always do, don't we?"

"Yeah. And between you and me, that's what Andrea hates about our friendship. She just doesn't understand us."

"Sometimes I don't either," Max said and laughed.

~~*

Robby's Testarossa pulled out of Cap Ferrat, turned right toward Beaulieu and took the first left marked Direction Moyenne Corniche. The middle road of the three corniches between Nice and Monaco is one of the more spectacular coastal roads in the Europe climbing from sea level to over 1500 feet at the top. Within minutes they could see the medieval Village Eze perched like an eagle's nest on a narrow rocky peak below the corniche, but still over a quarter mile above the Mediterranean. Stretched out below them was the Cap Ferret peninsula, looking like a giant topographical three-dimensional map.

Robby bypassed the arrows leading to the parking lot and ignored the signs reading *Ne pas entrer dans*. He gave the parking attendant a cursory wave of his hand, gunned the Testarossa and sped up the s short road squealing his tires around the switchback turn, then darting into an open slot in the small parking lot at the base of the wall reserved for VIPs and special permits. A short walk through the main gate opened onto the narrow stone pathway leading into the village. A fork to the left brought them to the Hotel Cheve d'Or which clings tenaciously to the rocky escarpment. Immediately below the hotel several garden terraces, like ramparts, step down the cliff replete with fountains, benches, tables and chairs creating secluded romantic retreats.

Robby requested a table at Les Ramparts – one of three restaurants in the hotel – overlooking the gardens below. Their conversation was mainly about the weather and the view. When the waiter arrived, they ordered a bottle of local white wine and both settled on the plat de jour.

Finally, Robby brought up the subject both had on their minds.

"Remember the other night when I told you I had learned Andrea was seeing a lawyer about a divorce?"

"I do."

"I've decided to let her go through with it."

"You serious?" Max did little to conceal his surprise.

"I am. Our marriage has been a coming apart for years. It's my fault, but..." he began to laugh, "... as you know, I'm not one to do much about correcting my faults. And, if I were to be completely honest, which I seldom am, I'd have to admit I have not been what you might call the most faithful of husbands," his guilty smile underscored the truth of his admission. "Given the emptiness of our relationship, I'd have to say a divorce would be best for both of us."

"You're bullshitting me, right? The other night you told me you would hate to lose her."

"The other night I was under the influence Shipwreck 1907. It is now..." he looked at his watch "... almost straight up noon and this is my first drink of the day. So you would have to say I am at this moment both sober and of sound mind. Am I going to hate losing her? Yes. But it's time. Anyway, truth be told, I lost her a long time ago."

"Have you said anything to her?"

"Not yet. From where I sit, the ball is in her court. It's her serve. If, as my 'eyes' have reported, she is talking with a divorce lawyer and she decides to file, and I expect she will, I won't contest it. We'll make it a clean break." Robby stared off in the direction of the Cap Ferret peninsula. After a moment he released a resigned sigh, then looked intently at Max, "Maybe my letting her go will put right what you and I did to her years ago."

"Meaning?" Max asked.

"I think we both know she never loved me as much as she loved you."

"Not sure about that," Max said. "She wasn't exactly decisive when it came to deciding between us."

"I guess we have to write it off to her age. At twenty-three, or whatever she was, Andrea was an impressionable, naive and very inexperienced young woman. Maybe... if you still have any feelings left for her... well... once she's free..." he made no effort to finish the implied suggestion.

Max began to wonder if this was some kind of calculated ploy on Robby's part in order to discover if he was, in fact, the 'someone' he suspected she was seeing. Max decided to say nothing.

"So," Robby continued, "bottom line: I'm ready to let her go if that's what she wants."

Max did his best to maintain an attentive, but non-revealing, expression on his face. In fact, he was near speechless. If Robby was telling him the truth... if he in fact did plan to agree to let her go... that would solve everything. Andrea could get her divorce, then they could, in a respectable amount of time, get married and Robby would never have to know he was the "someone" she was seeing. And his relationship with Robby? While it would never be the same, but maybe in time they could remain friends even if it was at a distance and intermittent. "If Andrea does file and you get a divorce, what will you do?"

"I haven't given it much thought. Maybe it's time for me to find something to do besides trying to make a third appearance on the cover of Sports Illustrated."

"You were on it twice, right."

Robby nodded, "Grand Prix Driver of the Year and once for climbing Everest. It might have been three if they'd gone to press with your fucking Picnic Mountain. It cost me a ton to get the story and picture killed. That was really shitty thing to do to me, you know it was, right?"

"Guilty. Too much over the top. But then, asshole," he said with a friendly grin, "per the rules of Le Jeu Ultime it was my turn." Max chuckled, "God, we pulled some idiotic stunts. Do you remember what the score was?"

"Thirty all." Robby said flatly. "Duce."

"It's been so long, I'd forgotten. I'm glad it ended in a tie."

"Except as I think Bear Bryant of Alabama said, 'A tie is like kissing your sister.'"

"Never had a sister, so never had to settle for that," Max laughed.

"Me either," Robby said.

Max looked up as the waiter approached their table with their lunch. "I was beginning to think they'd forgotten us." Both men gave their attention to their plates and Max hoped a comment on one of his new business ventures might be enough to move them off the subject of Picnic Mountain. Max sensed, as Andrea had told him, even after all these years Robby bore wounds that had not completely healed. Their conversation rambled on aimlessly for the better part of a half hour until they finally came back to Andrea.

Robby pushed his plate away and stared emptily out toward the sea. "I think once Andrea files for divorce, and I'm sure she will, I'd like to go back to the house I built in Malibu and make it my permanent base."

Max's thoughts drifted back to his first and only visit to Robby's Malibu estate. It was about two years after their wedding. After Max had had a moment to take in what purported to be Robby's basement, he said, "If I didn't know better, I'd think I was in a restored Pompeii."

"You like it? It's my version of an ancient Roman bath. Or maybe you could call it Baden Baden West."

"Without Lily Marlene, I hope."

"Listen, I'm sure I can have Lily flown in to join us if you like."

"I'll take a pass on Lily. Tell me about this place."

"I built this first and then put the house on top of it. Actually, there's almost as much square footage down here as there is in the upper part of the house."

Max looked around at the mosaic artwork embedded in the walls and the statuary standing next to small, beautifully lighted and flowing pools. "This is fantastic."

"I had really talented guys flown in from Italy. Told 'em I wanted this place to look like the baths of Caracalla. Smaller, of course."

"What's this?" Max asked looking at what appeared to be a model of a Roman bath sitting atop a pedestal.

"I had it made so my guests could get an idea of the whole thing." He proceeded to give Max a tour via the model. "Ok, we are here," he pointed to the room in the model in which they were standing. The next room the Roman's called their Apodyterium. This is where we'll dress and undress. Through that door," he said indicating the next room, "we'll go to the Frigidarium – which has a cold-water plunge. You'll freeze your ass off in there. Then we'll go to the Tepidarium, the warm room, and finally we'll really do some sweating in the Caldarium, the hot room. Like the one in Baden Baden. After the hot room, we'll take an immersion bath and then go back to the Tepidarium for a massage. And if, after all that, you'd like a nap, we have a Laconium."

"How long did it take you to learn all those Latin terms?"

"About a month," he laughed. "Never did get more than a C in Latin."

They left the model, Robby led them into the dressing room and took off their tennis clothes.

"Got any towels?" Max asked. "Or do we just drip dry?"

"On the way." The words were no sooner out of Robby's mouth than two attractive young women wearing sheer white togas, leaving little to the imagination, entered the room carrying towels." And those, shall we say, are traditional Roman comfort features."

"What's a Roman bath without some slave girls?" Max joked.

"Well, they're not quite slaves," Robby said. "I do pay them... and *very* well. If later you're up for it... and I do mean up," he added with a suggestive smile, "they'll give you a massage in the Tepidarium which I promise you will not soon forget." Robby took his towels from one of the girls and, as she turned to leave, gave her a pat on the behind. She looked back at him with an expression full of promises to be kept later.

Max took his towel from the second woman. "Why do I get the idea I wouldn't be likely to find Andrea in here?"

* ~ * ~ *

A breeze picked up off the Mediterranean and found its way up to Eze and ruffled the umbrella shading their table. Robby, who had been talking about his California retreat, looked at Max with a randy smile, "So many women on those Malibu beaches, so little time."

"Mae West said something like that about men."

"Poetic license on my part."

"Noted."

Robby stood up and said, "Back in a minute. I've got to hit the head."

Max found himself anxious to return to his villa and give Andrea a call. Things were working out better than either of them could have hoped. Since Robby did not plan to contest the divorce, it would be over and done quickly.

Music.

Like a waltz.

Where is it coming from? Max asked himself. The music seemed to be floating up from one of the several terraces below the restaurant. He looked over the railing and there, on the first terrace, was Mélisande. She was still wearing the white gown. Her eyes were closed and there was a dreamy look on her face as she swayed side to side in a trance-like fashion. *How the hell did she get herself up here?* As he watched her move from one end of the terrace to the other, past the fountains and the flowers, he said softly mostly to the wind, "Melisandre, what is going on with you?" If was as if she heard him. She stopped, looked up and motioned for him to join her. He held up his hand and waved as an indication he'd be right down.

"What are you looking at?" Robby asked as he returned.

Max turned away from the railing, "Come with me." He pushed back his chair, grabbed Robby's arm and hurried to the far side of the restaurant. "I want you to meet someone."

"Meet someone? Who?"

"Mélisande. My ethereal and mystical woman in white. She's on the terrace right below this one. Stairs are this way," he said pointing to the far end of the restaurant. They started down the narrow flagstone steps. "Do you hear the music?"

"What music?"

"Good grief man, get your hearing fixed."

As they stepped out on the terrace, the music suddenly stopped. "Where the hell is she? She was right here. Right here!" He repeated venting his frustration at not finding her.

"There's another terrace below this one. Maybe she's down there," Robby offered.

"No, she was here. Definitely here!" He made no effort to hold back his frustration. "Damn. I'm beginning to believe the woman has wings." Max noticed that a hotel employee was on his hands and knees weeding one of the flowerbeds. He walked over to the man. "What happen to the girl who was just here?"

"Je ne parle pas anglais."

"A women in white. Avez-vous vu une femme dans une robe blanche. She was dancing."

The man shrugged his shoulders, shook his head 'no' and glanced briefly at Robby.

"Don't understand. She wanted me to join her."

"She spoke to you?"

"No. You know, motioned for me to come down." He mimicked her gesture. "It couldn't have taken us more than a minute to get down here and she's..."

Robby gave him a skeptical look.

Max responded angrily, "She was here, Goddamn it! I'm telling you she was here! I don't know why the hell this guy didn't see her!"

"Maybe she wasn't here,"

"Oh, so I'm hallucinating?" he spat back.

"Hey, take it easy. That's your word, not mine." Robby chided unable to hold back a thin smile.

"How about adding delusional?"

"Whatever works," Robby replied.

"Well, I don't know where the hell she's gone, but she was right here."

Then with a look of growing concern Robby said, "I'd have to say it's a bit strange you're the only one who ever sees her."

"I guess I'm just lucky," Max was clearly irritated. "Let's get the check. I've got things I need to do this afternoon."

"Like what?" Robby asked as they climbed back up the steps to the restaurant.

"Like work." He said testily. "You know some of us just don't live off our old man's fortune and clip coupons. I've got businesses to run."

"Hey, why work if you don't have to? Gives me more time for fun."

They returned to their table, asked for the check and then made their way back down the narrow stone village pathway between the myriad Eze shops and galleries. They had to press themselves against the walls to avoid the crush of tourists who had just spilled out of a tour bus and we're invading the shops like hungry locusts.

The conversation on their way back to Cap Ferret was sparse and unrelated to Mélisande. When Robby finally pulled up in front of Max's villa, Max got out and as he shut the door, he said, "You don't believe me do you?"

"If you say you saw the woman, then I believe you," Robby didn't sound convincing. "Let's just leave it at that."

"I don't think I can."

5.

2 YEARS BEFORE THE MURDER OF ANDREA TRASK

Cap Ferrat, France

Max went into his library and found himself befuddled and consumed with thinking about Mélisande. Nothing seemed to make any sense. Of one thing was he certain; the woman was real and not a figment of his addled imagination. *But why this appearing and disappearing act? And why has she latched on to me?* If, as he suspected, she was probably under someone's care, why hadn't they come looking for her? Then there was the question of her mobility. No possible way she could have walked from Cap Ferrat to Eze. Something else. Robby had raised a critical question: Why had he been the only one to see her? There had to be some rational explanation. Finally, he decided the best thing to do was simply put her out of his mind. He owed Andrea a call. *Forget this nonsense with Mélisande; Andrea is the only thing that should matter to me.*

* ~ * ~ *

"We couldn't have planned this any better than if we'd written the script." The connection started to break up. "You still there?"

"Yes. Phones connections are not great here. But this is good news. Thank God. I don't think I could have handled a messy divorce. How do you think he'll take it when he finds out about us?"

"I almost believe he expects it."

"As I told you, I'm sure he knows."

"So what if he does? He's agreed to the divorce, so it doesn't matter. As of right now, you and I are looking at a whole lifetime together. And I promised you, Andrea, you will never regret being my wife."

"I believe that, Max. I truly do.'

"Now, let's talk about where we go from here. Even though Robby knows you've been talking to a lawyer, and he expects you to file, you or your lawyer have to let him know that you're actually going to do it."

"I'll tell him. I owe him that."

"Ok, have your lawyer start the paperwork."

"Since I'm not going to ask Robby for anything and if he's not going to contest it, getting the divorce shouldn't be all that difficult, should it?"

"It should be a heck of a lot easier and faster than any of mine. Of that I'm sure."

"How long do you think it will it take?"

"Comes down to what kind of backload the court has. Given you're both still residents of New York, and given their case load, it may take two to three months." Your lawyer will be able to tell you more."

"Oh Max, please tell me this is going to happen. That we really will be together. I'm so afraid something will go wrong."

"Like what? Trust me. It's all but done."

"I hope so Max. You have no idea how much I hope so."

~~*

It was after nine that evening when he ended the conference call with his staff and sent his last email to several investment bankers. Max had only poked at the dinner Jacques had prepared before he left for the night. *Need some air*, Max decided and made his way out to the terrace.

Dusk had given way to the edge of night. A heavy mist had crept up from the sea had draped itself over gardens. The heat of the day had been replaced with a definite chill. "I don't believe it," he said aloud to no one. What he saw looked much like a clichéd scene from a "B" horror movie where the mystery woman materializes out of the fog. Except in this case, what he was looking at was not a mystery woman, but Mélisande.

His first thought was that her thin white dress was not giving her much protection from the chill night air. His second was that it was time to end this appearing-disappearing act. *Enough*! This woman was beginning to act like some loopy stalker. *Maybe that's what she is*, he thought. At the same time, he found himself feeling sorry for her. Clearly, she needed help. It occurred to him the best thing he could do was to check her into a hospital. Nice had to have some kind of psychiatric unit. When she drew closer, he spoke her name as if greeting an old friend. "Good evening, Mélisande."

She looked up at him. "J'avais tellement peur que vous pourriez ne pas se souvenir de moi." There was a distinct stream of melancholy in her voice.

He answered her in English," Why were you afraid I wouldn't remember you? Sweetheart, you would be hard to forget. Was that you I saw up at Eze today?"

"Eze?"

"Village Eze. Up on the Moyenne Corniche."

"I was there?" she seemed confused.

"I think you were," he said kindly.

"If you say I was, then I guess it was. I don't remember," she answered vacantly.

"I wanted to talk with you. But when I got down to where I'd seen you dancing, you were gone."

"Où étais-je?"

"Good question. I don't know where you were." *I think a trip to the Nice hospital is your next stop, young lady.* "I have an idea," he said brightly, "why don't we go for a little ride?"

"Pouvez-vous me prendre à la maison?"

"Yes, I can take you home." *I wonder if she knows where home is.* "I can take you anywhere you want to go. If you want to go home, I'll take you there. Just tell me where it is."

She answered him without the slightest pause, "Près du Village de Chateaue du Lac? Savez-vous où c'est?

"I don't know where Chateau du Lac is, but my GPS will."

"Qu'est-ce que le GPS?" She asked

"Global Positioning System. It will lead us to there."

"Je ne comprends pas."

"Not important that you understand. I can find it. That's all that matters."

She switched back to English, "Once we get there, I can show you the way to my Chateau."

"You live in a Chateau?"

"For a long time."

"Will they be expecting you?"

"Who?"

"Your family or whoever's at your Chateau."

"Oui," she said brightening, "Pelléas has been waiting for me to come home. A very long time. I hope Goloud will not be there."

Let's hope they, whoever 'they are' at the Chateau, can help her. "If you're ready, I'm ready."

"Ready to...?" again, she seemed to have lost track of the conversation.

"To go home." Max took her hand and helped up the terrace steps."

"Why are we going in here?" she asked as they stepped inside the villa?

"It's shorter for us to walk through the villa to the front of the house." An idea. *Why not call Robby? Might be a good idea to have him along for the ride in case of...* He was not sure in case of what. But if Robby came along, there could be no question that he had not been imagining this woman. He stopped in the great hall in the middle of the house, pulled out his cell phone and motioned for Mélisande to wait, "I need to make a call before we go."

"Bon soir. Trask villa."

"Monsieur Trask, s'il vous plaît."

"Monsieur Trask n'est pas à la maison."

Max thought about asking when he'd be home, but assumed Robby was probably already out looking for someone to fill Andrea's bed – at least for the evening. *If I can't bring Mélisande to Robby, at least I can bring him a picture.* He selected the camera feature on his iPhone. "Mélisande, smile for me."

She turned toward him and Max took her picture. Immediately she recoiled from the flash. He started to take a second one, but she put her hands up in front of her face.

"What's the matter?" he asked.

"Non, non. J'ai peur. J'ai peur "

"Afraid of what?"

"Je ne sais pas."

"I don't know either." Max looked at the one picture he had taken. It was a good. Very good in fact.

"Why did you do that?" she asked pointing to his phone.

"Because I want to remember how beautiful you are."

She began to weep. "You will not remember me. You will forget. It is best you forget. Please, just take me home. I fear for Paellas. Goloud is so jealous."

Max was tempted to ask why Goloud was jealous but thought better of letting himself by drawn into yet another meaningless and disjointed conversation.

∼∼*

Max found the Village of Chateau du Lac on his GPS. It estimated it would take him about two hours. But then, his GPS didn't know he would be driving his Lamborghini.

The GPS led them north, off the coast, and wound through several small villages which, at that hour of the night, like most small French villages, were mostly dark with only an occasional streetlight or light in the window as proof they were inhabited. It was just after eleven when his GPS voice announced he had arrived in Chateau du Lac. His headlights pierced the darkness revealing what he could see of the small village. The buildings, dating from previous centuries, were set tight against the street as if determined to hold it in place. As with the other villages, the lack of any lights from residences suggested most everyone had long since gone to bed.

Mélisande had been strangely quiet during the entire trip. "Arrêtez-vous là, "she said breaking her silence.

"Stop where?"

"Là," she pointed to a small, lighted sign reading 'Tabac' hanging from one of the buildings. Lights glowed through the two front windows. Max pulled over to the side and parked next to the small bar and restaurant. Mélisande opened her door, got out and hurried inside. Max turned off the engine, took off his seat belt, open his door and followed her.

The restaurant had a bar with stools on one side of the room. On the other were several tables. It was empty except for an older man who appeared to have only a passing acquaintance with a razor.

"He is the proprietor," Mélisande said reverting to English.

The man stared at Max as one might look at someone who had just come face to face with a landlord about to deliver an eviction notice.

Not exactly the friendliest looking fellow, he thought.

"I have ordered you a coffee," she said. "A glass of water, for me. I need to go to..." She gestured toward the sign indicating the toilettes.

Max sat down at the far end of the bar and waited for the proprietor to deliver the coffee. The man slid the cup and saucer in front of him and, without a word, immediately retreated to the other end of the bar and began busying himself washing glasses.

"Open late tonight?" he asked before lifting the cup to his lips.

"Je ne parle pas anglais."

Max repeated the question in French, "Êtes-vous ouvert tard ce soir?"

The proprietor's response made no effort to hide his apparent irritation at having to answer what to him seemed obvious. "Si je ont été fermés, je n'aurais pas pu vous a servi du café."

Max looked down at his coffee cup, took a sip and smiled as he echoed the response, "True. If you were closed you could not have served me a coffee." *This man is not happy in his work.* It was a private observation.

When Mélisande reappeared, Max pointed to the glass of water the proprietor had placed on the bar. "There's your water."

"I'm not thirsty any more. Finish your coffee and let us go. My home is not far from here."

Max drained the last of the coffee as Mélisande left the restaurant. Max pulled out his wallet and looked toward the proprietor. "Combien pour le café?"

"Gratuit."

"Free?" Max did not expect that. "Merci. Not exactly a money-making enterprise, is this?" He put his wallet away

"Je ne comprends pas." The tone of his voice said more than the words. *I told you before I don't speak your fucking English.*

For good measure Max added. "Even at 'free' it's lousy coffee." Max left the restaurant, walked around the front of his car, opened the door, settled into his seat and started the engine. "Ok, where to from here? "

"Continuez tout droit," she said pointing straight ahead. "Je vais vous dire où tourner."

We're back to French. "Ok, I'll wait for you to tell me when to turn." Max figured they must have driven about five kilometers before he noticed a fog had begun to settle over the area rapidly making it more difficult to see the road.

"Allez à gauche, ici," Mélisande said pointing to the road coming up on their left.

Max made the left turn and began to shake his head in an effort to fend off the sudden urge to close his eyes. *Damn! Can't believe I'm so tired all of a sudden. No way am I going to be in any shape to drive home. Might need to find somewhere to spend the night. And given that we seem to be in the middle of nowhere, that's not going to be easy. Maybe I can stay at the Chateau. No. Not a good idea. I want to hand this woman over to her family or whoever lives with her and say 'sayonara, goodbye, and please stay out of my garden.' If I have to, I'll sleep in my car.*

Another two kilometers and she pointed toward two crumbling stone pillars on the right side of the road marking what once, he thought, must have been a grand entrance. *They look to be in need of a stonemason.* The driveway – it would be impossible to call it that – immediately became little more than a rutted and abandoned dirt road. He had not driven more than twenty yards when his headlights picked up a fallen tree blocking the way. It was not a big tree, but large enough to make it impossible to pass. "This can't be the way to your Chateau," he said. "Maybe we missed a turn."

"No," she said reverting to English, "This is where I lived." She opened her door.

Max was immediately struck by her use of the past tense 'lived.' But as he continued to fight the overwhelming desire to close his eyes, he did not give it any more thought.

"Turn off your headlights and look over there," she said pointing to his left. "My Chateau. That is where I lived." She got out of the car.

Again, why the past tense?

Max did as she requested. Beyond the fallen tree, the road – or what was once a road or a driveway or an approach – appeared to turn to the left. Max followed the road with his eyes and saw that it led directly to a large, three story castle-like structure bathed in an eerie dark blue glow. *Maybe fog filtered moonlight,* he thought. *Can't keep my eyes open. Gotta fight this.* As he stared at the chateau, he saw a light flicker in a window on the second floor. It grew brighter as if someone was lighting candles. "Mélisande, I don't know... ." *Where is she? There.* He saw that she was walking quickly toward the Chateau. He got out of the car and started to follow her. "Mélisande, he called, "Wait!"

Then he heard the voice of a man – a young man – calling from the Chateau, "Mélisande!" It echoed strangely through the woods.

"Pellias! Pellias! Je suis venue," Mélisande screamed. She pulled her dress up around her knees and began to hurry toward the Chateau.

Pellias, that was the name of the person she said she was looking for.

So tired. Max found he could barely put one foot in front of the other with any certainty. "Wait!" he shouted, struggling to keep himself from falling. She was running now. Her white dress trailing out behind her. He tried to follow, but his legs were lead and his feet felt as if they were mired in mud. He could barely move.

Again, the voice, "Mélisande!"

Again her response, "Pellias Jes suit venue!"

Max slumped to his knees as he watched Mélisande enter the Chateau. "What's wrong with me?" He asked aloud of the forest.

Then another voice from the Chateau. This one deeper, darker. "Mélisande! Vous êtes venus à temps pour voir Pelléas mourir!

What? You came in time to see Pelléas die? An agonizing cry from the younger voice followed by a painful and gasping, "Je t'aime, Mélisande!"

Flames!

A thunder crack and then an explosion.

Billowing smoke.

The room with the candle light had burst out in flames. The fire spread and quickly engulfed the middle part of the Chateau. He could hear the sound of falling debris. Mélisande screamed, "Pas Goloud, qu'avez-vous fait?" More screams and then... nothing.

Nothing.

Silence. Max lost consciousness and collapsed to the ground.

6.

2 YEARS BEFORE THE MURDER
OF ANDREA TRASK

Chateau du Lac, France

Cold. Damp with morning dew. Something hard under his back. Something poking him in the ribs. Slowly he open his eyes and stared first at the canopy of tree tops and then at the man, a hunter, standing over him, poking him gently in the ribs with a shot gun barrel as if testing to see if some hunted animal had any life left in it. The hunter removed the shotgun from his ribs and slung it over his shoulder. "Monsieur, vous êtes mort ou vivant?"

"What? Max asked trying to gather his senses.

"Are you dead or alive?" the hunter repeated.

"Not sure," he said putting his hands on his head.

"You're not French."

"No."

"English?"

"American."

"Good, I hate the English. What are you doing here? This is not a good place to sleep."

Max sat up trying to clear his head. "Where am I?"

"You are on the grounds of the Chateau du Lac... or what used to be the Chateau. It is a very good here for hunting deer. Not so good for sleeping unless you are dead." The hunter seemed to find this very funny and let out a loud guffaw. He stopped laughing only when he realized Max did not share his humor.

"Last night... I... I was bringing this..." Then it occurred to him not only was he not sure what had happened last night, but that any explanation to this hunter would sound wildly insane. Max turned and looked toward the Chateau. "My God, it's even bigger than it looked last night."

"Oh, it is very big, even bigger than what you can see from here."

"It looks... abandoned."

"Oui. For a very long time. And if you go closer, you can see it is crumbing badly. Once, many years ago, it must have been very beautiful. But now..." he shrugged, "It slowly falls in upon itself. It would take many fortunes to restore it. That will not happen. Let me help you up." The hunter took the shotgun off his shoulder, leaned it against a tree, then bent over to help Max to his feet.

Max stared at the Chateau which he guessed dated to the 16th century. The architecture was in the Renaissance style. Round towers anchored either end of the building and soared above the roofline topped with cone shaped roofs.

"According to what is known of the Chateau, it has suffered many evils, the last of which was a fire that killed the family living there."

"Fire? There was a fire?"

"So I am told."

"When?"

"Oh, maybe one hundred or more years ago. Maybe longer than that. Certainly long before I was born. If you believe the story, and I do not know if you can, it was very sad. Everyone in the Chateau died in the fire. They think maybe it was started on purpose. At least that's what my grandmother believed."

"Can you tell me what happened?"

"I can only tell you what was told me."

"That's fine."

"Well," he began in slow, measured tones as if he were doing his best to impress Max with his command of English. "In the house were two brothers. One much other than the other. The oldest one seems to have found this woman in some far-off place. No one seems to know exactly where she came from. Anyway, he falls in love and brings her back to the Chateau. And that's when it all started."

"What started?"

"The problem between the brothers. She fell in love with the younger brother whose name was... let me see if I can remember.

"Pelléas," Max volunteered

"That's correct. You know the story?"

"No, no, please go on."

"His name, as you said, was Pelléas. A very French name, but not very common today. And the woman, her name was ahhh... Mélisande. Yes, Mélisande. Same as my daughter. My daughter lives in Paris now and works for Gaumont. You know Gaumont? It is a motion picture company. She is very talented, though I am not sure what she does for them. My wife and I think one day she may even direct films."

"I'm sure she probably will but go on with your story." Max was growing increasing impatient.

"Ah, yes. I do get distracted at time. My age you know, seventy-three. Sometimes my wife says I have... what is the word? In French démence."

"Dementia. But go on. *And get to the point, for God sakes!*"

"Anyway, Pelléas and Mélisande fall in love. They tried to hide it from the older brother. If I remember correctly, his name was something like Golaud. Unfortunately, they were not as discreet as they should have been. So when Golaud finds out they have fallen in love, he kills his brother and to punish Mélisande, he sets the Chateau on fire. No one knows if he meant to kill himself, but he perished in the fire as well. According to people in the village, and you must understand, they are all very... what is the word? Ah, impressionable. They claim they see her ghost from time to time. She is dressed all in white and she appears in the Village asking for Pelléas."

This doesn't make sense. First, I don't believe in ghosts. Second, Mélisande was no ghost. The woman was flesh and blood. But this story? I don't know. It seems to be pretty much in sync with everything she told me.

"I think maybe you doubt the part about the ghost. I do too. I believe in what I can see and I have never seen a ghost. To tell you the truth, I sometimes wonder if people in the village have too much imagination. I think maybe they just like a good ghost story. Mothers like to tell about the ghost to young children as a way to discourage them from playing in the Chateau. It is in such bad repair it would be a very dangerous place for children to play." The hunter put his hand on Max shoulder. "Now, would you like me to take you home for breakfast? My wife makes wonderful brioche."

Max slowly nodded 'No.' "Thanks for the offer, but I think I'd better be on my way."

"Oh, I have been talking so much I have forgotten to ask you something. How is it you came to be sleeping here in the forest?"

"Not sure myself. But I wouldn't recommend it."

The hunter thought it was very funny and belched several linked guffaws.

He put his shotgun on his shoulder. "Au revoir," he said. "The deer await," and walked off into the woods.

Max got into his car and slowly backed up through the crumbling pillars and on to the road. It was a bright morning; the fog had lifted and he made his way back toward the Village of Chateau du Lac. *Didn't he say he was hunting deer? Yeah he did,* Max answered himself. *I know that gun. I have one. It's the most expensive turkey shotgun you can buy.*

* ~ * ~ *

Max drove into the village and parked across from the restaurant where he and Mélisande had stopped. He got out of his car and went inside. Several men were seated at the bar and a half dozen people occupied the tables

"Bonjour, monsieur," came the greeting from a middle age women of significant girth. "Café?"

"Oui." Max answered.

"Et quelque chose à manger?" She pointed to a tray with an assortment of croissants, brioche and pastry.

Max pointed to one of the pastry.

"Un ou deux?" she asked with a smile, her tongs poised to place his order on a plate.

"One," he answered.

"Bon," she said as she handed him the pastry. "Café noir ou café au lait."

"Noir. Is the proprietor in this morning?" he asked, inadvertently changing to English.

"My name is Michelle and I am proprietor. As you see I speak English," the woman answered proudly. "What I may do for you?"

"Last night... late last night, I was here and there was a man who said he was the proprietor."

She looked at him quizzically. "Here? In my restaurant?"

Max nodded, "Maybe your husband?"

The woman laughed, "Ha. My husband, he runs off with another woman. Une prostituée et d'une chienne, she added in French. And last night, we were fermé – closed."

"Michelle, nous avons besoin de plus de café," came a voice from one of the tables.

"Excusez-moi," she said. I must give them more coffee.

It was several minutes before she returned and Max had finished both his coffee and pastry. "What do you know about Chateau du Lac?"

"The village or the Chateau?"

"The Chateau."

"It is what gave our village its name."

"So I assumed. But what of the Chateau's history? How long has it been abandoned?"

"Since the war. The Vichy, those French who sold us out to the Germans, used it as one of their headquarters until the Allies drove them out."

"What happened to the people who lived there?"

"It was before I was born, but I was told the people who owned the Chateau were Vichy sympathizers and that they were responsible for sending many Jews to camps. At the end of the war, a group of men from the Village took everyone in the Chateau out into the forest and shot them. No one has lived there since. It is in very bad repair. Now, if you will excuse me..."

Max held up his hand asking for another minute. "Please, one more question. Has anyone here in the village every talked about the Chateau being haunted?"

"Haunted? By who?"

"A young woman and two men."

She made a dismissive sound with her mouth, "We don't believe in ghosts. The only things that haunt the Chateau are birds. And once or twice a year, the fire departments from all the villages in the area use it."

"The fire departments use it? How?"

"They set fires and practice putting them out."

"Any chance they might have been their last night?"

"She began to laugh." I don't think so. What we call le chef des pompiers, the chief of the firemen, was in my bed last night." She covered a smirk with her hand and began to giggle like a guilty schoolgirl. "I was putting out his fire." Realizing she might have shocked the American with her admission, she quickly pasted a proprietor-like expression on her face. "Now, I must see to my other customers."

"Yes, of course, I understand." Max pulled out his wallet and handed her twenty Euros – far more than needed to cover the bill." For the coffee, the pastry and the information," he said, then thanked her.

Her face lit up. "Merci, monsieur. S'il vous plaît venez à nouveau. Yes, come again."

Nothing was making any sense to Max. *I've got to go back to the Chateau. Maybe if I can take a look at where I saw the fire on the second floor I can figure out what...* He stopped mid-thought. He had no idea what he could figure out.

Max turned his car around and drove back to the Chateau. He pulled in between the pillars and parked only a few feet inside. It took him several minutes to make his way to the front of the Chateau. *What a great looking place to shoot a movie. As the hunter said, it must have been really something in its day.* A wide staircase led up to what had been the main entrance. To the right, a large arch lead to an inner courtyard. Slowly he climbed the steps and found the front doors hanging off their hinges. *A long time since these have been closed.* Carefully he stepped inside and found himself in what was once a grand reception hall. Plaster and wood debris from huge chunks of the ceiling and crumbling walls lay all around. *Maybe from the explosion last night? Then again, maybe not.* Michelle was right about one thing, it was home to dozens of birds that darted back and forth loudly complaining about the presence of an intruder.

Directly ahead, a sweeping curved staircase led to the second floor. From what he could see, it looked secure. He took the steps carefully and one at a time. After what seemed an endless climb, he stepped on to the second floor. A long hallway running in both directions provided access to over a dozen rooms. If someone had told him he was looking at the aftermath of an explosion, he would not have been surprised. As the hunter had said, it would take several fortunes to restore the Chateau. *The light I saw and the fire had to be in one of the middle rooms.* He selected a door and began his search for he knew not what.

~~*

It was a little afternoon when he returned to his car. He placed several small items and fragments he had brought from the Chateau on the passenger seat. As he looked at them, he felt sure they had the answer to what had happed the night before.

~~*

Max's cell phone rang. It was Robby. "Where the hell are you? I stepped by your villa this morning and Jacko said you didn't come home last night."

"I'm on the road. Heading home. Spent the night in the country."

"With a very attractive woman, I hope?"

"Yes, but not in the way you think."

"The way I think is there's only one way to spend the night with an attractive woman."

"Never mind, I'll tell you about it later."

"Ok. Now whenever you get back from whereverthehell you are, I want you to drop everything and get your sorry ass over here. I want my rematch. And this time bring your own fuckin' racket."

"Can't do it today. Maybe tomorrow. I've got some things I need to do."

"What can you need to do that's more important than my beating your brains out on the tennis court?"

"A long list of things, as it turns out."

"Oh, another matter. Andrea. Called me last night. As I suspected, she has asked me for a divorce."

"And...?"

"As I told you. I said I thought it was best for both of us. I told her I hoped we could remain friends."

"And...?"

"That was it. What has to be has to be. The lawyers will start on the paper work right away. She's going to stay in Anasara until it's done. In another week or two, I'll close up this place. We agreed to put the villa up for sale and split the sale fifty-fifty. As far as everything else, she takes what's hers and I take what's mine and we're splitsville. Clean, uncontested and we go our happy ways. Right now, I'm thinkin' the sooner the better. You have to admit, Max, this is a lot more civil than any of your divorces."

"A whole lot more civil," Max echoed.

"Ok. About our tennis game."

So much for any concern about the divorce, we're on to tennis. Clearly, Max thought, *Robby is not exactly heart-broken or shedding any tears over the end of their marriage. Actually, he sounded glad it was over., If he really is happy about the divorce, it will make it easier for him to accept that his best friend is the one removing the trophy from his shelf.*

"I'll let you off the hook today," Robby said. "But tomorrow, at eleven, I expect to see your ass on my court."

"I'll be there. See you then," Max said and hung up.

Max was back in his villa just after three. He told Jacques he did not want to be disturbed and immediately went into his library and closed the door. He sat down at this desk and laid out the items he'd brought from the house. He began by writing up a description of each and taking individual pictures with his iPhone. In one case, he wrote down the words he found on a scrap of paper. *Let's see, it's ten AM in New York and seven in L.A.* He began to make a list of the people he intended to call. Almost as an afterthought, he added Andrea's name. Then he logged on to his computer and began the first of several searches. What he found convinced him he was on the right track. *Love Google. This is going to be interesting.* He pulled out a pad of yellow lined paper and on four differed sheets wrote, Phase I, Phase II, Phase III and Phase IV. *I'll figure the rest out later.* Just writing the headings gave him a sense of organizational satisfaction. It was the same detailed, linear approach that he took to all his business decisions. It never failed him. *Yes, this is going to be very interesting,* he mused. *And dangerous? Maybe. Certainly, I'll have to do everything I can to reduce the risk.*

It was after nine when he finally put in a call to Andrea.

"Where have you been?" she sounded mildly frantic. "I've been expecting you to call all day. I tried this afternoon, but Jacques said you had asked not to be disturbed. What's going on?"

"I'm sorry," he said. "I should have told him to make you the exception. We've had a major snafu back in New York that's had me tied up all day." He felt guilty about lying to her, but there was no way he could go into detail about what happened last night or explain what had consumed his day, "I talked to Robby," he said at last. "He told me he agreed to the divorce."

"How did he sound?" she asked.

Max paused. *I don't think I want to tell her he sounded happy to have it over and done with. Not good for a woman's ego to think the husband is happy to be free.* "Very sad," he lied a second time "Obviously, he's not happy he's putting an end to this part of his life, but he's resigned in that he knows this is best for both of you. He's happy, things won't get ugly."

"Did you say anything about us?"

"No. No need to rub his nose in it. There will be time enough after your divorce is final for him to accept we intend to get married."

"Not that I owe Robby any consideration, but I guess you're right. We'll wait until the divorce is final."

"Robby said you planned to stay in Anasara."

"Yes, but I want you here with me."

"And I want to be there with you as well. As soon as Robby leaves Cap Ferrat, I'll come out to Anasara."

"Why wait? I want you with me now."

"Andrea, it's... well, it's cleaner this way. I don't want him to think I'm sticking it to him by jumping in bed with his wife before the divorce is done."

"Haven't we already done that?"

"But he doesn't know. I know you think he does, but, I'm not sure. Anyway, in two weeks, he'll have left and won't know, won't ask or even care where I am."

"Two weeks. And then you're here." It was not a request, but a demand.

"Count on it. We'll never get out of bed."

"Maybe for meals," she laughed.

"Not even for meals." he responded. "I love you Andrea. I am going to do everything I can to make up for lost time... for all those years that you should have been mine."

"You make me sound like a possession."

"Hey, like it or not. You are. A very beautiful one."

"Just as long as you don't put me up on your trophy shelf, like Robby."

"Not a chance. Gotta go. My head is splitting. Didn't sleep well last night."

"You were alone, I hope."

"Oh, very much alone, but thinking of you," he lied for the third time.

"Call me tomorrow."

"Will do. Love you," he said and hung up. He looked at his watch, Nine-thirty. One-thirty in L.A. He picked up his phone and pulled up the picture of Mélisande he had taken before they left for Chateau du Lac. He sent it to his computer and then attached it to an email address to three of his West Coast employees detailing a specific request. He tagged it urgent and requested a response within 24 hours. He did the same with the pictures he had taken of the items he found at the house.

"Ok, I think that's everything for Phase One. Tomorrow, Phase Two. Tennis at eleven."

7.

2 YEARS BEFORE THE MURDER OF ANDREA TRASK

Cap Ferrat/Chateau du Lac, France

Max woke at seven and immediately went into his library and logged onto his email. Responses to his requests the day before had arrived. *Good*, he thought. *It's what I suspected. Hard to believe after all this time. But there it is.*

Max had Jacques serve him breakfast at this desk as he sent replies to his emails. At just after ten he went upstairs to put on his tennis clothes. He would be in whites this time and he'd bring his own racket.

The match got out of hand early. Max was well off his game and down five games to two in the first set. Robby lifted a lob that normally Max would have easily put away as a winner, but his overhead smash sent the ball well out of bounds giving Robby the set at six-two.

Robby's tennis gambit, with players he knew to be better than he, was to talk his opponent into making bad shots. Today, he had said little to Max after the fourth game. "I don't know who I'm playing over there, but it's not Max Roarke."

"Yeah, I feel like shit today. My head's just not into it."

"Let's sit down. I'll get us a couple of waters." Max sat down on one of the chairs alongside the court as Robby went into his tennis shack and returned with two bottles of water. "Here ya go," he said handing one to Max.

"Thanks."

"I get the feeling my friend Max has a problem."

"I'm not sure what I've got. Maybe an over active imagination. Or maybe I'm just losing it."

"What are you talking about?"

"Robby, if I tell you something, will you take me seriously, or are you just going to start giving me the needle?"

He nodded his agreement. "I'm your friend. If you need to talk, I here to listen"

For a moment Max appeared to be gathering this thoughts, "It's about the woman in white that I kept seeing? I think she's dead."

"What?"

"Yeah, either that or she never existed."

"Sounds a little crazy, you know."

"I know. But let me tell you about the other night. I have a feeling you're not going to believe this, but I hope you'll trust I'm telling you exactly what happened... or at least what I think happened." Max began with Mélisande's appearance at his villa and her request to be taken to Chateau du Lac. Max told him about the bar and the old man who claimed to be the proprietor. He described driving into the Chateau, the downed tree, the voices from the house, Mélisande running for the Chateau, the explosion, the fire and passing out. He told Robby about what the hunter had told him about its history. He said nothing about the man hunting deer with a turkey shotgun, nothing about Michelle's very different story about how the Vichy sympathizers were taken out and shot.

When he finished, Robby asked, "Did you go into the Chateau? Check it out?"

"The hunter said it wasn't safe. You have to see this place. It's literary falling down on itself. Obviously, I didn't want to be inside if the roof were to fall in."

"No, you sure wouldn't," Robby said.

"I just don't know what to make of it all. I'm sure Mélisande was real. No figment of my imagination ever kissed me like that. Even though I blacked out at the Chateau, I'm sure I saw a light in one of the windows. And there was a fire. I could not have imagined that."

"If only someone else had been with you to see it." There was a brief cloud of doubt in his voice.

"What are you saying? That I imagined it all?"

"No, of course not. It's just..."

"You think maybe I've lost it?"

"No, not at all."

"Well," Max said lowering his head, "I'm beginning to wonder if maybe I have."

"What are you doing to do?"

"Not sure. Unfortunately, I have to go to New York for a couple of days, but when I get back... well, I'm not sure what I'll do."

"What if she shows up again?"

"Don't think that's going to happen."

"But if she did?"

"I'd tie her up, put her in a cage and deliver her to you. Then you could tell me if you think she's real or not."

* ~ * ~ *

Max let it be known he was off to New York for three days to attend to some pressing business. He never went. He had to do something he felt was more important.

* ~ * ~ *

Max picked up the phone. It was Robby. "You're back."

"But back to what? I really think I'm going crazy. I'm haunted by that night. I can't close my eyes without seeing Mélisande running toward the Chateau. The screams, the other voices and then the explosion and fire. I know what I have to do. And I want you to help me," he said his voice revealing just how distraught he was.

"Hey, whatever I can do."

"I want you to come over tonight about nine."

"What have you got in mind?"

"I'll tell you then. But I want to solve this. I honestly believe it's the only chance I have of saving my mind."

"Ok... hang in there. Don't do anything rash. We'll get this solved. See you at nine."

* ~ * ~ *

At nine Robby drove up and found Max in standing in the dark in front of his villa. Max got into the car. "Drive," he said.

"Where we going?"

"We're going to retrace that night. Same time, same roads... everything the same except I don't have Mélisande."

"Are you sure this is a good idea?" Robby asked, clearly reluctant to do as his friend had asked.

"If you're my friend, you'll do this for me," he said with grave intensity. Desperation crept into his voice. "You don't understand what this is doing to me. I've got to know."

"Know what?"

Max dropped his head to his chest and mumbled, "Just know."

"Ok, if you think this will help," he said. "How do I get there?"

"Just set you GPS for the village of Chateau de Lac. It'll take us there."

It was almost eleven when they entered the Village. The streets, as before, were dark save for two only streetlights set well part. The Tabac sign was dark. Max indicted for Robby to pull up next to the restaurant and stop.

"This is the place where you and Mélisande stopped?"

Max nodded.

"It's closed. But you said it was open that night?"

"It was. But you're right. No one's there."

"What now?"

"Straight ahead. I'll tell you where to turn."

Finally they arrived in front of the pillars marking the entrance to the Chateau.

"Pull in there and stop."

Robby did as instructed. Max got of the car and started to walk down the road toward the fallen tree.

"Where you going?"

"I've got to find Mélisande!" he said as he stepped over the tree. There was a slight panic in his voice, "I've got to save her from the fire!"

A scream. A woman's scream pierced the night.

"I'm coming Mélisande! I'm coming!" Max started running toward the Chateau.

"Max wait!" Robby shouted as he started to follow him. "Max! Stop! Max!" He was yelling at the top of his lungs.

"Mélisande! Mélisande!" Max ran up the steps of the Chateau and through the open doors.

Robby stopped running well short of the Chateau. "Max! Get out of there! Max!"

The explosion rocked the forest.

Leaves and branches rattled out of the trees cascading down around Robby. "Oh, shit! Max! Max!"

Flames leaped out from the front of the Chateau. There was the sound of crashing debris falling inside the building.

Robby froze, stood helpless, unable to believe what he was seeing. "Good God no!" he kept repeating sometimes as a shout sometimes just to himself.

Sirens!

Lights!

Shouts!

Robby turned around and saw several large vehicles bashing their way toward him down the old road. As they got closer, he saw that one was a water fire truck. A pumper. Behind him, two police vehicles. Robby stepped off the road and back into the woods to let them pass. The water truck pulled up in front of the Chateau. Fireman jumped out, attached hoses to the tank and started pumping a stream of water onto the fire. Within minutes the flames were out. Smoke rose up from the smoldering debris.

"Qu'est-il arrivé ici? Qui tes-vous? Avez-vous vu ce qui s'est passé? "a gendarme shouted at Robby.

"Robby could translate only enough to understand they were asking him what happened. Frantically he pointed toward the Chateau and shouted back, "My friend! My friend is inside!"

"Your friend?"

"Thank God, someone speaks English. Yes. He ran into the Chateau and it... it exploded!"

"What? That is insane. Why would he run into the Chateau? What was he...?" the gendarme stopped and looked suspiciously at Robby, "What were *you* doing here in the woods at this time of night? Eh?"

There was simply no way for Robby to explain and make it sound like something less than some sort of madness. Instead, he put a question to the gendarme, "How did you get here so fast?"

"We were on our way back from putting out a small kitchen fire when we heard the explosion. Lucky we were near. The whole woods could have caught on fire and then... I do not want to think about that." The gendarme looked intently at Robby for a moment, "But you have not explained to me why you are here." There was an accusatory sound to the way he asked the question.

Before Robby could answer, a voice rose above the din of the water truck's engine. It was from one of the firemen near the Chateau. "Nous avons trouvé un corps!"

"What did he say?"

"They found a body."

"Oh my God, no! No!" Robby cried.

Robby and the gendarme hurried in the direction of the fireman's voice.

"Par ici!" the fireman motioned for them to follow up the front steps. Once inside he pointed his flashlight toward the base of the staircase leading to the second floor. "Là, il est."

Robby slowly edged his way forward behind the policeman, stepping carefully over the rubble on the floor. The fireman's light revealed what remained of a totally charred body.

"Mon Dieu! I am not sure if it is a man or woman," the gendarme said.

The body was so badly burned it looked as if it had been pulled out in the middle of a cremation There was no way to identify who it was. Then Robby saw it. Next to what had been the person's right arm was a shiny object. "What's that? There!" he pointed.

One of the firemen leaned over and picked it up.

"Let me see that?" Robby demanded, holding out his hand.

The fireman looked at the gendarme as if asking permission to give it to Robby. The gendarme nodded.

"Oh, God no!" The wail of recognition filled the Chateau. It was a cigar cutter, sandwiched into a Napoleon coin. Robby turned it over. On the back was the inscription, '*Max Roarke Number One! Robby Trask Not Number One.*'

AN EXCERPT FROM THE DIARY
OF ANDREA TRASK

Two Days Before Her Murder

I was hysterical. I cried for days. My world, or at least the world I hoped would be mine, had suddenly and irrevocably been destroyed. Max was dead. And while I did not understand why at first, Robby claimed responsibility. 'I did it,' he said again and again. 'I killed my best friend.' I was too consumed with my own pain and heartbreak to even ask for an explanation. I believed then, as I do now, his remorse and pain were real. He had lost his best friend. I, of course, had lost the only man I ever truly loved. For a short while, a very short while as it turned out, I felt a renewed closeness to Robby as we endured our mutual grief. But later, at the inquest in Nice, I learned the truth. The short-lived emotional bond I shared with him was immediately ripped away and replaced with revulsion, disgust and yes, even hate. I lashed out at him with language I did not know was even in my vocabulary demanding an explanation, demanding to know 'why."

His response? "It was my turn."

Those were the same words he repeated at the 'enquête,' the inquest in the court in Nice. It was, to say the least, a bizarre performance by my soon to be ex-husband. The magistrate was clearly befuddled and unable to fully grasp the essential meaning or motivation behind Le Jeu Ultime. The name does not begin to describe their games which were, in fact, calculated humiliations. It was, ultimately, a fanatical, gross and vulgar combat on the basest level that could only have been enabled by their ability to spend any amount of money to carry out their manic obsession.

Listening to Robby's explanation and to the interpreter's attempt to convey it to the magistrate, I would have to say much was lost in the translation. For the reader of this diary I have included the court transcript.

MAGISTRATE
Correct me if I am wrong, but are you telling the court this whole tragic affair between you and the deceased was a game? A game of practical jokes?

ROBERT TRASK
We never thought of it that way. It was far more a than a game, it was a competition. One that demanded cunning and wits.

MAGISTRATE
Did it not seem a little senseless to engage in a competition of practical jokes when both of you were obviously aware of the other's intentions?

ROBERT TRASK
No. No. That's what made it so fascinating. To achieve a victory without being discovered was incredibly difficult.

MAGISTRATE
Tell me Mr. Trask, when did you first conceive the idea for this particular hoax? The one which resulted in the death of Mr. Roarke.

ROBERT TRASK
It was after Max had won a point making a fool of me after I climbed a mountain in Peru. It was a very difficult climb. I was the first to do it. But at the top, Max set up a prank. Not only did he win a point, but I became a joke at the Alpine Club. I was portrayed by various publications as the conqueror of Picnic Mountain. It was shortly after I began to plan what I would do for my serve... my turn. It took me a very long time to set up Chateau du Lac. I hired an actress to play Mélisande. I paid one of the world's great magicians to create illusions so that she could appear and disappear in front of Max's eyes. At the restaurant in the Village of Chateau de Lac, I arranged to drug his coffee so that later, during the fire, when his adrenaline began to flow, it would combine with the drug to make him pass out. I contracted with a motion picture company in Paris to create the fire and to produce the voices. I hired another actor to play the part of the hunter and made up the story for him to tell about the history of

the Chateau. I was there, that night, hiding in the woods to be sure nothing would happen to Max after he passed out. Everything worked exactly as I had planned.

MAGISTRATE
When did you intend to inform Mr. Roarke he had been the victim of your scheme?

ROBERT TRASK
I had arranged for dinner party at La Reserve in Beaulieu. There was to be an entertainment. The entertainment was to have my magician make Mélisande suddenly appear in the restaurant, have her jump into Max's lap and announce the score was now 40-30 in my favor.

MAGISTRATE
But, of course, that never happened.

ROBERT TRASK
No. I should never have let Max make me retrace the events of that night. He was obsessed. There was no way to talk him out of it. I figured we'd find the empty Chateau and go home.

MAGISTRATE
That is not what happened, was it?

ROBERT TRASK
No. Not what happened.

MAGISTRATE
One last question, Mr. Trask, how much time had elapsed between the practical joke he played on you in Peru and this hoax of yours?

ROBERT TRASK
About seven years.

MAGISTRATE
Seven years? May I suggest to you that considering the time it took for you

to take your turn, Mr. Roarke might well have assumed your game was over...
done?

ROBERT TRASK
It was my turn. He had to know that.

MAGISTRATE
Apparently, he did not.

To no one's surprise, the court did not press charges. Money does have a persuasive influence in French courts. I thought when the inquest was over that I knew everything there was to know about Le Jeu Ultime. I was wrong. Very wrong. And it was only when I learned the whole truth about what actually happened at Chateau du Lac and then what happened three months later in the Southampton cemetery that I knew that I – not either of them – had become the victim of their game.

It was then I decided upon a very special kind of revenge.

IV
THE HAUNTING OF ROBBY TRASK

1.

18 MONTHS BEFORE THE MURDER
OF ANDREA TRASK

Southampton, New York

Because of the Nice inquest and the time it took to finalize the paperwork necessary to ship the body back to the States, the funeral did not take place in Southampton until October. Of all the people who had claimed Max as a friend, of all the people who had benefited from his largess, Robby felt it disrespectful to Max's memory that only a handful of Max's friends found the time to attend the funeral. As it turned out, a dozen or so uninvited spectators, curious locals, found their way to the cemetery. Robby was sure they had come hoping to see someone important as it was known in Southampton Max had many famous friends, including a list of Hollywood names.

Robby looked over at Andrea, dressed in black, standing on the opposite side of the grave. She laid a single rose on the casket and dabbed at her eyes under her dark veil. Robby had asked her to stay with him at their East Hampton house, but she refused. Before the inquest in Nice, she had come to him for comfort – to share his tears. Afterwards, when she learned the truth about how Max had died, her only words to Robby were of condemnation. Her hatred for him had become palpable.

"Because God has chosen to call our brother, Maximilian Roarke, from this life, we commit his body to the earth," the minister intoned. "Earth to earth, ashes to ashes, dust to dust; in the sure and certain hope..."

"Max, you son-of-a bitch!" Robby shouted.

The mourners reacted in stunned silence as he darted past the grave and ran across the cemetery to where, not fifty yards away, a man was seen sitting atop a grave. "Goddamn you, Max! You fucker!" As Robby approached, the man turned his back, hiding his face. "You rotten bastard! I ought to kill you and put you in that box! Who the hell are we burying?"

The mourners at graveside looked at each other aghast. "The man's possessed," the minister mumbled.

"I think he's going mad," another said.

"What is he doing?" Andrea cried.

Robby was on the man now. He grabbed a shoulder and spun Max around. But it wasn't Max. Similar resemblance, but not Max.

"Oh shit! I'm sorry... sorry. I thought you were somebody else. You look so much like..."

The man on the grave marker stood up, not sure if he was going to have to protect himself or just run. On his shirt pocket the words, Southampton Cemetery.

Robby shook his head as he turned away repeating, "Sorry, sorry," and walked slowly back to Max's grave.

The minister began to read again, but at a much faster pace, as though he was looking to make fast work of the service. "So let us commend our brother Unto Almighty God we commend the soul of our brother departed, and we commit his body to the ground. Amen," he said and made a hasty retreat.

"That was certainly a fitting way to end the service," Andrea said derisively. The look she gave Robby was withering. "What was that all about?"

"That guy... I thought it was Max."

"Max? You thought it was Max? Have you lost your mind?" Andrea turned away shaking her head in disgust. She raised her veil and started to walk toward where the chauffeur had parked her limo.

Robby caught up with her. "You're staying at your grandmother's place, right?"

She nodded and kept walking.

"Can I take you?"

"My driver is waiting for me."

"I'd like to talk."

"No," she said sharply turning away from him. "We're done talking. Please go to hell!" she barked.

Andrea's words struck him like an icy blast, stopping him in his tracks. Robby did not move as he watched her chauffeur open the rear door of the limo and help her in. He was alone now, all but the man mistaken for Max and two other cemetery workers who set about lowering the casket.

Tears welled in his eyes as the coffin disappeared into the open grave. "Good bye, Max. God, I'm sorry. What the hell got into you? You had to know it was my turn."

2.

18 MONTHS BEFORE THE MURDER
OF ANDREA TRASK

Southampton, New York

It was over an hour after he left the cemetery when he found himself driving past Max's house in Southampton, past the beach where they'd first met Andrea and had their Kawasaki joust, and finally, past Marty's Lightfoot where Andrea's real age had been revealed by the police. He made up his mind that he had to find a way to shut out all those memories.

Within a few moments after leaving the village, his car was on the Montauk Highway headed for East Hampton. Even now, in early October, the two-lane highway was crowded and the speedometer on his BMW M6 never topped forty.

Except for his staff, the East Hampton house had been vacant for almost four years. Robby's financial advisers had suggested he sell it to take advantage of a surging market for waterfront property on Long Island, but he had ignored their suggestion. He had no idea why. Now, it only brought back memories of the summers he and Max had brought willing girls back to the house for carnal instruction.

Robby walked through several first-floor rooms. His thoughts drifted back to the night when he and Max had hidden the alarm clocks to assure his mother's wedding night with her new spouse would be a nightmare. *Wouldn't be surprised if a couple of the clocks are still hiding somewhere*, he thought.

It was May, fifteen years ago having barely accumulated the necessary credits, they both graduated. At about the same time, Robby's mother – who had divorced his father the year before – announced she was remarrying. Over the years, Robby had often talked to Max about how much he disliked both his parents. The senior Trask had made billions trading precious metals and oil. It was said of the man that the only thing more difficult than being one of his employees, was to be his son. From a very early age, Henry Trask and Robby lived as if they were in two armed camps continually at odds, never asking or giving quarter. His mother's main occupation in life was finding ways to have her picture show up regularly in *Town and Country* and *Veranda*. Robby, for the most part, had long been relegated to an afterthought in her life, an appendage to be tolerated and trotted out only when her role as a caring mother was called into question. When he discovered her new husband-to-be was an unemployed actor and fifteen years her junior, he decided she must have a truly unique wedding gift.

"Where do they plan to spend their wedding night?" Max asked.

"Our house in East Hampton," Robby said.

"You're sure?"

"Very."

"Question: As I recall there are at least twenty-rooms in your house, right?"

"And then some."

"Excellent." The idea blossomed full blown in Max's mind." I have the perfect wedding night gift for you to be giving your mother and new father."

"He'll never be my father."

"Well, whatever you decide to call him."

"Dickhead works."

"Sounds like it fits his personality."

"What have you got in mind?" Robby asked.

"You're gonna love this. We have some shopping to do."

Max and Robby visited dozens of appliance stores buying nearly one hundred wind-up alarm clocks. During the reception after the wedding, they set the clocks so that one would go off every three to four minutes from midnight to 6:00 A.M. Then they hid them like Easter eggs all through the house. That night, they sat outside in the shadows as the alarms went off. By one o'clock the buzzes and rings were accompanied by shouts, angry accusations, hysterical screams from his mother and stentorian curses from the actor.

Damn, that was fun, Robby laughed to himself as he recalled the night. *And Max's decision to leave ten-minute intervals between some of the alarms was a great touch. Every time they thought the ringing had come to an end, it hadn't.*

As he recalled how his mother and her husband had evacuated the house in a flurry of expletives, he began to laugh. He almost expected to hear an alarm go off as he passed through the main hall toward the rear of the house, stepped out on the terrace and sank into one of the chairs. His eyes roamed over the perfect lawn, the swimming pool and the tennis court that lay beyond. Dusk was giving way to night and he wondered when the last time was anyone set foot on the court. His staff had told him that once or twice they had found some young boys on the court and had to chase them away.

His thoughts wandered back to the time he and Max had occupied the court. The frustration, often bordering on anger, that he had felt every time he lost was now tempered by remorse. *The son-of-a-bitch was almost impossible to beat. And those few times I did win a set, it felt as if I'd won Wimbledon.* Robby went back inside and had his cook bring him something to eat. He walked into his poolroom, fixed himself a drink and picked up a pool cue. This was one game he had on Max. When it came to pool, Robby was the Willie Mosconi of East Hampton.

By his fourth Scotch, he could barely line up the cue stick with the cue ball. He tossed the pool cue on the table and shouted, "Shit! You fucker Max! What the hell got into you?" He waited as if he expected an answer. When none arrived, he left the room and went upstairs to bed.

* ~ * ~ *

He had been dreaming. He was in Hollywood with Max and they were on location filming a tennis scene for some movie t Max's company was producing. For some reason, one of the actors was having a problem hitting the ball back to the other. The director lost his temper. "Eric, I thought you said you played tennis? I wasn't talking about table tennis, you know."

Robby saw Max go over to the director and say, "Let me do it. Shoot me from the back and no one will know it's not Eric. Then cut in some close ups of his face swinging at the ball, add a sound effect and it'll look fine."

In his dream, Robby watched as Max had somehow changed into a tennis outfit and started a volley with the other actor. The rackets hitting the ball made a rhythmic 'whack' – 'whack' sound as the ball traveled back and forth over the net. At first, Robby assumed the sound was part of his dream, but as his eyes opened and he fought through the aftermath of his four scotches, he became aware the sound of the tennis volley was not coming from his dream, but from outside... from his tennis court. *What the hell?* He thought. *Kids playing on my court? In the middle of the night? Can't be. No lights on the court*. But there it was. 'Whack' – 'whack' one after the other – back and forth. He pushed himself up on one elbow and listened. *Somebody is on the court.*

He swung his legs out of bed and made his way to the open French doors that opened onto a balcony overlooking the backyard. The moon was not quite full but provided enough light to show him the court was empty. Still, the sound of rackets hitting a ball continued and then suddenly stopped. He told himself it had to be the residue of the four scotches. No sooner had he reached that conclusion than he was sure the heard Max's voice.

"Game and Set. Me!"

3.

18 MONTHS BEFORE THE MURDER
OF ANDREA TRASK

Southampton, New York

Robby sensed the effort would fail, but he felt he had to try. Andrea greeted him at the door, but the conversation never got beyond the front steps. "I'm told the papers are with your lawyer. I hope there won't be any delay," she said coldly.

"If that's what you want, I'll sign. I won't contest it. But I am here to ask... no, to plead with you to give us a second chance. I know I haven't been the best of husbands, but now with Max gone... well, I feel like I've lost my right arm."

"And what am I, your left? You want me to start playing your infantile game? I could, you know. I could be very good at it." The sarcasm in her voice was heavy and pointed.

"No, no, that's not what I'm saying. It's just..."

"Please Robby. This is a waste of time. I'll never forgive you for what you've done."

"But I'm ready to forgive you," he said.

"Forgive *me*? Forgive me for what? For putting up with your games all these years. For ignoring the other women?"

"No, I'm ready to forgive you for sleeping with my best friend this summer." His attempted defense only added to her bitterness.

"What are you talking about?" she said blanching.

"Don't try and deny it. I know. Just as I won't deny there have been other women. But, you have to understand, they meant nothing to me."

"Nothing? Just a wham, bam, thank you ma'am one nighter? And the fact they meant nothing justifies it?"

"I'm not saying that."

"Then, what are you saying?"

"Just those women... well, you didn't know any of them. It wasn't like I was having an affair with your best friend."

"My God listen to yourself, Robby. Are you saying it's ok to sleep with someone... anyone... so long as they're not one of your wife's friends?"

"No, I'm just saying neither of us has any right to criticize the other."

"There was one major difference between your one-night bimbos and Max. I loved Max. Our marriage was a mistake from the very beginning. What I mistook for love was really just fascination. I liked you. I liked you a lot. Maybe at some time, when we were all chasing around Europe, I even thought I loved you. But I never felt about you that way I did about Max. He was my first the summer I was twenty-one and I had hoped he would be my last."

Her admission caught him by surprise. "Your first? He never told me."

"Why should he have? It didn't concern you. Anyway, it's past history and I don't want to talk about it. All I want is for you to sign the divorce papers so we can both get with our lives."

The news that Max had been the first to sleep with her was like an attack of acid reflux. *That son-of-a bitch. He lied to me. Can't believe Max didn't tell me he'd slept with her back then. We had a bet. Wasn't like him not to collect on a bet.* Robby looked up at Andrea and was about to say something more about her not telling him she'd slept with Max, but when he saw the look in her eyes confirming the obvious, he realized it didn't matter now. It was over with Andrea. He nodded and mumbled a contrite "Ok, I'll sign the papers."

"I wish I could say it's been fun, Robby, but it really hasn't." With that she went inside and closed the door.

Robby stared at the door for a moment, then walked back to his car which he'd parked by the curb. As he was about to get in, two teenage boys on bicycles raced past him in the street. One of the boys put on a burst of speed and he was reminded of how Max had passed him in their Tour de Francis before his tire exploded. He had never told Max the truth about his accident.

He remember how after they'd agreed to make Andrea the prize for winning a bike race, he had almost immediately found himself regretting it. He had no idea how good Max would be in a bike race. For all he knew Max might have lied to him about not being on a bike since he was ten. While he'd won many trophies for Formula One events and for the horses he owned that had raced at all the major tracks, no prize meant more to him than Andrea. *This is one trophy I have to have on my shelf and I will do whatever it takes to get it.*

Having volunteered to provide the bikes, Robby immediately found an elite bike source in Paris and bought two Enigma titanium bikes at $15,000 each. The thought of losing Andrea to Max loomed more and more like a real possibility, especially after he discovered Max was somewhere out on the French countryside, on a bike, getting himself in shape for the race. Robby knew he could do the same and would, but even in top physical shape, things could happen to a rider during a road race. It was that possibility which gave him an idea. One that would guarantee his victory.

He removed the rear wheels of both Enigmas and, after what turned out to be a difficult search, located a man who could assure him of a win. He was told it would take a week to rig the wheels with a small, remotely detonated explosive embedded in the tires. There would be one wireless remote for each bike, and the only danger, he was warned, would be mixing up the remotes when it came time to blow the tire. Robby solved that by marking each tire and remote with a different color. Max's choice of bikes would determine which remote Robby would take with him during the race.

The day before the race as they checked into the Hôtel le Vallon de Valrugues in Saint Remy, Robby had a tinge of guilt. For a moment he thought about throwing away both remote detonators. But as he and Max ate dinner together, he sensed if they were to call off the race and leave it to Andrea to make a choice, she would, eventually choose Max. That realization was enough to push any residue of guilt out of his mind.

For much of the race, they took turns in the lead, allowing the rider in the back to benefit from the draft created by the man in front. It was on the Avenue Vincent Van Gogh about three kilometers to Saint Remy Max broke away with a burst of energy that stunned Robby. Within minutes, he lost sight of Max who he guessed had to be at least a quarter mile ahead. He reached into his pocket and pulled out the remote detonator. For a moment, he hesitated and thought about what he was about to do to the man he claimed to be his best friend. It was, he decided, a Hobson's choice: *Win Andrea and lose Max or let Max win and lose Andrea.* He made his choice.

As Robby approached Max, he saw that, as intended, the explosive charge had blown his rear tire. Max was sitting in a ditch next to his bike. As Robby rode by he looked at Max whose expression already reflected his defeat. "Tough luck, Max," Robby shouted. "You'll still be my best man, right?" he chided.

As he rode on, he thought he heard Max shout something, but he was too far away to make out what he said.

* ~ * ~ *

Robby visited Max's grave after he left Andrea and then drove aimlessly around the eastern end of Long Island for several days intent on paying a last visit to all the places he and Max had claimed as their special haunts. Several times he was sure he saw Max, once darting into a store, another time getting into a car, but each time found he was mistaken. Once, while he was seated at a bar in Bridgehampton nursing a drink, Max's face had appeared, but for a fleeting moment, on the television screen over the bar. Or was it Max? Max was everywhere, but he was nowhere and Robby began to wonder why his mind seemed to be conspiring to let Max haunt him.

* ~ * ~ *

It was late in the afternoon when his pilot called to confirm his plane was ready for the fight to Los Angeles. Robby had just walked out of the real estate office where he had left instructions to sell the house, unload it, at whatever price they could get and to do it within the next two months. "Give it away, if you have to. I want it out of my life." No sooner said than he found himself laughing at the thought of a broker giving his house away. *Not much of a commission in giving it away. No, they would probably over-price it in hope of making a quick killing.* It was a spectacular house and some Wall Streeter would certainly appear to snap it up. *Whatever, I just want it out of my life.*

As he pulled into his driveway, he saw her at the last moment and slammed on the brakes. *Where did she come from?*

The woman was standing with her back to him in the middle of his driveway looking at his house. She looked to be elderly and as if she had chosen her wardrobe out of some charity's free clothing box. Nothing seemed to fit. Several ragged scarves hung off her shoulders. Her shoes looked as if someone had crafted them from cardboard. Her curly, untamed, oily-looking locks were partially held in check with a blue headband. *Don't think she's come to buy the house.* He chuckled at the thought.

Robby beeped his horn briefly, but she did not move. Slowly he edged the right wheels of his car off the driveway onto the grass to get around her.. He stopped when his window was next to old women and rolled it down. "Can I help you?" he sounded more like an inquisitor than someone offering assistance.

The woman continued to stare at the house. "I have a message," she said in a low gravelly voice that spoke of far too many cigarettes.

"A message? For who? One of my staff?"

"No."

"Who then?"

The woman turned, looked at him with a toothy grin. A dental nightmare. She handed him a piece of paper.

Robby took it and looked at one side then turned it over. "It's blank."

"But is it? Wait," she said enigmatically. Then suddenly she became very business-like: "Now, you must pay me fifty dollars."

"What?" *Crazy old bitch.* "Get lost!" he said emphatically. "And get off my property or I'll call the cops." He gunned his car leaving her quickly behind. He began to laugh. *In New York*, he thought, the *street baggers ask you for a buck. Out here they want fifty. Talk about inflation. I guess the cost of living for panhandlers is a hell of a lot higher in the Hamptons.* He pulled up in front of his house and turned off the engine. *Have to figure what I am going to do with this car. Sell it? Ship it to the coast?* Robby reached over for the piece of blank paper he had tossed on the passenger seat and was about to crumble it up when he noticed that two words had appeared on the paper. They were small and he had to look closely to read what they said.

My Turn.

"What the hell?" He got out of his car and looked back at the old woman who was about to step onto the street. "Who gave this to you!" he shouted. The old woman appeared not to hear him. Again, "Where did you get this?" he shouted holding up the paper. Again no answer. Robby glanced down at the two words and when he looked up again, she was gone. He crumpled the paper dismissing it as someone's sick joke. *But who?* He wondered, and *why?*

4.

18 MONTHS BEFORE THE MURDER
OF ANDREA TRASK

Malibu, California

"He never saw it coming," Robby smiled at the guests around the table as he transported himself back to Baden Baden. He really hadn't intended to tell anyone about Le Jeu Ultime, and he certainly hadn't expected, or even remotely desired, to become the center of attention at the dinner party. It proved to be unavoidable. He had succumbed, if not to a command performance, to the table's pressure for an explanation.

Just the day before, his plane had taken him from the Islip Airport on Long Island direct to the Santa Monica Airport where his chauffer had driven him west on the I-10, then turned Northwest on the Pacific Coast Highway to Malibu and delivered him to his palatial house on Cliffside Drive. When Anson Fuller, the President of Max's film company, learned that Robby was back in town he and his wife Marianne arranged for a dinner party at their home. The intent, ostensibly, was to help him put Max's death and his upcoming divorce in his rear-view mirror. The Fullers were in their sixties and Marianne, Robby knew, had been a surrogate mother to Max after Mrs. Roarke was killed in the car accident.

There were fourteen people around the dinner table initially bent on maintaining the most banal and purposeless conversation so as to avoid any mention of Max's death or of Robby's pending divorce. Robby sensed almost from the moment they sat down what was on their minds and he found it uncomfortable and a bit unnerving. Just before the desert was served, he decided to pop the bubble of communal avoidance. "Folks, if I may? You don't have to tip toe around what's just happened in France. It was what it was. As for my wife and the divorce, it happens to the best of us. As just about all of you here know" it was a pointed barb at what he knew to be a collection of multiple marriages. "my split from Andrea is without contention. I want you to know I will always regard her as one of the most special women I have ever known. At the same time, I will be the first to admit she deserves a lot better than me. As for Max, he was my best friend. He was my only competitor in just about everything outside of business. We never mixed business with the rest of our lives. He was a *player*. A player in a league limited to only two people. No one else had either the genius, the audacity or, most importantly, the money to join us."

"If it's not too... well painful," Marianne asked, "can you tell us what this game was the two of you were playing? The article I read – and I'm somewhat embarrassed to admit I saw it in the National Enquirer – wasn't very clear."

Robby smiled, "Ah, yes, the journal of fabricated credibility. Any unfounded gossip that fits the print." He sighed, paused for a moment and then, like a tired father being pressed for a bedtime story, offered an abbreviated explanation of the game they had created in Harry's New York Bar. It was when one of the guests asked for an explanation of 'a turn' that he was commanded, or more accurately socially coerced, into telling them how he'd scored his first point at Baden Baden.

After Robby had finished telling them about Max's surprise at finding the sign indicating the score was 15-love, a very Anglo-looking woman in a sari asked, "Why would a transvestite let you tie a sign to his penis?"

"I didn't tie it, he did?" Everyone in the room but the woman laughed.

"But why did he do it?" she pressed.

"Money is a great persuader." Robby said confirming the obvious.

"So what happened?" Anson asked.

'Max pulls on his pants – didn't bother with his shirt – and comes flying down to the casino like Batman chasing the Joker. We're in the bar laughing our asses off."

"I imagine he wanted to punch you," the facelift said.

Robby looked at the woman as if she had just accused him of a major breach in etiquette. "No. Of course, not. In fact, Max congratulated me on winning the first point. We were friends. You don't punch a friend on the tennis court when he serves you an ace. And we would not have done it in our game. For the rest of the night we drank and laughed. As we left the bar to go upstairs to bed, Max just looked at me, smiled and said. 'And now, I believe, it's my serve'."

"But this last... whatever you called it... 'game' you were involved in. Didn't it get a little out of hand? I mean, your friend died. "

"I think we've pressed Robby enough for one evening," Anson Fuller injected hoping to rescue his guest from an inquisition.

Robby held up his hand indicating he did not need Anson's help. Robby glared at the woman. "It should never have happened. I don't know what got into Max. It was not like him to react that way." The intensity in his voice floated down over the table like a billowing shroud. "I was ready to claim a victory and he .. he just went crazy. I know a lot of people blame me for his death." His voice rose defensively. "But what they don't understand is I had played by our rules. What they, and I suspect you, don't understand is I had every right to take my turn. He had gone way out of bounds with the Peruvian mountain climbing thing he did to me. Way out."

Robby was sure he detected condemnation behind the fabricated smiles on the faces of several of the guests. He continued to defend himself, "I was ridiculed on the cover of every sport magazine and even that rag Newsweek. No one, other than me and one or two of our friends, knew what happened with the transvestite. And even when you consider what I did to him at National Museum of Art unveiling, he never personally suffered. Embarrassed a little maybe, but not humiliated. No, the game was meant as a mano a mano challenge of wits and cunning. It was never meant to humiliate the other guy... to destroy his reputation in front of the whole fucking world."

Robby could no longer keep his anger in check as he sensed their readiness to reject his defense of Chateau de Lac. "I deserved my turn... no matter how long it took. Yes, I wanted to pay him back for Pinnacle Cumbre. But, even my win would never have humiliated him in public. Not like what he did to me."

Every eye at the table had drifted away from Robby to shield their own embarrassment at witnessing a troubled man tossing himself over a psychological cliff. Then, almost as if he had flipped some internal switch, the rage was replaced with remorse and his words became barely audible. "Not only did I not get even, I lost my best friend."

Anson looked desperate to save Robb by diverting his guests' attention. The staff appeared with the plates of dessert. "Ah, Tiramisu, my favorite. Marianne has this special place Italian place she knows." It was a feeble effort, but it offered the first opportunity to derail the conversation. "Oh, if any of you would like coffee..."

"How about a toke?" the only man not in a sport coat asked.

"Sorry," Anson responded with a weak laugh, "our dope peddler missed our stop this week. Police picked him up," he laughed again and several others joined him.

The other guests immediately began finding something intensely important to share with their dinner partners. The common goal of the impromptu conversations appeared to make it seem no one was going to give a second thought to Robby's outburst. The only guest not to join in the small talk was an extremely thin woman, wearing an Oscar de la Renta topped with several strands of South Sea pearls. She stared at Robby with a piercing, analytical look from behind the not so handy work of a plastic surgeon that looked to have used a nine iron rather than a scalpel to rearrange her face.

"Mr. Trask, I am a fully accredited psychiatrist. And if I may be so presumptuous, I would say you, as a result your recent situation with your friend, plus the added burden of coping with a divorce, are exhibiting signs of a classic rage/guilt psychological cycle."

"A what?" Robby asked, clearly annoyed at this off-the-couch analysis.

She continued, "I sense, from your conversation, that you are assuming an irrational blame for your friend's death. Hmmm?" She lifted her eyebrows by way of asking for confirmation. "This can, and in your case possibly has, engendered unbearable emotions of guilt, anxiety, shame, remorse, and loss. It is not uncommon for a recipient of such displaced blame to manifest feelings in the form of rage. Thus the rage/guilt cycle which, I sense, is what I'm observing in you. The danger to someone in your condition is the possibility of an emotional spiral into an emotional abyss from which you may not be able to escape."

Robby's did his best to mask his resentment at being subjected to this dinner table shrink. Curbing his urge to offer a primal response, he did his best to make light of her remark, "Am I going to receive a bill for this?"

The woman returned his question with a thin, supercilious and patronizing smile. She reached into her purse and produced a business card. "Here is my card. You may find it beneficial to call my office and arrange for a visit. I'm quite sure I can help you though this."

Robby was tempted to tell her she could cram her business card into a dark place, but out of consideration for his hosts, said, "This is the first time I've ever had therapy served up with Tiramisu. Doesn't add much to the flavor, does it? But then, I've never had much of a taste for psychobabble."

From that point on, the dinner party was socially, if not technically, over. Within a quarter of an hour, all the guests had found reasons to leave. Once the last of them said their good nights, Anson turned to Robby, "Sorry about her," he said referring to the psychiatrist, "If I'd known Marianne had put her on the guest list, I'd have crossed her off. In her world, everybody needs to spend time on her couch."

"Forget it. We are in California, after all."

"Cigar?"

"Definitely."

"Let's go out on the terrace."

"Looks like we missed the sunset," Robby said.

"Well, we probably didn't miss much. Every time I think we're going to get a beautiful sunset, the fog bank forms up and the sun gets swallowed."

Several minutes passed before Marianne made her appearance. "Robby, I want you to do something for me."

"Sure. Name it," he said.

"I want you to talk to Max."

"What?" Both Robby and Anson asked in unison.

"You're not...?" Anson challenged.

"But I am." There was a 'don't-try-to-stop-me' determined look on her face.

"What are you talking about? What do you mean 'talk to Max'?"

"Come with me," Marianne said taking Robby's hand.

Dutifully Robby followed her back into the house. Anson trailed behind. "This is not a good idea," he muttered.

"Where are we going?"

"Just into the library. I'm set up in there," she said.

"Set up for what?"

"Robby, I apologize in advance. She's got her Goddamn Ouija board out."

"Ouija board?" Robby echoed. "That's a kid's game, isn't it?"

Marianne was deadly seriousness. "Not at all. A friend and I use it all the time to..." she paused and glanced at her husband as if daring him to contradict her. "...to talk to the other side."

"Marianne, I love you, but this is nonsense." Robby said kindly.

"You've got to do this. You've got to know that Max forgives you."

"Forgive me for what? Ending his life at thirty-seven? For preventing him from marrying Andrea? Even if you were able to..." he could not believe he was about to say was he was thinking, "... *communicate* with the dead. There's no forgiving."

It took her another few minutes of pleading, but finally she prevailed.

Robby, Anson and she sat down at a small game table on which she had placed the Ouija Board and the planchette.

"All we are to do is let our fingertips lightly touch the edge of the planchette," she instructed. "At first we have to move the pointer in circles around the board to get it warmed up." She began to move the planchette in circles while Robby and Anson did their best to keep their fingers in place. "Ok. Stop. We're ready for you to ask your first question."

"I think I'll leave that up to you," Robby said making no effort to hide the fact that he could not take the board or Marianne seriously.

Marianne closed her eyes as she asked the first question. "Ouija board, will you help us contact a spirit?" For a moment nothing. The planchette appeared frozen in the middle of the board."

"I guess no one's home tonight." Anson said.

"Shhh," she demanded. Another moment passed and slowly the pointer began to move.

What's making this thing move? Robby wondered. *I'm not. It has to be Marianne.*

The planchette found its way to YES.

"May we give you a name to contact?"

The pointer went to YES.

"Maximilian Roarke." She said.

The pointed moved slightly and then returned to the center of the board.

"Have we contracted a spirit?"

The point quickly moved to YES.

"What is your name?"

The planchette moved from YES to M then to A and finally to X.

"Are you Max Roarke?"

The pointed slid up to YES.

"Come on, Marianne. You've got to be moving this thing," Robby said.

"No," she answered softly. "I promise you I am not. Please. Let's just concentrate."

"You really believe he's talking to us through this board?" Robby made no effort to conceal his doubt.

"Yes."

"I don't."

"Why don't you ask him a question that only you and Max would know the answer to."

"Good idea," Robby said,

"That should convince you this is real."

Robby looked at the board and asked, "What was our nickname for the headmaster at Ambary Prep?"

"The pointer paused then moved to H-E-A-P.

"Heap," Marianne said aloud. "Is that right?"

"That's right." *How did Marianne know about old Heap?*

"Where are you?" she asked the spirit.

The pointer quickly spelled out the answer. H – E – R – E.

"Do you understand that what happened at the Chateau was part of your game?"

The pointer moved rapidly to YES.

Do you understand that Robby is grief stricken over what happened to you?

Again a YES.

"Can you forgive him?"

For a moment, the pointer failed to move. Then slowly it went first to 'I" followed by T then D-E-P-E-N-D -S.

"Depends on what?" Robby asked. .

It took almost half a minute to deliver the answer. Marianne repeated the words as they were spelled out, "On... having... chance... to... take... my... turn."

Robby's blurted response was reflexive, "But how can you take your turn from where you are?"

The planchette moved very quickly: I W-I-L-L F-I-N-D A W-A-Y.

* ~ * ~ *

"Thank you for the dinner, Marianne." Robby said as headed for the front door. "Not sure I can say the same for the Ouija Board session."

"Don't be a stranger." She gave him a slight goodnight peck on the cheek.

"Let me walk you to your car," Anson Fuller said. Once they were through the front door Anson looked back at his house to be sure Marianne hadn't followed them. "It's all bullshit, the Ouija board thing. As far as I'm concerned. Marianne has let herself get hooked on just about anything having to do with the occult." Then almost absently, "Is that grounds for a divorce?" He laughed to indicate he wasn't serious.

"Doubt it. But I will have to say it was... well, strange."

"Between you and me, I think Marianne forces the pointer. I have to believe she's controlling it."

"Maybe, but how would she have known about our nickname for the Amberly Headmaster.' Heap' was not just a lucky guess."

"That I don't know. I'm only sorry she put you through it." Anson watched as Robby opened his car door. "Something I should tell you. Don't know this means anything, but then again it might. I guess it was several days before Max died that he emailed me a picture of a woman. A young woman. Blond. Very pretty. Asked me to have our casting department search our picture files to see if she might be an actress. I think we must have every pictures of every actor and actress who ever had their picture taken."

"And?"

"They found the woman and I sent the information back to Max."

"Do you happen to remember her name?"

"I recall thinking it sounded a lot like the French actress Jeanne Moreau. It was Jeanne Malveau. She's French but speaks good English. Not sure why he was looking for her or what it might mean to you, if anything, but I thought I'd let you know."

Robby's thoughts were spinning, but he managed to contain them. *He knew! The son-of-a-bitch knew Melisande was an actress!*

He got into his car. "Thanks again for the diner," he said absently.

"If you're up for it, let's do lunch sometime," Anson said. Robby nodded an acceptance, closed the door and pulled out of the drive.

If he knew, why didn't he say so? Doesn't make sense. All he had to do was call a service fault and he'd have won the point. That would have made the score 40-30 in his favor and it would have been his turn. He would have been one point away from a win. "Max," he asked aloud as if Max were in the back seat, "are you playing games with me?" No answer came back. He would have to give what Anson told him a lot of thought.

5.

18 MONTHS BEFORE THE MURDER
OF ANDREA TRASK

Malibu, California

The phone rang in Robby's Tepidarium. "I'll take it," he said to the masseuse. She handed him the wireless phone and left the room. "Hello?"

"Mr. Trask, this is Jeanne Malveau. I have to talk with you."

Robby immediately recognized the voice of the actress he'd hired to be Melisande. *Is this just coincidence or is part of Max's plan?* "You got your money, right?"

"Yes. But, I am not calling about that. It is Mr. Roarke. He has come back."

Robby wasn't sure he'd heard her correctly. "What did you say?"

"He's come back. Mr. Roarke has."

Robby detected a good deal of stress in her voice. "What are you talking about?"

"I think he wants to punish me for what I did."

He sensed she was barely maintaining control. "Jeanne, no one, least of all Max, wants to punish you," he said calmly.

"No, you do not understand!" She was crying now, "I think he has come back from the dead. He wants revenge for what you made me do to him."

The woman was clearly on the edge. *Borderline delusional*, he thought. *Like the Melisande character she played.* The thought echoed, *Like the Melisande character she played.* "Jeanne, let me ask you a question: Did Max ever take your picture?"

For a moment, she said nothing then, "Once he did. The night we left for Chateau du Lac. He used his cell phone. Why do you ask?"

"No reason," he lied. His mind quickly began to review what he knew: *Max sent the picture to the head of his production company to see if they could identify her. That meant he had to suspect what was going on. But if he did, why wouldn't he have said something? And if he knew, or at the very least had suspicions, why did he take me back to the Chateau and run into the house, unless...? Unless Max was planning to take his serve without calling a fault. Unless he is not dead. But then, the body, the cigar cutter? How do I explain that? Max if you...* Jeanne was talking to him again. He decided to think about those questions after he dealt with her. "You said he has come back. Did you actually see him?"

"Yes, but not like you think. I have an apartment off of La Cienega and each night I see him just outside my window. And I am on the fourth floor. Sometimes he comes through the walls and floats in midair at the bottom of my bed. I can see right through him. He is not real. I just scream for him to get out. But he does not. He just stands there looking at me. Then finally he just fades away… disappears right when I am looking at him. Last night he spoke for the first time."

Jeanne, he said to himself, *are we playing another role here? Has Max put you up to this?* Robby decided to say nothing and see where she might be going with her story. "What did he say?"

"Tell Robby I want to talk." He just kept repeating those same words. "You have got to help me Mr. Trask," her voice was frantic. "I am very afraid. I cannot sleep. I cannot eat. I am afraid to stay in my apartment any longer. You have got to help me. Maybe I could come stay with you for a few nights. Maybe if I am not home, he will go away."

He found himself speculating: *Could finding a way to put her under his roof be part of Max's plan? Depending on what he was up to, that would make sense,* he thought. *Then again, what if she is actually seeing things? Dealing with a delusional woman is way above my pay grade. Ok,* he decided, *she's obviously looking for me to bring her here, whatever the reason. I guess I better figure out what it is.* "Jeanne, if you think it would help to stay with me for a few nights, I'll send a car. Maybe if the ghost, or whatever it is you're seeing, does not find you in your apartment, it'll move on. I have a guest house you can use." He found he was unable to resist the thought, *and maybe I can use you a couple of nights.* He chuckled to himself at how his mind never strayed far from his zipper.

"Oh yes. If I could just get away for a little while." She sounded instantly relieved. Almost too relived, like someone who has just made an important sale but doesn't want to gloat about it. "I hope he will not find me at your house."

Not likely, Robby took her address and hung up. *Max, you bastard, I know you're taking your serve. I know you are. Well, I'm not about to let you get away with it. What's the score? If he claims a fault point for figuring out Chateau du Lac it's 40-30 his favor. But now, if I get a fault point for blowing up this little charade of his, we'll be at duce, 40-40 and my serve.*

"Ok, Max where the hell are you?" he asked the empty Tepidarium. "I'm going to find you and call your serve a fault. Do you hear me Max?" It was as if he almost expected an answer. Then a totally uninvited, and what his rationale mind labeled ludicrous, thought popped up demanding his consideration. *But what if he really is dead? What if what Jeanne told me is true; that she really thought she saw Max?* He was at once perplexed by his inability to dismiss the questions and angry that he had even asked them. He called for his masseuse. *I'll think about it after my massage.*

6.

17 MONTHS BEFORE THE MURDER OF ANDREA TRASK

Malibu, California

Robby rolled over on his book and woke up. His bed light was still on and he realized he'd fallen asleep reading. He stared up at the ceiling and found himself wondering when and how Max would come at him to declare victory. *If he's alive.* Then he added an admonishment for doubting what he was sure he knew to be true. *Don't be a jerk! Of course, he's alive. This is La Jeu Ultime.*

What time is it? The clock on his nightstand read 3:25. *Music?* Awful, discordant, grating music. *Where's it coming from? Sounds like it's coming from downstairs.* He got out of bed and made his way down to his living room trying to determine the source. He stopped, listened, and then realized it was coming from the basement. He walked down a hall off the living room to the door that led to his Roman bathes. As he opened it, the music grew louder, piercing. He reached for the switch to turn on the lights. But there were no lights. Instead, a blue glow rolled in at the bottom of the spiral staircase like a release of steam from a broken pipe.

"Who's down here?" he tried to shout above the music. Slowly, he made his way down the stairs. At the bottom, he saw both the source of the glow and the music appeared to be coming from the Tepidarium . The door was partially open. Again he shouted, this time louder and in the threatening voice. "Who the hell is in there?"

Smoke?

Smoke!

The smell from whatever was burning had a terrible stench to it, like decaying flesh. Robby gagged and covered his nose and mouth with his hand. Suddenly, the music stopped. Dead quiet.

Robby pushed open the door and in the faint light he saw Jeanne's body sprawled on the floor. The sheet on top of the table was smoldering as though something had been set fire on top of it. He walked over to the table and saw what appeared to be an image burned into the sheet. It was too dark to make out what it was. Jeanne began to stir and sat up. He went back to the door and fumbled for the light switch. An electronic dimmer brought the room to the subdued and relaxing glow he had programmed for the Tepidarium. "Are you ok?" he bent down to help her up.

She nodded. "It was horrible!" There was a terrified look on her face.

"What was?"

"When I came in here!" She pointed toward the massage table. "There was a body on top of it. It was burning!"

"A body? You saw a burning body?" his response was a combination of shock and doubt.

"Look," she said pointing at the sheet, "It's the image of a man."

Robby walked back to the table and looked down at the sheet. The black image looked like a charcoal drawing of a man lying on his back. It reminded him of pictures he'd seen of the Shroud of Turin. And the face? It was unmistakably Max.

"My God! My God! "She cried. She looked up at Robby." What is that? What does it mean?" she was sobbing.

Having no answer, Robby, let his temper flare, "How the hell do I know?" Then an obvious question, "What were you doing in here? It's the middle of the night."

"I was in my room in your guest house and I heard this horrible music. I went out on my terrace and it sounded like it was coming from your bathes. I thought maybe you were in here. The door was open. I came in and all I remember is... is... I do not want to think about what I saw. I told you. He has come back to punish us." She was frantic.

Robby took her hand and said, "Come on, let's get some air. It's going to take me forever to get the stink out of here. *I don't know how you did it Max,* he said to himself, *but it looks like you're pulling out all the stops.* As they walked out of the bathes toward the beach, Robby saw that, except for a thong, she was naked and shaking. It was not from the cold as it was over eighty outside. *One thing I'm sure of, it wasn't real,* he told himself. *Somehow, Max set it up. But how? No one gets in there without my letting them in. Jeanne? Could she have...?"*

She interrupted his thoughts, "Has he come back?" She asked as if afraid to hear the answer.

"No, he's not come back." There was a definite note of dismissal in his voice.

"Then, what did we just see?"

"An illusion. A trick. Nothing more."

"How can you be sure?" she cried.

He could see she was frightened and appeared emotionally crumbing. "Let just say I'm sure... pretty sure anyway." He was surprised to hear himself express even the slightest amount of doubt.

For several minutes Robby stood looking at the sea. Slowly, Jeanne came up beside him, "Please hold me."

Her body felt good pressed into his and for a moment he wondered if this might be invitation. No, she was scared – or at least was pretending to be scared – believing what she had witnessed was real. Sex was most certainly not on her mind.

"A friend of mine told me that if you talk to a ghost and ask it to forgive you, it will leave you alone."

"You're friends are delusional There's no such thing as ghosts." He was tempted to add, there's no way to talk to Max accept on a telephone. But decided not to say anything about what he suspected. If she was working for Max, he wanted to know for certain before he said anything.

"No, no you are wrong. There are ghosts. And there are people who make it possible for us to talk to them."

"You mean a medium? Sorry to disappoint you, but they're all phonies."

"Not all. Not all. Not the real ones. The real ones have spirit guides that help them contact the dead and it is through them maybe we can talk to Mr. Roarke."

"Sweetheart," he said in a weary and deprecating tone, "That only happens in movies. Like the one with Whoopie Goldberg and Patrick Swayze. Enough of that talk, ok? I'm going for a walk on the beach. Why don't you go back to your room and get some sleep? "

"I would like to stay with you," she sounded like a child looking for parental protection from the boogie man.

"Suit yourself."

They walked along the water's edge past all the sleeping houses facing the ocean. Not a single light. No sign of anyone stirring."

Neither spoke for several minutes. Then, "Can I ask you something?"

Robby just nodded.

"Can I bring someone to your house?"

"Who?"

"His name is Harold Gresham.

"Who's he?"

"You won't get angry/"

"Can't promise that."

"He's a medium."

"What did I tell you about mediums?"

"No, no. Not this one. He is very famous and very successful. He says he can contact Mr. Roarke for me. I must ask him to forgive me before I go out of my mind."

For the first time, Robby saw what he perceived to be a woman on the edge of hysteria. But then he wondered if, in fact, that's what he was actually seeing. *Is this all part of her act? Is she playing a California version of Melisande? If she is, there ought to be some type of Oscar for her performance. On the other hand, if what I'm seeing is real, it's not going to take much to push her over the edge.*

"You do not understand, Mr. Trask, I cannot take this. The guilt is killing me. Somehow I have got to make him stop." She grabbed Robby's arm and held so tight it felt like someone had just applied a tourniquet. "Oh please, please let me bring this man here. If he cannot help. If he cannot contact Mr. Roarke, I promise to leave and never brother you again. Oh, please." She was frantic.

The last thing I need right now, he decided, *is to have to deal with a mostly naked woman about to go nuts on me. Then again, if as I suspect she's acting, I should probably toss her out. But no. Don't want to do that. Not yet, anyway. I've got to see if she's eventually going to lead me to Max.* "Ok, invite Mr. Gresham to the house. I don't have to be here, right?"

"Oh, I think you should. I realize I am not very intelligent. It is easy for people to fool me. If this man is what you say, a phony, you will know. I may not be able to tell. Also, I have never met this man and I would not like to be alone with him. Maybe if you are just in the house when he comes, that will be enough."

Maybe she's right. I should at least be in the house. For all I know the guy might decide to rob me, rape her and God knows what else. No, I'll be there. He chuckled. *Be honest with yourself Trask. You want to be there so you can prove to Jeanne, and maybe even to yourself, this guy is a fake. If Max is alive, and I'm sure he is.* He interrupted himself. *Why do I sound like I'm trying to convince myself? I know he's alive. He has to be. Which means there won't be any spirit for the medium to contact.*

7.

17 MONTHS BEFORE THE MURDER OF ANDREA TRASK

Malibu, California

Except for the long frizzy hair, he looks normal. As Robby shook the medium's hand he thought, *I look forward to exposing you.*

"Thank you for coming, Mr. Gresham," Jeanne said." Will there be a fee?"

"No," the medium said. "I was given a gift and I feel obliged to share it."

The man has to be phony if he does this kind of nonsense for free.

"Where should we do this?" Robby asked.

"Anywhere you feel comfortable. I would like for us sit so that the both of you can face me."

"Why don't we go into your den, Mr. Trask? We can sit at your round table."

"Find," Robby said and led the way.

"Jeanne has told me about the man you want to contact. I must warn you, sometimes when a person suffers a violent death, as I understand was the case with your friend Mr. Roarke, my spirit guides find the person reluctant to talk.

Already giving himself an out, Robby thought. "So how does this work?" Robby asked as they sat down at the table.

"I want you to imagine your friend is standing directly behind you. If he arrives, that's exactly where he will be. I will see him, but you cannot. Nor will you be able to hear him. Only I can do that. But, he can hear your questions. When he answers, I will repeat what he says." The medium stopped and looked critically at Robby, "I sense, Mr. Trask, you have doubts about my ability to contact your friend. You should. There are many charlatans who purport to have powers like mine. But as you know, they do not. May I suggest two things? First, try to keep an open mind. If I am a fake, you will know soon enough and you can ask me to leave. Second, once I make contact, ask some questions to which only you and your friend could know the answers. That should be proof enough we have contacted Mr. Roarke."

Wasn't that the same thing Marianne asked me to do on the Ouija board? Must be standard procedure for doubters. "Fair enough." Robby said.

"This will take a moment," the medium said staring at a spot over and beyond Robby's head. "When I speak, you can begin to ask questions."

A full five minutes passed and then the medium said, "He says 'Hello, Robby.'"

"Is that you Max?"

"Yes," the answer came back through the medium.

"I want to be sure it's you."

"It's me," again the medium's voice.

"I'm going to ask you to prove it," Robby said.

"How can I do that from where I am?"

"By answering some questions."

"Ok."

"What was in the paper cups we gave Perkins at graduation?"

There was a moment hesitation. "Empty Superglue tubes."

Robby was taken aback. *How the hell would the medium have known that?*

"Is that right Mr. Trask?" Jeanne asked.

Robby stared at the medium and nodded then asked a second question, "What did we do the night of my mother's second marriage?"

Again, there was a pause before the medium repeated what Max said, "Set one hundred and six alarm clocks."

Robby was not sure what to make of the medium's performance. If he were a believer, he'd have to be impressed. *Wait,* he thought, *this can't be real. There has to be some kind of trick. Maybe the medium has a device in his ear and Max is feeding him the answers.* "Harold, may I call you Harold?"

"Yes, of course."

"Would you turn your head and show me your ears?"

"My ears?" The medium gave him a quizzical and confused look.

"I just want to be sure you're not wearing some type of hearing device."

"Why would I be doing that?" he asked, turning to his right and then to his left.

Too much hair, he decided. Short of pulling back his hair and using a doctor's otoscope to look into his ears, there was no way of telling if he had inserted some sort of receiving device. "Just checking."

"Mr. Roarke, it is me Melisande. My real name is Jeanne. Will you forgive me for what I did? I did not ever think anyone would be hurt. Mr. Trask just said it was a prank. Please, I need to know you forgive me."

"What's to forgive?" Max answered through the medium. "You did what you were paid to do. My friend Robby is the one who broke the rules."

"Broke the rules?" Robby shot back at the medium. "What are you talking about?"

"You let it go on too long. You should have claimed your victory and ended it when I came back from the Chateau."

Robby decided that whether he was talking to Max via some electronic ear device or, in the unlikely possibility, to Max on the other side, he was going to defend himself. "I wanted to claim a victory. I was going to do it during a dinner party at La Reserve. But you left Cap Ferrat for a few days before I could. When you came back, you insisted on going to the Chateau. When the hell did I have time to claim my point?"

"There was time. You let it go on too long. And the fire..." The mediums voice reflected the sadness in Max's answer.

Robby was totally on the defensive now. The feelings of guilt over what he had done at the Chateau was bubbling up as rage and, just as the psychiatrist had predicted, he was spiraling down into an emotional abyss. "Bullshit! Max, I had nothing to do with the second fire. I have no idea what caused the explosion. The firemen didn't either. I never thought..."

"No, you never did."

"So what now?" Robby was nearly shouting. "If this is not some fuckin' trick, and I know it is, why don't you go to hell and leave me alone?"

"I want you to join me. We can finish the game over here.""

"If you really are dead, you're crazy too." Robby was on the edge of losing it.

"But I will have my turn." The medium repeated the words so that they sounded like an unveiled threat.

"So what are you going to do, haunt my house?" Robby's anger was unchecked.

No answer from the medium.

"Max you son-of-bitch, answer me!"

No answer.

"Your friend is no longer here," the medium said.

"Bastard!" Robby spat.

"Did you hear what you wanted to hear?" the medium asked quietly.

"Not exactly."

* ~ * ~ *

After the séance, Jeanne offered to walk the medium to his car. She never came back. A day later, she left a voice mail on Robby's phone saying she was moving back to La Cienega since she felt sure Mr. Roarke would no longer be haunting her apartment

That absofuckinlutely proves it! The whole thing with Max was nothing more than part of Le Jeu... his serve. While he had failed to detect it, he felt sure Harold had used some type of electronic hearing device so Max could feed him the answers. That was the only logical explanation. Now, there were only two questions: Where was Max and when did he plan to claim his win? *Can't believe it won't be soon,* he thought. *Have to believe after all this he's got something planned. He's going to try to stick it to me. But he won't, because I won't let him. I wonder if Anson Fuller knows what he's up to? Doubt it. And Marianne? She was like a mother to him after his own mother died. Could she be in on this? If she is, she's not about to tell me. No, I've got to figure this out myself.*

He didn't have to. The answer arrived in call from New York.

8.

16 MONTHS BEFORE THE MURDER OF ANDREA TRASK

Malibu and Southampton

Mr. Trask, the voice on the phone said. "I'm Willard Watson. I was one of Mr. Roarke's lawyer's and my bank, The Morgan Bank, is serving as the Executor of his estate. I've been trying to contact you for several weeks and it was only when we located Mrs. Trask in Anasara, Italy that she suggested I'd probably find you in California. On the one hand, I'm happy to inform you that Mr. Roarke left you his entire estate in his will."

"He did what?" Robby's surprise was genuine.

"As I said, he'd left you his entire estate and all his holdings. A considerable inheritance I might add. But there is a one potentially major issue which must be dealt with."

Why am I not surprised? Robby thought.

"As you might expect in an estate as large at Mr. Roarke's there are a number of parties, mainly ex-wives, contesting the will. This is not surprising as the alimony payments Mr. Roarke agreed to pay his ex-wives were legally bound to expire upon his death."

"You mean they no longer get to feed at the Roarke trough?"

"That's one way to put it. Plus someone, we suspect an ex-wife, has contacted the authorities here in New York and suggested Mr. Roarke's death was not the accident the French court reported it to be. They even questioned if it was Mr. Roarke's body we buried. Unfortunately, it's gone so far at this point the District Attorney for Long Island has authorized the exhumation of his body so that a full autopsy can be performed. It was suggested a DNA test be performed to prove that the body is indeed his. But this will not be possible as Mr. Roarke had no living issue or relatives."

"So what's the bottom line here?" Robby asked impatiently.

"I'm getting to that. The District Attorney's office – and I for that matter – would very much like to have you come back to Southampton when they exhume the body to see if you can identify it as Mr. Roarke's."

"As Max's lawyer you have to know, as well as I do, his body was burned beyond recognition. I'm not sure there's anything left to identify."

"You may be correct, but our hope is there might be something about the corpse you'd recognize and be able to confirm that it is the body of Mr. Roarke. They will, of course, go ahead with the autopsy, but based on what we know and what you told the French court – I have the transcript – it will prove only that he burned to death. Nothing more. Please, your presence at the exhumation could very well help us fend off those who are contesting the will and facilitate your receiving control of Mr. Roarke's assets. I'm sure you don't want there to be any doubt Mr. Roarke's death was, in fact, an accident. As I'm sure you're fully aware, a public figure such as yourself is always considered fair game in the tabloids. Particularly if it is suggested you declined to cooperate with the Long Island authorities. May I count on you to be here next Thursday? So far December weather has been relatively mild, not California weather, but mild for us."

Robby's mind was spinning. *Is this for real or part of Max's game. Is this lawyer for real or is he someone Max has hired to impersonate one? And if I didn't show up, am I the front-page story on the supermarket tabloids? First thing I need to do is to confirm he's who he says he is.*

"Mr… I'm sorry, would you mind giving me your name again?"

"Willard Watson, I'm a VP here at the Morgan bank."

"Let me check my schedule for next Thursday and call you back. Where can I reach you?"

Willard responded with his phone number and extension.

"I'll get back to you shortly." Robby said and hung up. He immediately googled Willard Watson at the Morgan bank in New York. Somewhat to his surprise, google confirmed Watson was both a VP at Morgan and a lawyer. But, he asked himself, is that really who I was talking to? He called information and found the number he'd been given was in fact the same number at the Morgan Bank in New York. He dialed and when a woman's voice announced he had reached the Bank he said. "I'm trying to reach Willard Watson and I have his extension as 1023, but I thought I'd better check."

"Yes," came the voice, "that is his extension, shall I connect you?"

"Yes, please."

There was a slight delay and then the sound of the phone ringing. On the second ring the phone was picked up, "Willard Watson."

Robby recognized it as the same voice. "This is Robert Trask, I find I can make it. Where would you like us to meet?"

"Well you can come to my office on Park Avenue or, if you prefer, we can meet at the cemetery. Whichever is more convenient for you. I'm told the exhumation with take a few hours, but the body should be ready for your inspection by four o'clock. The authorities from the District Attorney's office will be there at that time."

"I'll come direct to the cemetery. I'll have my pilot land at the Islip airport and arrange to have a car meet me."

"As you wish. I know this is a large inconvenience, but if we can wrap up the identification and autopsy we can deal with those contesting the will and get this resolved without any unnecessary, shall we say, complications."

"See you next Thursday," Robby said. *His whole estate? I can't believe it. But then who else could he leave it to? None of his ex-wives. They hated him and I don't think he had any love for them. Or is this just part of the game?* Then it occurred to him to call one of his own lawyers and have him see if he could confirm what Watson had told him about the contested will and the demand for exhumation. More questions needed to be answered before Robby could be convinced what Watson had told him was fact.

As his G-550 took off from L.A. International Robby looked through the reports from his lawyers. Their investigation seemed to verify everything Watson had told him. In a matter of hours he would see Max again – or what was left of his charred body. A grisly prospect and one he was not looking forward to. But if that was what it was going to take – that and the autopsy – to remove any suspicion that he had somehow purposely caused Max's death and to release Max's estate, then the trip would be worth it.

As fate would have it, his plane was late getting to the Islip airport. He called Watson's office and told his administrative assistant, to get word to Watson he'd be an hour or so late, but that he was definitely on the way.

Once on the ground and parked in front of the general aviation hanger, the car he had arranged was brought plane-side. He immediately left the airport and headed for the cemetery. The clock on his dash board read just after six and it was already dark. He was much later than he'd expected and hoped Watson and whatever authorities were involved in the exhumation would have brought some lighting equipment.

As he drove into the cemetery and made his way along the thin strip of roadway that led to where they had buried Max, he saw that a number of cars were parked near the grave site. *Good, everyone's still he*re, he thought. *Want to get this over with.* He parked his car behind the others and approached the grave which, he was glad to see, was being lit by some portable lights. A man stepped out of the group and offered his hand as Robby approached..

"Mr. Trask, I presume. William Watson. The casket is out of the grave but they've not yet opened it. I asked they wait for your arrival."

Another man stepped up. "Mr. Trask, I'm with the District Attorneys. office, We're the ones handling the investigation. All we'd like you to do at this point, if you can, is confirm the body is that of Mr. Roarke."

"You realize, of course, his body was very badly burned and there might not be much to identify."

"We'd like you to try anyway. Possibly upon a close inspection you'll find something on the body what will help you confirm it's Mr. Roarke."

Two men approached the coffin which was now at ground level. Slowly they release the bolts holding the lid and opened it. Immediately they were greeted by the grotesque sight of a burned and decaying body. One of the men turned quickly away and started to wretch.

"Mr. Trask," asked the man from the District Attorney's office. "is that Mr. Roarke?"

As Robby stared down at the corpse it appeared to be slowly rising out of the casket.

"Am I seeing things?" Watson asked, his voice trembling. "It looks like it's floating."

"Gas," one of the men who'd opened the casket replied "When the body starts to depose, gas is often formed and it's not unusual for the body to fill like up like a gas balloon and begin to swell. When there's enough gas inside it will actually begin to float."

"I've never heard of anything like that," Robby's tone was more a challenge than an admission of ignorance..

"How much experience have you had exhuming dead bodies Mr. Trask?"

Robby said nothing but kept staring at the rising body which was now clearing the side of the casket. "Good God, shouldn't someone push him back down. Put a rock on him or something."

"Is this Mr. Roarke?" the voice of the man from the attorney's office intoned.

"I don't know. I can't' tell. But it has to be. We buried him in that casket."

Now the body was floating nearly a foot above the casket.

"Push him back," Robby shouted. "Push him back."'

"Don't touch him," a voice commanded. "If we cause the gas to leak out, the smell will be more than any of us can stand."

Higher and higher the body floated until it was a good three feet above the casket.

"Please, take a close look. Is this Mr. Roarke?" Robby bent close and was about to pull back from the casket when the body sprang into a sitting position and threw its arms around Robby.

"Of course it's Mr. Roarke. And the score it Game, Set and Match." Max was jubilant.

Robby pulled away and looked at Max as he climbed out of the casket and pulled off the rubber mask covering his face.

"You rotten son of a bitch," Robby shouted. "You no good bastard. I should kill here and now and push you back in the grave."

Ah... but that's against the rules. The one you insisted on. Not allowed to kill the other guy."

The men who had been part of the elaborate ruse began to fade away. Some laughing and muttering comments that Robby could not make out, but presumed they were at his expense. A few others walked away shaking their heads in mild disgust at the grotesqueness of the prank.

"Next time new rules," Robby countered.

"Won't be a next time. Le Jeu Ultime is fini. Game over."

~~*

Three hours later Max and Robby were sitting in Max's Southampton house nursing glasses of single malt Scotch. Robby's anger had all but abated, but he still had to tamp down the gnawing fact he had been humiliated once again and Max had won Le Jeu Ultime.

"You son-of-bitch, I was sure you were alive, I was sure until I saw you in the coffin. God, I believed it was you. You looked just like what we buried. All that crap you pulled on the West Coast with the Ouija board and the psychic. You bastard. Can't believe I let myself get suckered into coming out here. And the funeral last fall, I was almost sure somehow that wasn't you we buried. By the way, who was it?"

"A cadaver donation from the Paris School of Medicine. Gave it to me in return of a sizeable donation. Same guy you found in the Chateau."

"Ok, so you had me at the grave site. But what I want to know is how did you know? Where did I slip up at the Chateau?" Robby asked.

"The hunter."

"The hunter?" Robby echoed. "How did he...?"

"You don't hunt deer with a shot gun created for turkey shoots. I own three of those."

"That's what tipped you off?" Robby was incredulous.

"No. But that's what started me thinking. When I left the woods, I drove back into the village to the restaurant and the real proprietor told me a completely different story about Chateau du Lac. I went back to the Chateau, went inside and found what turned out to be pieces of lighting equipment, a piece of paper with the name of Gaumont, the motion picture company on it. Right away, I figured this was not what it appeared to be. When I called Gaumont and told them I wanted to create a special fire effect for a film I was producing, it didn't take long for me to find the guy who'd set up the effects at Chateau du Lac."

"And I paid the SOB not to say anything to anyone."

"I guess you didn't pay him enough. Then, before I took Melisande to Chateau du Lac that night, I took her picture. At first, my intention was to use it to prove to you she was real. The next day, when I began to put the pieces together, I sent it to Anson Fuller and asked him to see if the casting department could identify her. In less than an hour they found Jeanne Malveau, French born actress with almost zero film credits. Finally, just for the hell of it, I googled the names of Pellias and Melisande and guess what I found?

"I know what you found, the characters in the Debussy opera that had almost the same story. I figured since when it comes to opera you think Pavarotti is something to eat, you'd never make the connection."

"Well, I'll concede my lack of operatic knowledge. But it's amazing what Google can tell you."

"There's one other thing," Robby said, "You broke the rules. Once you knew what I was doing, you were supposed to call a fault."

"Yeah, I know. I should have. But when I saw an opportunity to turn your little prank around and maybe double my points, I had to do it. Plus, I figured since my *best friend...*" there was an edge to 'best friend,' "...since my best friend had waited almost seven years to get even for Picnic Mountain, I was entitled to bend the rules a little. Hell man, I didn't even realize we were still playing."

"Remember, we agreed: No time limit," Robby said.

"Yeah, I remember."

"I still contend when you figured out what I was up to, the rules said you should call me on it." He sounded as though he was about to bring in an arbitrator to adjudicate the issue.

Max was not about to argue. "Look, if it will make you feel any better, I'll take a penalty and give you the point."

"That would make the score duce, right?" Robby brightened as he accepted Max's concession.

"That will make it duce," Max confirmed. "Now, let's get on with our lives." The look on his face was not unlike that of a child on the playground who has given in to a friend in order to avoid an argument.

For a moment both men decided to focus on their single malts. Then Robby posed a question, "Do you know where we went wrong with Le Jeu Ultime?"

"Yeah, deciding to do it."

"No, we let it complicated. There are dozens of actors in Hollywood who pull pranks on each other. But not like ours. Our first couple of pranks were clever, but basically simple. They didn't require a lot of preparation and we sprang them on each other before either of us knew what was happening. But with these last two. Too many moving parts. Took too much time and too many people involved. We should have kept them simple. And that shit you did to me on the mountain," he said making no attempt to mask his bitterness.

"You're right... we let it get out of hand. Much too complicated. More scotch?"

Robby held his glass up, "Don't be stingy." Max filled it to the top.

"You eaten?"

"Not hungry." Robby nodded toward his glass, "I think I'll just drink my dinner."

"Hope you plan to let someone drive you home."

"I don't have a home here anymore. Sold it. You're putting me up tonight." Then a question popped into his head," Have you talked to Andrea?"

"Not yet."

"So she doesn't know that it wasn't you we buried." He waved absently in Max's direction.

"No, I guess she doesn't," he said his voice laced with guilt. "I know I should have at least told her I was alive. But, we both know she'd never have gone along with what I'd decided to do. Andrea's not a game player. I know she never really approved of Le Jeu Ultime. Especially after your wedding night. And on that subject, what's the status of your divorce?"

"Final. Done. You can step in and take my place any time."

Max's expression asked question he did not need to put into words.

"How did I know? Robby responded. "She told me everything before the funeral. As I told you, if she was going to leave me for anyone, I'm glad it's you."

"Let's see," Max said looking at his watch. "It's about five in the morning in Anasara. I'll call her in a few hours."

"Don't be surprised, if..." he stopped himself and sipped his scotch.

"If what?"

"I hate to say it old buddy, but I think you've really fucked up your relationship. I mean, it's not exactly a good idea to let people think you've died and *not* tell the woman you love you really didn't. Andrea's not about to laugh that off. You don't know 'pissed' if you haven't seen her pissed. She can get ugly. I know."

Max nodded as concession to Robby's prediction. "Yeah, but if I did screw up, and I probably did, it's all your fault. No way could I let you get away with the Chateau thing. I know I should have called a fault, said "fuck you" and taken off for Anasara to be with Andrea." Max thought for a moment then said, "You know, I actually tried to warn her."

"You tried to warn her? How?"

"The afternoon before I drove you up to the Chateau, I called her and said I had some business to take care of. Told her it might mean I'd be out of touch for a little while, but to keep in mind that no matter what she heard, things are not always what they appear to be."

"Based on her reaction at your funeral, she either didn't understand what you were talking about or never really heard you."

"I kept thinking I should call her, but I knew if I did, she'd have thrown a fit and probably said something to you before I got a chance to get even. I'd made up my mind to give it back to you in spades and go one better." Max said nothing for a moment as he began to assess what he'd done to his relationship with Andrea. "As you said, I've probably fucked up with Andrea. I'm in very deep shit right now. Or will be when I call." Then he sighed the sigh of a man confronting the aberration of his bizarre obsession. "I really got my priorities bass-ackwards."

"Both of us did. But in your case, all you had to do was call a fault on me when you figured out what I'd done at the Chateau. You'd have won the point and it would have been your turn. You could have walked off the court and I might even have agreed. Game over."

I know," Max said staring into his glass. "But once I figured what you'd done and saw an opportunity to win Le Jeu, I couldn't resist. You may have taken the Tour de Francis, but Le Jeu Ultime was going to be mine." Max took a long drink of his scotch. "God, I sound obsessed. Maybe I was." Then added, "Am. What the hell am I going to say to Andrea?"

"More important, what the hell is she going say to you?"

Max shook his head. "It won't be pretty."

"Let me just say I don't think I'd want to be on your end of the conversation," Robby said. "

They fell into an abyss of silence that lasted several minutes. Finally, Robby raised the question that had become the elephant in the room. "So where do we go from here?

"Nowhere. As far as I'm concerned it's game over. We're done."

"You're saying you want to call it quits?" Robby asked.

"That's what I'm saying, but it takes two to put an end to this."

"So we're leaving it at duce and calling it over and done. An end. As in now? Today?" Robby could see Max was slightly irritated.

"Maybe I should say it in French," Max said. "C'est fini. Or at least jai terminé

Robby shrugged to indicate his acquiescence, "My French has gotten so good I know exactly what you're saying. French or English, we agree."

"Let's shake on it and make it official."

Robby stood up and extended his hand. As both men shook, he sensed Max was actually sincere about bringing Le Jeu Ultime to an end, but Robby found himself asking, *is a hand shake really all that binding? What if I decided to renege?*

It would be many months before they saw each other again. And when they did, it was totally unplanned. At least by them.

5.

AN EXCERPT FROM THE DIARY OF ANDREA TRASK

One Day before Her Murder

At first, I was ecstatic, delirious with happiness when I got the call from Max that morning. But almost immediately, delirium turned to anger. No, rage is a better word. All I could think of was how much I hated him for letting me believe he had died. How much I wanted to find some way to hurt him more than he had hurt me. I hung up. There was no way I could have talked to him then. Here was the man I had loved since I first saw him that summer so long ago. Here was a man who had asked me to marry him once my divorce was final. Here was the man who I was sure could give me the happiness, the love and the understanding I never had with Robby.

And what did Max do? He chose to play his infantile Le Jeu Ultime rather than starting our lives together. Without ever being asked, I was made an unwilling spectator at a game in which I would never have agreed to participate and most certainly did not approve.

Max continued to call almost hourly. He pleaded to let him come to Anasara to talk. I made it very clear, I did not want to see him, ever. Like his game, we were done. Over. I refused to accept dozens of his apologies and his vapid excuses for not telling me he was alive. The last thing he heard from me was some very unladylike language telling him what he could do with his apologies.

A week later he arrived, uninvited, in Anasara. I instructed my staff not to let him in and that if he persisted, to call the Anasara police. I learned he remained in the village for several days pleading with people – almost anyone who would listen – to please beg me to meet with him. I never did.

There have been many letters from him since then that I have not read. Phone calls I have not answered. Once, we nearly bumped into each other in Paris. Luckily, I saw him before he saw me. You may ask, why have I steadfastly refused the entreaties of the one man that, even today, I love more than any other man I have ever known? The answer is simple: He has broken my heart and left a deep wound that, at least until now, has refused to heal.

And of Robby? Our divorce became final, of course. While I will admit to having some sweet memories during my years with him, the fact that I spent all those years as nothing more than a much-neglected trophy served only to replace the sweet with the sour.

For a while, I felt liberated, free of them both. I did my best to put them out of my mind. To bury the past completely. However, I discovered I am not one to forget or forgive easily. The thought of how I had been made the real victim of their games gnawed on my psyche. The incessant urge to find a modicum – no, correct that – to find a major form of revenge took root. Juvenile as it might sound, I wanted to make them both suffer. It took time for me to decide how. Now, I have found a way. Tomorrow my game begins. I have made my own rules. I will not bother to share those rules with either of them. I will have my revenge... and die to do it.

V
REVENGE IS A DISH BEST SERVED COLD

1.

THE DAY OF THE MURDER
OF ANDREA TRASK

Anasara – A Tuscan Island – Italy

The letters to Max and to Robby were nearly identical.

Dear Max

I need to see you, desperately, here in Anasara. I haven't much time left.

I've arranged for you to be picked up by private seaplane at Porto Santo Stefano at 10AM on August 26th – my birthday. It will be the last time we will ever be able to celebrate together. Use my name at the port office and they'll direct you to the plane which will fly you here. One of my staff will meet you at the port and bring you to the Villa de Anasara.

Please Max, for all that we once meant to each other, I pray you will not disappoint me. I will be waiting.

Love,
Andrea.

Dear Robby

I need to see you, desperately, here in Anasara. I haven't much time left.

I've arranged for you to be picked up by private seaplane at Porto Santo Stefano at 9 AM on August 26th – my birthday. It will be the last time we will ever be able to celebrate together. Use my name at the port office and they'll direct you to the plane which will fly you here. One of my staff will meet you at the port and bring you to the Villa de Anasara.

Please Robby, for all that we once meant to each other, I pray you will not disappoint me. I will be waiting.

Love,
Andrea.

Max was taken from the dock by the Porto Santo Stefano launch to the waiting seaplane. The trip to Anasara took less than twenty minutes. As they neared the island, Max understood what Andrea meant when, years ago, she had described the island like a pearl in an oyster cradled by warm blue seas. Max looked down at the letter from Andrea. On the one hand, he hoped that it might represent a thaw in the icy barrier she had erected to keep him out of her life. On the other hand, he was desperate to find out what she meant by 'I haven't much time left.' In a few minutes, he would know.

The plane landed outside the Anasara harbor and was able to taxi to the end of a long wharf jutting out from the center of town. Once the plane was made fast, the co-pilot opened the door and Max was greeted by an older man in a formal dark suit and chauffeur cap.

"Senior Roarke?"

"Yes."

"Welcome to Anasara," he said and took Max's suitcase from the pilot.

"You speak English."

"Many years ago Senior Speganni sent me to school in England."

To Max, the part of the town that hugged the small harbor looked as if it deserved to be featured on a postcard or in a book of best kept secrets in Italy. The ochre, beige, yellow and red one and two-story buildings displayed their business names on myriad signs hanging over the front doors to serve as tourist magnets. It looked like the kind of place people sought when attempting to escape the hustle of the Italian cities. From where he stood, Anasara appeared to be a town that, even in this morning hour, had yet to get serious about the day's business. Andrea had once described the village as having a docile facade that, when scratched, revealed a population possessed of a strong, even fiery sense of independence. "It is," she had said, "a collective personality that provides a communal cohesiveness and singular pride in their island." She had told him that in addition to their affection for the island, the people cherished a deep sense of appreciation for Andrea's step father, Arturo Speganni. He had almost single-handedly restored the island to fiscal solvency after the deprivation it had suffered in the Second World War. When Speganni died, Andrea maintained his largess and the town, in turn, transferred their affections to the new benefactress and mistress of the Villa de Anasara.

"How far is the villa from here?" Max asked.

The driver simply pointed to the huge towering structure high on a hill over-looking the port. This was the place Andrea had told him she considered her retreat from the temporal world.

"It's beautiful."

"It was once a military post," the driver said happily assuming the role of tour guide. "but in the 18th Century the owners hired one of the most renowned architects of the time to redesign and convert what was then called a castle into an enormous luxury villa. Inside you will see beautiful frescoes in the Great Hall. The Signora is kind enough to invite the people of Anasara there for concerts."

It took only a few minutes to drive through the port and up the winding road to the villa.

"I will take care of your luggage," the driver said. "You are to wait for the Signora in the Great Hall. Through there," he said pointing to the ornate entrance.

"Thank you," Max said, and entered the villa. Inside he found himself on the balcony overlooking a magnificent, two-story room that was even more impressive than the driver had described. *Big enough for a basketball court*, he thought. For a brief moment he found himself hoping Andrea would appear, if not with open arms, at least with a welcoming smile. She didn't appear. "You're not exactly what I expected," Max made no effort to hide his surprise.

"I could say the same thing." Robby said.

"What are you doing here?

"I suspect the same thing you are," Robby answered

"Then I assume you got a letter from Andrea asking you to come."

"I did. It was the first time I'd heard from her since the divorce was final."

Why would she invite us both? Max wondered.

"Stairs are to your right," Robby said.

As Max stepped into the great hall he looked at Robby who had made himself comfortable on one of the many couches. "I don't understand why she sent us the same letter."

"Did yours say she needed to see you desperately?"

"Yes, and that she didn't have much time," he said finishing the line in her letter. "Whatever that means."

"Do you think she's... well, sick or something?"

"God, I hope not. Have you seen her yet?" Max asked.

Robby shook his head." No. No sign of her. When I arrived, the driver took my bags and I was shown in here and told to wait. At least I think that's what the butler, or whatever he is, said. My Italian is about as good as my French."

"Which is non-existent." Max chided. "Maybe we should ask somebody where she is."

"But who?"

"There has to be a staff."

"Maybe, but I haven't seen anyone."

"Really? Nobody?"

"Nobody," Robby answered.

Max began to pace around the great hall looking at the frescoes and the impressive art. After several minutes he sat down opposite Robby. "Does this seem a little strange to you, Andrea not being here?"

"More than a little, to tell you the truth."

"So what do we do?"

"Wait until she shows up."

The two men sat staring at nothing in particular, looking like two strangers waiting in an empty bus terminal. Finally, Max broke the silence. "It's been some time."

"Almost two years." Robby said.

"What have you been up to that I haven't read about in the scandal sheets?"

"I think they've covered it all. Climbed some mountains, drove some cars, raced my horses and worked in a few compliant ladies in between."

"In between the sheets, no doubt."

"Who needs sheets?" He laughed. "What about you? Any more centerfold women?"

"I've lost interest in those." What Max did not say was his only female interest was the one that lived here in Anasara. Clearly, Robby's presence dashed any hope he had that Andrea's invitation meant she was ready to take him back.

"When was the last time you talked to Andrea?" Robby asked.

"Right after my resurrection. She suggested I might think about an extended visit to hell."

"Not surprised. Knew she would be pissed. You haven't talk to her since?"

Max shook his head. "Tried many times, but she's refused."

A door at the opposite end of the hall swung open and two maids, dressed in black, rolled in two small service tables and placed them in front of Max and Robby. Each table had a selection of cheeses, bread, several different fruits, prosciutto and a bottle of wine.

"Pranzo," one of the women said and, with the other, turned to leave the hall.

"I think she said 'lunch.'" Robby said.

"I guess this means we won't be having lunch with Andrea."

"Looks that way."

"Mi scusi," Max called to the maids before they reached the door. "Dove si trova la signora?"

"No," came back the answer.

"What'd you ask?"

"If they'd seen her."

"Well, at least we've got something to eat." Robby picked up his wine bottle and looked at the label, "Brunello di Montalcino. A first-rate red."

"The woman does know her Italian wines," Max added.

Robby picked up the knife on his cheese tray, "Look at this. When was the last time you saw a seven-inch blade on a cheese knife?"

"I've got one too," Max said holding up a similar sized knife. "Looks like you could cut branches off a tree with this."

"Well, at least if we get attacked we'll be able to defend ourselves." He added a short laugh.

It was about fifteen minutes later the maids returned and began to remove the tables. "Ahhh... I'm not finished," Max said. The maids paid no attention and began pushing the tables toward the door. "Well, it appears I am finished." Max was somewhat bemused by the abrupt end to his lunch.

"I guess you have to eat fast here," Robby added, grabbing the wine bottle and his glass before it rolled away.

"Il Signora. Quando?" Max called.

"Subito," one of the maids answered.

"She said Andrea will be here soon."

"How soon is soon?" Robby wondered aloud.

"Who knows? If she doesn't show up in the next few minutes, I think we should go look for her," Max said.

"I agree. This is ridiculous." Robby stood up and began to pace. After several minutes he said, "Let's see if we can find her."

"Since you've been here before, lead on."

They hadn't taken but a few steps toward the nearest door when they heard a creaking noise from overhead. They looked up in time to see a long, narrow trap door open and a large video screen lowered into the hall stopping about six feet off the floor. Immediately, the screen began to flicker and the head to toe image of Andrea appeared against an empty white background. It was not the same woman either of them had known. She looked tired, deathly tired. Her face was drawn, dark bags hung under her eyes. The once light brown hair with the touch of red had turned mousey and partially gray. She had tied it back in a careless knot. Her dress, looking like something she might have borrowed from one of the maids, totally obscured what had once been her inviting body. *My God, what's happened to her?* Max wondered.

"I hardly recognize her," Robby said.

"She looks very ill to me. Terrible."

Andrea started to walk slowly, even haltingly, toward the camera. She had a thin, enigmatic smile on her face that was at once plaintive and disturbing.

"What's this all about?" The question was directed to Max, but Robby's eyes never strayed from the screen.

"I have a feeling we're about to find out," Max said.

It took Andrea several minutes to walk up close enough to the camera so that only her face appeared on the screen. The smile faded and there was a sense of melancholy in her voice as she spoke. "Hello, Max. Hello, Robby. I'm sorry I cannot greet you in person, but as you'll learn shortly, that would be quite impossible."

"Do you think this is a video tape? Or is this being shot live?" Robby asked while staring at the screen.

"Has to be tape," Max answered.

"First, let me say how pleased I am to have you both here before..." she did not finish her sentence. "I thought it might be fun, as a kind of finale to our relationships and to celebrate my last birthday, if we played a little game." There was a strange, detached look in her eyes.

"A game? What the hell is she talking about?" Robby looked baffled.

Max just stared at the image on the screen unable to make any sense of what he was seeing. "Something is really wrong with her."

"Yes, I said 'a game.' Since I know how much you two like games, I thought you might like to join me in playing one of my own creation. It's called 'Murder at the Villa'. Sounds very Agatha Christie, don't you think? Now, to play Murder at the Villa, all you need to know is that a murder has just been committed. And the victim, in this case, is me. Yes, that's right, me. I was murdered less than an hour ago. Brutally stabbed. At this moment I am lying somewhere in this villa quite dead."

"Has she gone nuts?" Robby could not believe what he was hearing.

"Look at her eyes," Max said. "You may be right." As he watched Andrea, a psychotic smile crept over her face.

She continued, "What makes this game interesting, as you're about to discover, is all the evidence points to you." She punctuated the statement with a short unnatural sounding laugh. "The object of the game is for you to try and prove you're innocent. You'll have to convince the police those are not your finger prints on the oversize cheese knives you used a few moments ago. Of course, they are your fingerprints."

Both men stared at the screen. They were simply speechless.

"Unless you can find some way to prove you did not murder me, you're going to find justice in Anasara is very swift, very thorough, and very, very final." There was an ominous, threatening tone in her voice. "I suppose, about now, you must be wondering why I am doing this? The answer?" There was a long, pregnant pause. "Revenge. Retribution. Reprisal. Call it what you like, but this is the only way I know to pay you back for all the terrible pain, the hours of tears and the unbearable heartbreak the two of you caused me while I was alive. And what better way than with the kind of game you, more than anyone else, will appreciate."

"Oh, what are the rules, you might be asking? Truth is, there are no rules. And because there are no rules, I will be the winner and you will be the painful losers."

"Painful losers? What the hell is she talking about?" Robby had had enough of her 'game.'

"I think we've lost her... mentally," the distress in Max's voice spoke to more than just what appeared to be the reality of her condition. It spoke to his guilt and the possibly of having lost the one person he truly loved.

"My only regret is that I will not be able to celebrate my victory with you in person. I would have liked a chance to gloat. But, unfortunately, as I've explained, that won't be possible. Enough explanation. It's time to play Murder at the Villa. I'd wish you luck, but sadly, when it comes to this game, you won't have any luck." She paused, the thin, oddly detached smile returned momentarily. "Goodbye." The screen faded to black.

"What in the hell was that all about? The woman has gone bonkers!" Robby was beside himself.

"Remember, in her letter she said she didn't have much time left? You don't suppose she knew she was losing her mind or that she's dying? Maybe that's what made her decide to punish us for..."

"Oh, stop!" Robby snapped angrily. "You don't believe all that nonsense she handed us do you?"

"About her being dead or about us being accused of her murder?" Max asked.

"Both. She's playing some kind of game. Andrea's not going to kill herself," Robby said confidently.

"You think that was a sane woman we just heard? I don't."

"It could all be part of her game. There's only one problem."

"Which is?"

"To make her little game work, she needs a body."

"What if there is a body?"

Suddenly Robby turned and glared at Max. "What a minute. Wait one fuckin' minute! Nice try, Max!" He seethed." How dumb do you think I am?"

"What?" Max had no idea what he was talking about.

"You bastard! What are you and Andrea up to? You cooked this up! You couldn't leave it at duce, could you? Had to take one last shot at me!"

"What in hell are you talking about? Are you nuts?" Max shot back.

"It's obvious. You and Andrea planned this so that you can go one up on me with Le Jeu! Admit it!" Robby said with certainty.

"If you think Andrea and I had anything to do with... that," he pointed toward the blank screen, "you're crazier than I thought. Maybe the both of you need a shrink. How could she and I have planned this? I haven't seen her or spoken to her in almost two years. Even if I had, there is no way she would ever agree to anything like..." Max stopped himself in mid-sentence. "Of course. I get it now. You're the one playing games. You accuse me as a way to hide the fact it's *you* behind this Murder in the Villa nonsense!"

"Bullshit! Do you think Andrea would ask me to help her with something like this? And maybe you forget, we agreed to end Le Jeu Ultime."

"Yeah, but how do I know you meant it." Max fired back

"I gave you my word."

"And what's that worth?"

"Go fuck yourself." Robby shouted.

"Up yours, asshole!"

"I'm outta here!" Robby started for the stairs leading to the balcony and the front entrance.

He made it only to the first step before the screams cascaded down into the hall. "Assassini! La signoria è morto! Morto! Assassini!! Morto!"

"What the hell!" Max was shocked.

"What are they screaming?"

"They're screaming 'killers, Andrea is dead.'"

"Oh, shit! Come on," Robby shouted. "The screams are coming from somewhere up there." Robby indicated the balcony.

They took the steps two at a time. When they got to the balcony they were blasted with more screams coming from a hallway that ran off to their left. They ran down the hall, through a door opening on a large sitting room.

"La signoria è morto! La signoria è morto.

Max slipped but caught himself before he fell. "Blood!" he said as he looked at a pool of red on the floor.

The door to the adjoining room was open.

"That's her bedroom," Robby said.

Inside, police and two maids were standing next to a large canopied bed. While Max and Robby's view was partially blocked, they could see a bloody body lying on the bed. A man with a stethoscope around his neck and a black bag pushed them aside and hurried to the bed. For a moment, all attention was on the doctor and the body.

"Morto!" he said gravely. "La signora è morta."

The two maids who had served them lunch turned away from the bed and, seeing Max and Robby, began to point and scream, "Assassini!! Assassini!!"

Before either could react, the police were on them, pushing, shoving and wrestling them to the floor. Their arms were pulled behind them followed by the click of hand cuffs. Max lifted his head in time to see two men with a stretcher enter from a door on the other side of the room. As they lifted the body off the bed, he caught sight of her blood-soaked dress. Her head fell slightly to the right."

"My God, it's Andrea!" Max cried out.

The screams from the maids continued. "Assassini!! Assassini!!"

"Let me up!" Robby shouted at the police holding him down. "I don't believe it! I want to see her. She can't be dead."

As the stretcher carrying Andrea disappeared out of the room, a policeman with several stripes on his sleeve identifying him as the officer in charge, indicated for his men to help Max and Robby to their feet. Once they were standing, he stared first at one and then the other with a hard, hostile look. "Si macellai vili!" he said through gritted teeth.

"Vile butchers?" Max was sure he understood. "No! No!"

"Io ti arresto per l'omicidio della signora Trask." Then he told the officers to 'take them away.' "Portateli via!" Max protested as two policeman pushed Robby and him down the hall.

"Wait a minute! Listen to me! Listen to me! "Robby shouted as they forcibly force them out the front door.

Either the police had no intention of listening or they simply did not understand English. Either way it made no difference.

2.

THE DAY AFTER THE MURDER
OF ANDREA TRASK

"This is bullshit! This is bullshit!" Robby kept repeating as he was returned to the cell the police had put them in.

"Stop! Will you? I'm tired of listening to you. Tell me what happened with the phone call."

"When they were fingerprinting me, I found one guy who spoke a little English. I told him I was entitled to a phone call. I intended to call my lawyer in Nice. But the damn phone connection was so bad we couldn't hear each other. When I said I wanted to try and get a better line, they said, 'No. That was your one phone call.' This is bullshit!"

"Damn," Max said, "I wish I spoke better Italian. I'd like to find out what the hell they intend to do with us."

"Other than the guy who fingerprinted me, I haven't seen anybody to talk to. I don't know about you, but I'm not particularly fond of the idea of having to make this dungeon my home for any length of time. I expect to see scratches on the wall from the Man in the Iron Mask."

"I just can't believe Andrea would do this? I don't blame her for hating me. But this is insane. Maybe I drove her to it."

"Even if you did, we didn't kill her. We never got out of that damn room."

"I can't get over how bad she looked. I wonder how long she's been ill?"

They looked toward their cell door at the sound of keys in the lock. The iron bar door opened and a smallish middle-aged man with a briefcase entered. The door was closed and locked behind him.

"Who the hell are you?" Robby asked.

"My name is Vittorio Mario Franechelli."

"You speak English." Max said.

"Yes. Very well, I think."

"What do you want?"

"I have come to tell you your trial has been set for tomorrow. I have been appointed to be your lawyer."

"If it's all the same to you, we'd rather call our own." Max said.

"And we'd like a phone that works."

"Oh. That is not permitted," he sounded apologetic.

"What's not permitted, the phone call?" Robby asked.

"Not the phone call. Calling an outside lawyer. We only allow lawyers from Anasara to appear in court."

"That's not right." Robby said.

"In Anasara it is."

"What if we wanted to find another lawyer here in Anasara?"' Robby asked.

"That would be difficult."

"Difficult? Why?" Max asked.

"Because I am the only defense lawyer in Anasara."

Max let out a short disparaging laugh, "Doesn't give us a lot of options does it?"

Vittorio sat down on one of the beds and opened his briefcase. "Would you like me to review the evidence they have against you?"

"What evidence?" Robby asked. "First of all, we didn't kill her. We never left that great hall from the time we got there in the morning until we heard the maids start to scream."

"Can you prove that? Do you have any witnesses?"

"The chauffer, the maids, and we have each other," Robby said.

Vittorio shook his head, "That might not be enough."

"Wait a minute," Max said. "The video! Andrea was on a video that was shown to us. The TV screen came right out of the ceiling. If you can find the video, it will prove we had nothing to do with her murder."

The lawyer shook his head, "The police found the video. But I don't think you want it shown in court."

"Why not?"

"Because on the video the Signora says she fears for her life. And it is the two of you she fears the most."

"What?' Max was taken aback.

"This is crazy?" Robby added. "That's not what she said on the video we saw."

"Well, I am sorry, but that's what the police showed me."

Robby said, "The video was nothing fearing for her life. In the one we saw she explained she was planning this whole thing."

"Well, let's hope I can find it." He fumbled though his papers. "There is more evidence against you."

"Like what?" Robby asked making no effort to hide his irritation.

"The Signora was stabbed many times with a large blade or blades. They found two large knives – eight-inch knives with blood on them and... this is very bad... your finger prints were on them."

"Those cheese knives," Max said. He turned to Robby, "She said we'd have to be able to explain how our finger prints got on those knives."

Vittorio looked surprised, "She said that?"

"In the video. That's exactly what she said."

"She's really set us up," Robby said "Perfect way to get our finger prints."

"And then there are your clothes."

"Our clothes? What clothes? These?" Max gestured to what he had on.

"No, the ones they found in your rooms with blood on them. And there was blood in your bathrooms. They claim you tried to wash it off your hands and left stains on the towels."

"This is ridiculous," Robby was angry. "If we were trying to cover up a murder, we sure as hell wouldn't have left bloody clothes lying around or blood-stained towels hanging in the bathroom. We are not killers, and if we were, we wouldn't be that stupid."

"Plus, we never had rooms," Max said. "We were shown right to the great hall."

"The driver who brought us from the port said he'd take care of our suitcases. He, or someone, had to put the blood on them." Robby looked over at Max and shook his head in resignation, "This whole thing doesn't make sense, unless... unless..."

Max could see that something had occurred to him, "Unless what?"

"Unless Andrea is just playing with us."

"That's kind of what she said she was doing," Max said.

"And unless she's not dead."

"But we saw her in the bed."

"But, did we really see what we thought we saw?"

"Excuse me," Vittorio said. "What are you talking about."

"Nothing," Max immediately realized this was something he and Robby should talk about in private. "Do they have any more evidence?" Max spit out 'evidence' as though he was trying to rid his tongue of a bad taste.

"No. But in order to convict you, they must prove a motive."

"There was no motive," Max protested. "Neither of us has seen Andrea in almost two years. She invited us here. So what possible motive could we have had?"

"The prosecutor will tell us," Vittorio said.

"Tell us what?" Robby asked.

"I don't know. All I know is he has some someone who will testify to establish a motive."

"Who?" Max pressed.

"I don't know. Under Anasara law, we are not permitted to know who will testify against the defendant."

"What kind of law do you people have here?" Max could barely contain himself. "I don't pretend to be any kind of expert in Italian law, but I do know the defense is allowed to know who is going to testify against them."

"Well, this is not Italy, this is Anasara."

"What are you talking about? You're a part of Italy."

"Yes, but we don't pay much attention to what goes on in Italy. And they don't pay much attention to us. Rome has too many problems. The whole country has too many problems to care about or even notice what goes on in little Anasara. If we were on Sardinia or Elba or even Capraia, those are big enough for them to care about. But Anasara? They forget about us. That's why we have our own laws and do things the way we want to do them."

"Wonderful," Robby said derisively.

"This doesn't look good," Max added.

Vittorio shrugged and shook his head "Yes, I am afraid it looks very bad for you."

"Vittorio, did you know Mrs. Trask?" Max asked.

"Yes. Everyone in Anasara knows her... or knew her," he said correcting himself.

"On the video we saw, she looked very ill and... well, not quite herself," he said choosing soft words for mentally disturbed.

"Oh, yes. It is very sad. She was such a beautiful woman, but then she became ill and..." he shrugged, "something happened to her. Up here," he pointed to his head. "She was very strange at times. Walked around her villa like she did not know where she was. Very confused and so much crying. Naturally, because she meant so much to Anasara, we were all very concerned. People wanted her to go to Rome or maybe New York to see a doctor. In Anasara our doctors just deliver babies and fix broken bones. They do not fix heads. But she would not go. Said she would not leave us."

Max was devastated. "That's awful. That's awful," he repeated several times. "I can't tell you how much this hurts. I truly loved her and to think she... she has just crumbled physically and mentally in only two years. Maybe it was me or maybe..." he left the maybe up in the air. "It's just terrible to think what's happened to her."

Robby looked askance at Vittorio, "I find it very hard to believe our Andrea would deteriorate so fast."

"I would too," Max said, "except some pretty unexpected things can happen to people. Sometimes faster than we can imagine. To me what Vittorio has told us explains a lot of what we saw and heard on the video."

"Possibly."

"What do you mean 'possibly?'"

"Let's just say I'm basically a cynic. I sometimes don't believe all of what I see and even less of what I hear. But leave my doubts for later. Let's get back to this sham trial we're facing."

"I do not understand this word 'sham,'" Vittorio said to Robby.

"Bogus. Not real. Part of her game."

Vittorio at first appeared confused, then his expression turned darkly serious. "Let me assure you, this trial is no game. It is very real and could go very bad for you."

"So, what do you recommend?" Max asked.

There was a blank look on Vittorio's face suggesting he had no idea. All he could offer was, "I'm afraid we will have to take our chances at the trial."

"And what if they find us guilty? What then?" Robby asked,

He lowered his head to avoid eye contact, "You don't want to know."

"But we do," Max demanded.

Vittorio looked at both men and then said, "They hang people for murder in Anasara."

"Bullshit." It was a futile protest.

3.

TWO DAYS AFTER THE MURDER
OF ANDREA TRASK

The Anasara court had all the characteristics of a building left over from the 16th Century Italian Inquisition. The crowds that pressed to get inside looked like refugees imported from the French revolution calling for the Guillotine!

Shouts of "Assassino! Assassino!" filled the courtroom. Max and Robby stayed very close to Vittorio as they walked in and sat down at the defendant's table. When the judge entered, everyone stood up and then sat down after he did.

He began to address the court in Italian.

"What about a translation?" Max asked.

"Translation? You want a translation?" Vittorio seemed surprised at the request.

"It would be nice for us to have some idea of what he's saying," Robby said sarcastically.

"Do not worry," Vittorio assured them. "I will translate if he says anything you need to know."

"That's comforting," Max said feeling no comfort at all.

After a moment a door opened, twelve people entered the courtroom and sat down in the jury box. They stared grimly at the defendants.

"That's an ugly bunch. Who are they?" Robby asked

"The jury."

Max nudged Vittorio, "Don't we get a chance to voir dire the jurors?"

"Not here. Not necessary. We always use the same jury."

"They look like they're ready to find us guilty before we even begin." Robby said.

The judge offered a few more comments and then nodded toward the prosecutor seated at the table next to Max and Robby.

Vittorio leaned over and whispered to the two men, "The judge said, 'Let's get started.'"

"I sort of figured that out all by myself," Robby said.

The prosecutor got up and addressed the jury. He spoke for almost twenty minutes using wild gestures, all manner of invectives, his voice ranging over an octave of shrill accusations. At one point, he appeared to be having an emotional breakdown and had to ask a juror for a handkerchief to wipe away the tears. He blew his nose in it, then handed the handkerchief back to the juror, returned to his table and sat down.

"Nothing like sharing your germs," Max said in disgust.

Robby turned to Vittorio "What the hell did he say?"

"Usual kind of thing," Vittorio answered.

"Usual?" Max echoed.

"He told them you were guilty of killing Signora Trask and that you should be hung."

"It took him twenty minutes to say that?" Robby looked incredulous.

"Well, he repeated himself a lot."

"Great," he said sarcastically.

The judge indicated Vittorio could now make his opening remarks. Vittorio stood up and looked at the jury." I miei clienti non sono colpevoli. Almeno io non credo che siano," he said and sat down.

"That's it?" Max asked. "That's it! What did you tell them?"

"I told them that I didn't think my clients were guilty."

"I'm sure your little speech must really have convinced them." Robby said. The inflection in his voice making no secret of what he thought of their lawyer's performance.

"Always better to be brief with our jury. They don't like long speeches."

"But the prosecutor went on for twenty minutes," Max pointed out.

"That is different. He is a friend of theirs."

"And you're not?"

"I am new in Anasara," Vittorio looked embarrassed at this admission.

"Oh, God, this gets better all the time," Robby said.

Once the prosecution began to call its witnesses, the pace of the trial picked up. Andrea's maids were called and identified Max and Robby as the killers. Next, a policeman produced the two cheese knives and testified that Max and

Robby's finger prints were found on them. This was followed by what the prosecution told the court was an expert who swore Andrea's blood was found on the killers' shirts and pants.

From what little Max could understand of the testimonies, and judging by the reactions of the jury, he was convinced Vittorio's cross examination had probably done a better job of supporting the prosecution's case than the prosecutor.

"Your honor," the prosecutor said speaking in English for the first time, "we have one more witness. Because this witness does not speak Italian, I request the court permit us to proceed in English. This witness will provide the motive for this heinous crime."

"Granted," the judge said.

"I call Jeanne Malveau."

"What in the...?" Max spun around as Jeanne walked in the rear door of the court room. "Where did she come from?"

"How the hell did Andrea find her? I don't believe this." Robby said, "Luigi Pirandello couldn't have written a better farce than what's going on here. Talk about theater of the absurd."

Max watched as Jeanne walked up to the stand. He leaned over to Robby, "How is she supposed to supply the motive?"

"Depends on what script Andrea gave her."

"You really think Andrea.is alive and in complete control of this whole thing?"

"Absolutely," Robby said with conviction.

"I wish I could believe that," Max said softly.

"Trust me. You can believe it. She's probably hiding somewhere in this courtroom laughing her ass off."

Jeanne Malveau was sworn in and asked a few preliminary questions as to how she knew the deceased and the defendants. "They were friends. I knew them socially."

"Socially? She was nothing more than an actress for rent," Robby said to Vittorio.

The prosecutor finally asked her the number one question: "Can you think of any reason, any reason at all, why the two defendants... the two men you see seated at the table, would want to kill Signora Trask?"

"Yes," she responded simply.

"And what reason would that be?"

"She was going to expose the truth about them. Andrea Trask threatened to reveal the one secret she knew would ruin the reputations of both men. The one thing that, if it were made known to their friends and to the gossip columns, would totally humiliate them. It is the one thing they have desperately tried not to reveal all their lives."

"And what, may I ask, was this secret?" the prosecutor queried.

"Max Roarke and Robert Trask are homosexuals!"

Max and Robby bounced out of their chairs, but Vittorio gestured for them to sit down. The two men were speechless.

"Is that true? " Vittorio asked.

"Fuck, no!" Robby fired back.

"How can you prove it is not true," Vittorio asked.

"Maybe the jury would like to see us screw her here in court." Max said sarcastically.

"We're a lot of things, but I can line up a hell of a lot of women who will testify that homosexuals we're not." Robby added.

As Jeanne left the stand, she passed close to the table where Max and Robby were sitting, leaned over next to Max and said quietly: "Souhaitez-vous deux comme pour dîner un jour? En supposant qu'ils ne vous raccrochez." Then walked away.

Robby turned to Max, "What did she say?"

"She said she'd like to have dinner if they don't hang us."

"What a nice invitation," he said facetiously. Robby then whispered to Max, "I'm telling you, Max, this is all bullshit. It's not real."

"Then why do I have this sinking feeling in the pit of my stomach? I mean, this is all going way too far just to be some kind of prank."

"But that's what it is. Andrea is trying to take our Le Jeu Ultime to a whole new level. I'm sure of it."

Max moved uneasily in his chair, "I hope you're right."

First Robby, then Max were called to the stand. They both told, in detail, essentially the same story of what had happened at the villa. While their testimonies were in English, there was no translation. Max was beside himself realizing the jury had no idea what they were saying. He raised an objection to his own testimony. "Your honor, how the hell is the jury to know what we're saying if it's not translated? Do they speak English?"

"No," the judge answered.

"Then I object!"

"Obiezione respinta," the judge said.

"Did he say what I think he said?" Max asked Vittorio.

"Your objection was overruled."

When Max returned to the table he said to Robby, "They didn't understand more than ten words of what we said."

There was a look of supreme confidence on Robby's face. "You're probably right. But it doesn't make any difference. It's all part of the farce."

"You keep saying that."

"And you should start believing it."

The judge asked for summary arguments, in Italian, and then sent the jury out to deliberate. They filed out of the court room and were gone for no more than a couple of minutes before they came back in. The verdict was no surprise. The people who had crowded into the courtroom cheered when the foreman said, "Colpevole!" The loud and raucous celebration was permitted to last several minutes before the judge graveled for quiet. He immediately handed down the sentence. And he did it in English. "It is the decision of this court that the prisoners shall be taken from here and tomorrow, at 11AM, hung by the neck until dead." More cheering.

"Wait a minute!" Max bounced out of his chair and shouted at Vittorio over the clamor, "He can't do that. Italy doesn't have a death penalty."

"Anasara does," Vittorio said matter-of-factly, then started to pack up his brief case.

"How can that be?" Max was mad. "Rome may not pay you any attention, but this is still Italy!"

"Yes, but here in Anasara, we do things our own way. You have to understand the Signora was much loved. For most of the people who live in Anasara, she is, or was, their benefactress. They are not happy, in fact, they are very angry that you killed her and want you punished."

"But we didn't kill her!" Max yelled.

"I believe you, but the jury didn't and these people don't."

"But the judge..."

"If it had been anyone but the Signora, he might have been lenient and sentenced you to maybe twenty years of hard labor. But, not in this case. The judge is no fool. He knows the people might attack him and burn down his house if he let you off by just sentencing you to prison."

"I can't believe this is happening," Max sank back in his chair.

"Max, trust me. I'm telling you, this is not real. It's a game. You watch,

Andrea is going to show up and prove I'm right. Actually, I thought she might come back with the jury so that everyone could laugh it up."

"Laugh it up? You think all these people..." he waved his hand at the people who were still milling about in the courtroom, "...that everyone in Anasara is in on this?"

"Wouldn't surprise me at all. As Vittorio said, Andrea is their benefactress. And for that reason, you've got to believe they'll do anything for her, especially if she's paying them."

As the police approached the table to take Max and Robby back to their cell, Vittorio said, "Some good news for you, I hope."

"Good news will be nice for a change," Max said.

"Tomorrow morning they will be burying Signora Trask. Tonight her coffin is lying in the church. If you like, I can arrange to have you taken from your cell to the church tonight to pay your respects."

Robby jumped at the offer, "I'd like to do that. I want to see a body." Robby leaned close to Max, "I'm betting they won't let us within fifty feet of the casket."

"But if, let's say, she really is dead, what difference does it make how close we get?"

"Because it's hard to fake being dead close up. I'm telling you, she is not dead."

* ~ * ~ *

It was after nine when guards appeared at the cell door. "Andiamo alla signora in chiesa."

Robby and Max were handcuffed and leg irons were put on so there was no chance they could run.

"Do you get the idea they're afraid we might try to escape?" Max stood up and discovered just how difficult it was going to be to walk.

"Hell, even if we could escape, the mainland is a little too far for us to swim." Robby said.

The church in Anasara was a source of great pride to the villagers. It had been built by 15th century artisans. With the help of people like Andrea and her step-father, the church had been brought back to its original grandeur. Max and Robby were driven the short distance from the jail to the church. Doing their best to cope with the leg irons, they waddled their way up the steps of the church. As they entered, they could see a coffin on the high alter surrounded by candles. Slowly, accompanied by their police guards, they made their way down the long aisle. The bier on which the coffin sat was large enough to make it impossible for them to get closer than about three feet from the body.

The coffin top was in two sections and only the top half of her body was exposed. She was dressed in a white gown and someone had put a diamond Tiara in her hair. A thin, transparent veil had been placed over her face. Even with no other light than that supplied by the candles, they could see it was the same, drawn and sickly face they'd seen in the video.

"It's really her!" Max whispered to Robby.

"Maybe. I'd like to touch her. That way I'd know if it's her body or if we're looking at a very good dummy."

"A dummy?" Max needed an explanation.

"Look, you know better than I do that movie special effect people can create some very lifelike dummies. Their skin looks very real, but once you touch it..." Robby slowly extended his manacled hands out toward the coffin. He immediately felt a club smash across his forearms. "Non toccare il suo!" the guard said.

"He said, 'Don't touch.'" Max translated.

"Yeah, I got the message," Robby grimaced. "Damn, that hurt."

Max looked at Andrea for a moment," I think it's her." Then he whispered, "I'm so sorry Andrea. I was a fool. I got carried away. What I did, what I put you through, was unforgivable. I only wish you would have let me apologize. I would have spent my life making it up to you." Max backed away from the coffin. Robby continued to stare at the body, then stepped back and joined Max. "I'll admit she looks dead but, I'm not convinced. There are ways she could fake it."

"How could she fake being dead?"

"There's this drug, it's a very real drug that can make you look dead. It was what the character of Lord Blackwood used in a Sherlock Holmes film I saw a few years back to fake his death. As I recall it's called something like Graytox or Grayantox... no, it's Grayanotoxin."

"How would she know about something like that?"

"She's smart. She could easily have done some research."

"I think we have to consider that she could really be dead. I mean, you saw the video. Not only didn't she look very well physically, but I saw a very psychotic woman talking to us. God knows what she was capable of doing, especially if she felt she had to get revenge."

"Sorry, I don't accept that. She's alive. She knows exactly what she's doing. She's orchestrating this like a symphony conductor."

As the guards nudged them to leave the altar and start walking out of the church, Robby nodded toward the guards and said, "Think we could bribe these guys to let us go?"

"Who knows? The only problem is I don't know enough Italian to offer them a bribe."

"I thought you spoke Italian?"

"Only enough to order a meal or ask directions. No way can I negotiate a bribe."

"Maybe they speak English."

"Mi scusi, non uno di voi parla inglese?"

"Non parla inglese," they responded.

"They don't speaka-da English, right?" Robby confirmed.

"Right. Any other ideas?"

"I'm thinking."

"Well, don't think too long. We've got about twelve hours to figure out something or the nice people of Anasara or going to..." he paused, "I don't want to think about what they're going to do."

Once they were returned to the cell, they realized there would be no further contact with anyone until the next morning. Max looked out the window of their cell. The full moon illuminated the square in the street below. In the middle, surrounded by bleachers, he could see gallows had literally sprung up since the end of the trial. There were two ropes. Two trap doors. "Come here. Take a look."

"All part of her show," Robby said still exuding confidence.

"If so, where's the director? Where's Andrea?"

"That I don't know." A trace of concern crossed his face.

Max shook his head, "I think they're going to hang us."

3.
THREE DAYS AFTER THE MURDER
OF ANDREA TRASK

It was a mostly sleepless night. Their meager breakfast was never touched. From just before nine, they stood at their cell window watching the crowd form below around the gallows.

"God, they want blood," Robby said.

"No, just our heads."

"So much for Andrea showing up this morning at our cell door."

So maybe now you think all this might be for real?" Max left the window.

"Maybe." For the first time, Robby looked worried. "The hell of it is, we're not guilty!"

The sound of a key in the door.

Andrea?"

No. Vittorio.

"Come to see us off, have you?" Robby's forced jovial greeting was undercut by the cynical look on his face.

"I have been to see the judge this morning. I was hoping to convince him to delay your execution so that I could have more time to investigate. But he said 'no.'"

"Vittorio, what's it going to take to buy our way out of this?"

"What are you talking about? A bribe?"

"Exactly. We can make a lot of people here very rich if they can put us on a boat back to the mainland."

Vittorio began to shake his head. "A bribe? Not a good idea."

"Why not?" Max asked.

"They punish people in Anasara for offering bribes."

Robby laughed derisively. "Punish people! For offering a bribe? Since when do Italians not accept bribes? And how much worse can the punishment be than hanging?"

Suddenly they heard a commotion in the square below. All three went over to the window. Below they could see two men struggling with the police at the base of the scaffold.

"What's going on?" Max asked.

"Oh, they are hanging those two men. I guess they figured since they'd built the gallows they might as well use it for other criminals as well."

"We're not criminals! We didn't murder Andrea!" Robby protested angrily.

"What did those two do?" Max asked.

"One is a very bad thief. Incorrigible. Many times in jail. I guess they figured since he won't change his ways, they would just hang him." He began to laugh. "That will cure him of being a thief, all right. The other is a man who shot a friend of his in a duel over the other man's wife. We don't permit duels in Anasara."

They watched as the two men climbed the steps and took their places over the trap doors on the scaffold. A priest said some last words then hoods were placed on their heads and ropes were put around their necks.

"I don't think it is a good idea for you to watch," Vittorio said pushing the two men away from the window.

They didn't resist.

Moments later there was a loud 'ca-chunk'.

"What was that?" Max asked.

"The trap door. That would be the last thing they heard. It is over. It was very quick. You can take a look now, if you like," Vittorio said as he stepped back from the window." They are taking the bodies down."

"I'll pass," Robby said lowering his head and sitting on the edge of his cell bed.

"Well, I just want to say it was nice meeting you and I am sorry I could not have been more successful," Vittorio offered his hand but neither man took it. He turned to the cell door, "Sono pronto ad andare," he called to the guard. As the door open he turned back and looked at both men and said "Adio" and left.

"Sort of final, wasn't he?" Robby said.

"The only good news is that he didn't give us a bill for his services."

Robby lay back on his bed for several minutes then sat up and stared at the floor. "I'm beginning to doubt myself." His words were barely audible to Max. "I'm beginning to believe this is what it appears to be. Maybe Andrea really was looking for... how'd she put it? Revenge. Retribution. Payback. If she were... well, if she were normal, I'm talking mentally normal... there's no way she would have done this. But, if for whatever reason, she had become psychotic... it could be that..." he didn't finish the thought.

"If she were alive we'd have either seen her by now or someone would have slipped up and said something. No way could all those people in court or the police keep this game of hers a secret. Somebody would have tripped up."

"And now with Andrea dead, they've lost their checkbook. Their benefactress is gone with no one to replace her."

"Hell, we could!" Robby said. "We could fuckin' buy the whole Goddamn island. What if when they take us down there we offer them a billion dollars? Somebody has to speak English. They're Italians! They understand money."

"The only problem is I don't have a billion dollars on me right now and I forgot to bring a check." There was a heavy mordant tone in his voice.

Robby sat down and mumbled, "This can't be happening."

Max went back to looking out the window. "Hell of a crowd we're drawing. Too bad we can't charge admission."

"Robby looked up at his friend, "So what are we going to do?"

"Not much. Except wait to get hung," Max sounded as if he were resigning himself to their fate.

"No Goddamn it!" Robby exploded and stood up. "We didn't kill her! I'm not going to let them put me on that scaffold without a fight!"

"Fight with what? Suddenly I have a lot of sympathy for Richard the Third."

"What! Who?"

"You know. Shakespeare. A horse, a horse, my kingdom for a horse."

"How about 'A boat. A boat. My Malibu house for a boat."

Max let a small grin escape, "Ah yes, a little gallows humor courtesy of Mr. Trask"

Suddenly Robby's body tensed and he had the look of a man about to enter a street brawl. "I'm going to fight 'em, Max. I'm not going to make it easy for them."

"While you do that, I'm going hope you were right about this being a farce. I'm going to pray that either before they come for us, or maybe once we get down there, Andrea will show up and claim her win."

$$* \sim * \sim *$$

At just after ten-thirty the guards came for them. They approached Max first, turned him around and tied his hands behind his back with rope. He made no effort to resist. Robby, on the other hand, immediately made it clear he was not going to go easily. "We're not guilty! You're going to have to drag me down there! This whole thing has been a sham. Where the hell is the Signora?"

That the guards understood and answered grimly, "Morto! Morto!"

The words stuck home and for a brief moment, Robby appeared ready to accept Andrea was really dead. But that in no way made him any less innocent. It in no way lessened his determination to fight his jailers all the way to the gallows. "No, Goddamn it. I don't want to die! We didn't do anything. For God sakes, don't you understand? She did this to herself to get even. She had to be insane!"

The guards did not appear to understand a word.

It took four of them to get Robby out of the cell, down the stairs and to the street. Max did not offer any resistance. What for? There was no way he could reason with them, no way for either of them to escape. The nightmare – bogus or not – was about to come to a painful and abrupt end.

Max was led to the scaffold and, because his hands were tied, needed help up the steps so as not to lose his balance. Robby continued to make himself difficult. "You bastards! You can't do this! I am not guilty of anything!" He struggled not to climb the steps. "No. I'm not going up there." But the guards paid no attention. Finally, after an extended struggle, Robby was standing on the scaffold.

On the platform hung the two ropes. A priest in full clerical garb, holding a Bible and a crucifix, stood between the ropes..

"What the hell is he here for?" Robby barked.

"Last rites," Max answered.

"Fuck that! I'm not a Catholic!"

As black hoods were slipped over their heads, the priest uttered a final prayer: "Dio di compassione, preghiamo per coloro che stanno per morire. Che possiate ricevere nel vostro amore che perdona. Amen."

The ropes were place around their necks. The crowd which was now filling the square was chanting: "Hang loro. Invia all'inferno." Hang them. Send them to hell!

Robby was crying. Shrieking! Max waited for the door beneath his feet to open and drop him in the abyss of death. He hoped it would be quick.

"Ora" a voice yelled out.

Max heard the sound of the lever controlling the trap doors. The floor fell out from beneath his feet and he was falling.

Falling!

Falling into what felt like a pile of straw. It smelled like straw. And it was straw. He heard the crowd let out a rousing cheer followed by laugher, guffaws, hoots, cackles and whistles of celebration. He lowered his head and shook off the hood.

"Signori, buon giorno." He looked up at one of the policemen who had taken him to the scaffold. He was carrying a large knife and for a moment Max thought he meant to use it on him. He did. He cut the ropes binding his hands and then moved on to Robby. When he'd finished, he stepped back and looked down at them with a toothless grin, "How you say in America? Have ee nicea day." He laughed as he left.

"I'll give you a nice day," Robby threatened while pulling off his hood. "I'll kill these bastards! And I'll kill that bitch as well! I knew it! I knew she wasn't dead!"

Max turned to look out toward the crowd which continued to laugh and point at the two men. It had been, as Robby suspected, an enormous sham. And then he saw her moving toward them though the crowd which, as if on cue, parted to let her pass. She walked up to the scaffold and stopped just short of Max. This was not the Andrea of the video. This was the Andrea of his memory at Cap Ferrat. There were no signs of illness. She looked quite sane and very much in control. The sun at her back made her white dress appear almost transparent and brought back memories of that day in Southampton when they saw what looked to be a naked woman walk out of the sea. Max had never seen her more radiant. She was triumphant in her bearing – buoyant with her victory. As she stood looking down at the two of them, sprawled as they were on a mound of straw, Max tried to stand, but his legs failed him. Robby moved not at all. He was mad, but his tongue was frozen in his mouth.

Max looked up into her face – it virtually glowed. She paused, looking first at one and then the other. Andrea took a short breath and spoke, "I just thought you should know that three can play your game. And the score? My murder made it 15 – Love. The trial and your conviction: 30 – Love. Your visit to my not-so-dead body in the church: 40 – Love. And now this," she glanced up at the gallows. "I believe this is Game, Set and Match."

With that Andrea turned and walked away. Max could not help but marvel how regally she carried herself. The sun-promoted silhouette of her body lurking below the white dress erupted passions in him that had lain dormant for far too long. *Look at her, she is absolutely magnificent*, he thought *I've got to get her back.*

Max pulled himself to his knees and watched as Andrea made her way triumphantly up the cobblestone street. People from the village – apparently all in on the hoax – poured out from every door, every side street and began to follow her forming a kind of victory processional while showering her with an unintelligible flood of praise. She was, after all, their benefactress and, as she had once suggested, they would do anything for her or old Spaghetti.

She is all I ever wanted, he thought. *How could I have been so stupid to...?* He did not have an opportunity to finish his thought.

"The woman is sick! How could she do this to us?" Robby shook with rage.

"Give her credit," Max said. "She beat us at our own game." He looked up the street where she had paused momentarily. "What a fantastic woman."

"Yeah, well I'm going to get even with your so called 'fantastic woman' if it's the last thing I do!"

Max spun around and looked threateningly at Robby. "Oh, no you're not." He stood up. "I love that woman. I don't care how long it takes, I'm going to win her back." He glared at Robby, "The game is over. She won." He turned away and began to run up the narrow street toward the crowd "Andrea, wait!" he shouted. "Wait!"

Max ran through a chorus of the jeers, past the pointed laughter of the people lining the street. When he finally caught up with her, out of breath, he touched her arm and said, "Andrea wait. Please stop." She did and looked at him without showing any emotion. His words rattled out quickly between gasps for breath. "I admit to being all the terrible things you said I was two years ago. I was stupid, inconsiderate and the world's number one fool. Now, I'm asking you to give me a chance to prove how sorry I am. If you do, I will spend the rest of my life making it up to you. You will be the most adored and loved woman in the world."

"And your trophy?"

"No, no," he protested. "A woman I will love forever. Please, can we at least talk?" He had run out of pleas and waited for a response.

Andrea looked at him for several moments. He thought he detected a softening in her face, even the start of a slight smile. She reached out and touched his hand for a brief moment. "In the morning," she said finally. "Sit across from me at breakfast. We'll talk." With that she walked on, the crowd falling in behind their beloved benefactress. Max did not attempt to follow, but stayed where he was, watching until he could see her no more. "Breakfast," he said smiling. "I love breakfast," he called after her.

* ~ * ~ *

"Damn, I think I broke my ankle. Or at least sprained it." Robby grabbed on to one of the scaffold supporting pillars and pulled himself to his feet. His body ached from the fall through the trap door. He brushed the straw off his shirt and pants, then watched as the last of Andrea's procession turned a corner. Max, he could see, was now standing alone in the street watching the disappearing crowd.

There was a curious look of anticipation on Robby's face as he shouted to the empty street. "It's not done! It's not over!" Then, as if sharing a secret only with himself, he said quietly, "New game! My serve."

CPSIA information can be obtained
at www.ICGtesting.com
Printed in the USA
BVHW070042060619
550247BV00001B/57/P